DESTRUCTION

J.M. MADDEN

Copyright © 2018 by JM Madden

This book is licensed for your personal enjoyment only. This book may not be resold or given away to other people. If you would like to share this book with another person, please purchase an additional copy for each recipient. If you're reading this book and did not purchase it, or it was not purchased for your use only, then please return it and purchase your own copy. Do not take part in piracy. Thank you for respecting the hard work of this author.
This book is a work of fiction. Names, characters, places and incidents are either the product of the author's imagination or are used fictitiously, and any resemblance to actual persons living or dead, business establishments, events or locales is entirely coincidental.
Any logistical, technical, procedural or medical mistake in this book is truly my own."

Cover by Octopi covers

Editing by MegEdits.com

❀ Created with Vellum

A NOTE FROM THE AUTHOR

The Dogs of War

If you haven't read the prequel, Genesis, and book 1, Chaos, first, I STRONGLY suggest that you do. These books take place in a very short span of time and they are tightly woven together.

You can find links to every platform on my website JMMadden.com .

And PLEASE sign up for my newsletter! I very rarely bother you, only with truly important stuff.

www.jmmadden.com/newsletter/

ACKNOWLEDGMENTS

I have to acknowledge my reader group. I love you guys! You make me so happy to be doing what I'm doing!

Family, you are awesome, of course.

Sandie, thank you for being the cheerleader that you are! You brighten my days!

Meg, excellent job, as always!

Sharon Griffiths Woodside, there's something in here for you. Let's see if you notice it. Lol!

Band Boosters, you all rock! Don't freak when you read the book!

FONTANA

Going back into the torture camp where he'd been so brutally abused is the last thing Navy SEAL Drake Fontana wants to do, but if there are other men being experimented upon he has to be the one to get them out. And he has to give them an option other than to be test subjects for the Silverstone Collaborative, the pharmaceutical company carrying out the diabolical experiments.

If he had his way, Fontana would go in alone, but he's assigned a team of retired, disabled military from the Lost and Found group. They all have strengths, but he hates being responsible for their safety. The most vital of the team is Jordyn Madeira. Scarred, the woman has fire in her blood and her heart, and she has contacts in the Amazon he could never find on his own.

More than that, though, Jordyn holds an immediate, dangerous attraction for Fontana. As the team crosses the jungle finding research camps and searching for survivors, he realizes that she is what his heart has always been longing for. Home. But Fontana has always had to fight for everything he's gotten in life, and Jordan's damaged heart will be no different.

CHAPTER ONE

Fontana woke early, knowing that his life was going to go to hell today. Perhaps literally.

The thought of returning to the jungle chilled him to the bone, but he didn't know any way around it. His life was the most fluid of the three remaining Dogs of War. Right this minute, he had the most freedom to go back to the camp to check for survivors.

As he blew out a slow breath, he tried to appreciate the irony, but it was hard. The camp where he'd been held prisoner for eight months, and where heinous things had been done to him, might hold other men right now, just as desperate to escape as he had been.

The four of them— Aiden, Wulfe, Rector and Fontana— had broken out almost two years ago, but he could remember the smell of the moist, loamy dirt beneath his bare feet, and the feel of the textured paint on the floor of his cell. He could remember the cold steel cuffs biting into his wrists and ankles as they abused him, knowing he was powerless to stop them.

Lifting his phone, he turned off the music app and

unhooked the power cord, then pulled the earbuds from his ears. His ear canals flexed and relaxed. If he could come up with some other way to go to sleep, he would because he knew it wasn't best for security, but it had to work for now. If the music was loud enough it would drown out the screams in his mind, and he had to have sleep. He'd been running almost constantly for the past few days as the Collaborative got closer to catching him.

Usually when he woke Aiden was already sitting at his computer console going over information, but he'd spent last night with Angela at her place. Fontana looked at his phone, wondering if Aiden had messaged them. Nope. Nothing. Wulfe was stretched on the couch, his long legs hanging over the edge and propped on the coffee table. His long arms were crossed over his broad chest and he slept with a frown on his face.

Fontana rolled up, stretching his back muscles. Normally he didn't mind sleeping on the floor, but the past couple of nights he'd been restless. Too much crap going on. It would have been nice to sleep in an actual bed. Maybe he could have relaxed.

He rolled to his feet, his right leg aching like a son of a bitch. It took a minute to get it loosened up. He glanced out the window on his way to the bathroom. It wasn't even dawn yet. His phone had said five-thirty on the dot, exactly what time he'd wanted to wake up. Their meeting at the Lost and Found offices wasn't until seven, but he needed some time to build momentum today. He wanted to be wide awake and completely coherent when he walked into that meeting room.

He had a feeling he was going to have to fight today, and he wanted to be ready. No one was stopping him from going back to Brazil. If there were men in that jungle, he was going to make sure they got out.

Jordyn didn't normally get nerves, but there was a different kind of energy in the building today. There was change in the air, heralded by the message from her boss Chad Lowell. He'd met her late last night when she'd come on station to change into her surveillance gear. He'd asked her some odd questions, but nothing she wasn't willing to talk about, and after he'd left she'd been scratching her head in confusion. He'd explained that it was in relation to a new op they were planning, and not to be surprised if she got called in for another meeting in the morning.

At 6 am, just before she'd gone off shift, the big boss, Duncan Wilde, had requested her presence in the big meeting room. Jordyn knew she'd been doing a good job, but anxiety still rolled through her. It wasn't very often that you got called in for meetings like this.

"No word on what it is?"

She looked at Drake Hardwick, also known as Zero, and shrugged. "I just know there's been a lot of activity through here recently. Not sure what it has to do with my mother's service in the Venezuelan army, though. We don't do out of country assignments, do we?"

Zero shrugged and scraped a hand over his nearly bald head, something he did often. The former SEAL had a few quirks, but he'd always given it to her straight up. Not that he had a whole lot more experience than she did at LNF. He'd been here six months, and she'd been here five. But she couldn't recall any out of state assignments, let alone out of country.

"I've never heard of any, but the company has been in business going on ten years. I'm sure they've done more than the mundane stuff we've been assigned."

Pulling his locker door open, he grabbed his tablet and truck keys, shoving them into his jeans pockets. It was a long drive to Colorado Springs where he lived with his new fiancée, and Jordyn knew he liked to listen to podcasts as he drove.

He shut the locker and turned to her, resting a hand on her tense shoulder. "Whatever it is, you'll kick ass like you always do. If you need anything, let me know."

She nodded. "Thanks, Zero."

Jordyn watched his strong back as he left the locker room, the handle of his large Bowie knife breaking the line of his shirt. The man was a hoss, big and muscular, and an invaluable addition to the graveyard shift. Scary smart, as well he should be; he'd been in the SEALs for fifteen years before joining LNF last year and he'd automatically settled into an instructor-type mentality. Nothing shook him, and he moved like he had hours to do anything. But he got every job done more quickly and easily than expected.

When Jordyn had hired on, she'd been tightly wound and anxious, but working with Zero over the months had mellowed her, if that were possible. She was naturally a busy person anyway, but he'd made her slow down and do things more economically.

She glanced at the black waterproof watch on her wrist. Ten more minutes. Maybe she should wander that way early. Fuck, the meeting room was twenty feet away. It wasn't like it would take her long to get there.

It just took her that long to gird herself for what was to come.

It had been four years since she'd been injured and left the Army. Four years of adapting to the changes on her face and body as the scars healed. Sometimes when she looked in the mirror she was taken aback, because she'd forgotten about it for just a moment in time. Then someone would do a double-take, or their mouth would drop open, and she'd remember all over again. When she met new people, she'd learned to just expect the horror-filled looks. It made it easier. The people that looked at her with acceptance in their eyes were few and far between.

Lost and Found was the first place where she didn't feel like a side-show freak. There were other men here with injuries similar to her own, as well as other women vets, and they'd all found a place for themselves here.

The guys here were all good guys and she'd gotten used to their looks. But she also knew that right now there were other men around the office that didn't work at LNF. And she'd heard through the grapevine that there was something big going on but no one had any details. It was just like the Army. Let the grunts run around in the dark while the top brass hoarded the flashlights.

She felt bad thinking that almost immediately. Duncan had been a better boss to her than that and she had no room to bitch. He'd made every accommodation to her needs he could, and she truly appreciated that.

It was just a hard transition; she'd *liked* the Army, the life of a soldier.

Staring at the clock, Jordyn counted down the time till there was less than a minute to get to the conference room. Straightening her black t-shirt in her BDUs, she strode down the hallway, then paused. She shook out her hands and knocked on the door. It was opened almost immediately by a tall, good-looking man with thick black hair and pale silver-blue eyes. Jordyn couldn't remember ever seeing him before. Walking past him, she surveyed the room.

There were six men total in the room, counting the door man, and one woman, Shannon Palmer. She only knew three of the men— Duncan Wilde, Chad Lowell and John Palmer, the three partners of the Lost and Found Investigative service. The other three men she didn't recognize, although one looked remarkably like John Palmer, with dark hair and dark eyes. There was also a startlingly handsome man sitting at the table, turned toward her. He had a thick head of golden curls and bright green eyes. There was brown stubble across his clamped jaw, like he hadn't shaved in the past couple of days.

There was also a manic intensity in his eyes that put her on guard. She wasn't sure what his deal was, but he looked like he was about to jump up and grab her and shake the crap out of her. She watched him out of the corner of her eye as she circled the table toward the friendliest face.

Shannon smiled at her as she slid into the chair and some of Jordyn's tension eased. Shannon had the kind of womanly personality that was built to nurture, and it wasn't just from having the twins. It seemed completely innate, and Jordyn admired that.

Shannon's energy was a nice buffer against everything else that was rolling toward her.

Chad caught her eye. "Thanks for coming in again, Jordyn. I hope we're not disrupting your schedule too much."

She shook her head, tucking her short hair behind her ear. "It's not a problem at all. I am curious why I'm here though."

Chad turned to look at Duncan, and the older man smiled at her, his brown eyes kind and watchful. "Chad tells me your mother was a helicopter pilot in Venezuela."

Well, that took her by surprise. "Yes, she was. She was a national hero for several years after she rescued the sitting president and most of his cabinet during a violent coup. The *presidente* was very appreciative, both of her looks and her skill, and turned her into a spokeswoman for the bravery of his administration."

"That must have been an interesting childhood," John murmured, his dark, dark eyes looking for her reaction.

Jordyn shook her head. "I wasn't even around then. It was many years before I was born here in the States." She could see the question forming in John's expression. "My mother fell in love with an American journalist and emigrated to the states decades ago, though she maintains dual citizenship, as do I."

"Does your mother still fly?" Duncan asked.

"Every day. She owns a private charter company out of San Diego."

The three partners shared a look, but it was Duncan who spoke. "Do you think she would be willing to fly an operation for us into the Amazon?"

Jordyn frowned, glancing at the faces along the table. If anything, the blond male's aggression had ramped up. He almost seemed to be vibrating in his chair.

"What is this for?"

Duncan sighed, looking at the man who looked so similar to John Palmer. The man nodded as if giving permission and Duncan turned back to her.

"We're planning a covert insertion into Guyana, Venezuela and Brazil to look for," he hesitated, moving a hand, "prisoners of war."

Jordyn scowled. "American?"

Duncan nodded, his expression grave. "American servicemen, as well as those from more than a dozen other countries, were forced to take part in an operation to create super soldiers, using a plant only found in the Amazon. Aiden, Wulfe and Fontana," he pointed at each man individually, "all broke out of the Brazilian camp almost two years ago. They took vital information that the company needs to continue producing the serum."

Jordyn held up a hand. "Wait. What company? I thought you said 'government'?"

Duncan gave her a slight smile. "The Silverstone Collaborative has been working with the government, well, ours and others, for the past several years. We weren't sure who exactly was involved until we had a final piece of information the men stole from the camp when they escaped. We've gone through the information and now know who is involved here stateside, as well as names of the servicemen roped into Project Spartan, as well as the locations of the other camps—there were three that we know of—where they were conducting the experiments."

Jordyn shook her head, stunned. "Are you serious?"

"I am," Duncan told her. "But we're on a time crunch right now. We have a small amount of lead time and we want to take advantage of it. Right now the company has no idea that we know about the other camps. We want to insert a team into the jungle to check for survivors."

Jordyn's mind raced to catch up with what he was saying. "Are we expecting combat?"

Duncan glanced at Aiden, who shrugged. "We hope not," the other man said, "but the teams are going to go in loaded for bear just in case."

Her adrenaline spiked at the thought of direct action. She'd been a damn good soldier and the thought of taking part in this got her blood pumping. Even when she'd been in the Intelligence Bureau she'd been in places she probably shouldn't have been. Arrangements would have to be made depending upon how long the operation went, but they couldn't have asked her to do this at a better time.

Wait, they hadn't asked for her. They'd asked for her mother.

"Well, my mother won't be able to do it. She's in Italy right now."

The men looked at each other, frowning.

"When will she be back?"

That was from the guy on the end, the blond that seemed

so tense. Rough and clipped, his voice grabbed her attention His fists were in front of him on the table, his knuckles turning white from the pressure.

The lights above them flickered and she glanced up, but they didn't do it again. "She won't be back for another month."

The lightbulb in the fluorescent light above her head exploded, raining glass down upon her. Shannon cried out and jumped away from the table. Jordyn covered her head instinctively, praying that that was the only thing that was going to happen. She waited, breath held, expecting the light fixture to fall on her head or something, but after the initial pop of explosion, nothing else happened. She lifted her head, surveyed the scene, then leaned over the carpet to shake glass out of her short hair. It was still all over her, though. Sliding out of the chair she stepped away from the table to shake out her clothes, careful not to get cut.

The three Lost and Found partners were looking at the other three men on the opposite side of the table, and Jordyn got the feeling that something was going on. Aiden and Wulfe, two of the men she didn't know, muscled the blond out of the room, and it looked like it took every bit of strength they had to do it. The big man was staring at her, his expression an odd mix of contrition and frustration and anger.

Jordyn straightened, planting her hands on her hips. "Pardon my French, gentlemen, but what the fuck just happened?"

Chad scowled and got up from the table to come around and make sure she was glass free. Jordyn didn't mind that he brushed a few flecks of glass from her shoulders and back.

Duncan was the one who cleared his throat, drawing her attention.

"Well, to put it bluntly, some of the experimentation that the company did was a success."

She stared at him, unwilling—unable— to believe what he was telling her.

"Are you saying that one of those men *made* that light fixture explode over my head?"

Duncan gave her a single nod. "They have developed some mental capabilities that no one has ever seen before and I believe that when their emotions are heightened, that power can leak. If I was to guess I would say that Fontana let a bit of his control slip. He's the most... determined to return to the jungle to check for survivors."

"Fontana, the blond," she clarified.

"Yes."

Jordyn stepped back, crossing her arms over her chest. Shannon sat tentatively in one of the chairs the men had vacated, her notepad ready. Chad used a yellow legal pad to sweep the remaining glass on the table into a waste basket before he went back to his chair.

Jordyn wondered what the hell she'd gotten herself into. LNF had seemed like a pretty plum job, working with other vets. No one passed judgement on her as soon as they saw her, and she was regarded with respect, which shouldn't even ever be an issue as a vet, but it was.

Duncan sighed and rocked back into his chair. "I guess we've kind of wasted your time this morning, Jordyn, and I apologize for that. It was a bit of a Hail Mary pass anyway, hoping that we had that kind of resource at our fingertips. You can go ahead and go home. We'll find another pilot. It was presumptuous to hope that your mother would help us anyway."

"Oh, I have no doubt she would have if asked, regardless of the political issues it could get her into." Sighing, she planted her hands on her hips. "My mother can't do it, but I know someone who will. I think I can even get you a chopper."

Duncan leaned forward, tilting his head. "You know someone who would be willing to do this?"

He didn't get it. "Yeah, me."

CHAPTER TWO

Fontana jogged on the treadmill, leg screaming with pain, trying to burn off some of his anxiety. For some reason it had peaked, today, and he wasn't sure exactly why.

Actually, he did, but he hated to admit it to himself. It was the woman. She'd knocked him off his game.

As soon as she'd walked into the room, he'd felt a charge go up his spine. He'd latched eyes on her and he'd been unable to look away. And it hadn't been because of her scars, which she had to be thinking.

The woman was a compact package of kinetic energy. She couldn't be more than an inch or two over five feet, tiny, but she was built strong. Her t-shirt strained over her upper half and there wasn't an ounce of fat on her. The lower half of her body looked just as strong, but curvy, her hips rounded nicely and her thighs looking long and athletic in spite of her height. She wore black BDUs, and a black t-shirt that hugged her full breasts. But even as strong as she was, she still managed to keep her femininity. Her thick blue-black hair was perfectly cut, longer in front and very short in the back, and her fingernails... he'd never been one to notice that kind of thing on a woman, but today he did. They were squared off and painted a deep burgundy-purple.

Fontana was drawn in by her eyes, though. They were thick with black lashes, and the iris was a rich hazel green color. Army green. Arched brows curved over her eyes, sleek. Her face was lean with high cheekbones, her lips surprisingly lush. Her coloring spoke to some type of Hispanic influence. In spite of her clothing and her attitude, she was most definitely all woman.

The burn scars that ran down the right side of her face spoke to a devastating injury some years ago. Dangerously close to her eye, the scars tugged the corner of the eye back, making the symmetry of her face a little off. The skin around her right ear was malformed, partially burned away at the top, but there were little diamond studs in the lobes. Her perfectly cut hair seemed to be a bit longer on this side, covering a patch of hairless skin on her scalp just above the ear. The rough scar tissue ran down her neck and beneath the collar of her t-shirt, and he wondered exactly how far the scarring went.

Fontana had seen injuries like that before on veterans, but never on a woman. His heart gave an unexpected twinge of sympathy for what she had to have gone through. He'd developed a callousness over the past few years and not a lot affected him, but the thought of her being damaged in some way made him curl his fists.

She'd walked across that room like she owned it, though. It was obvious she'd had to deal with stares for a long time and she'd learned to power through it. He loved the confidence it took to do that and he could feel the determination in her heart.

There was something more, though. She had a confidence she had fought for, over and over again. Being that diminutive in the Army she'd surely gotten some ribbing from Basic on.

Sitting at the table, she'd given them all considering looks. For the briefest moment her eyes had met his, and it had shaken him. There was something about the woman that roused him. He *wanted* her to notice him. Was that why he'd slipped? To draw her regard?

No, that didn't seem right. He wanted her to see him but he certainly didn't want to hurt her.

That was a little fucked up, Aiden murmured internally, looking up at him from the weight bench.

Fontana punched the button on the console to stop the belt. He stepped off the machine.

Yeah, it was fucked up. "Not sure what happened," he panted.

And he didn't, really. One minute he was ready to leap out of his chair and go kill something, and the next he was wondering if the woman's hair was as soft as it looked.

He needed to apologize to her, even though she couldn't help them.

With that thought in mind he turned toward the conference room. Wulfe stepped in front of him, hand up. "Where are you going, *hitzkopf*?"

"I'm just going to apologize, Wulfe, let me by. I've cooled off."

"I don't know," he said slowly, not budging an inch. "I think you are tired, yes?"

Fontana blinked, taking stock of his body. Yeah, he was feeling tired, and not just from the treadmill sprint. He was still tired from fighting Priscilla Mattingly and all of her mercenaries in the train depot two nights ago. That had taken a lot out of him, using that much mental and physical power. But they didn't have time to rest just yet. They needed to move while the Silverstone Collaborative was still reeling from Priscilla's death.

"I'm fine," he told his friend softly. "I'm more in control

now. I need to apologize to that woman. She might be the only way we can get into the country."

Wulfe shook his dark head. "No. If she doesn't work, we will find another way. Even if it's just you and I going in, we won't lose this opportunity."

Fontana eased back, reassured that he wasn't the only one pushing for this op to work. He just needed to remind himself that he wasn't alone.

As if in answer to his thoughts, Wulfe reached out and squeezed his shoulder, even going so far as to give him a back-slapping hug. Fontana took it, appreciating the big German's zeal.

"Get a drink, then we will go back."

They crossed to the coffee machine together and each poured a cup. Fontana dumped in sugar and an obscene amount of coffee creamer until the liquid almost overflowed the cup, then he slurped in a drink. As soon as it hit his stomach he was reminded that he hadn't eaten anything recently. Turning to the vending machines he looked for something to eat, but nothing really appealed to him.

Anxiety churned in his stomach like he was in trouble with the teacher again, or something. He slurped down more coffee. Then, looking at Aiden, he nodded. *I'm good to go.*

For a long moment Aiden just stared at him, then nodded and they headed back down the hallway.

When they walked into the conference room, his gaze immediately went to the compact woman across the room. She'd moved from her spot, obviously, and had a notepad in front of her. Her eyes turned guarded as they skimmed over him and she sat back in her chair, waiting.

"I'm sorry about that," Fontana told her softly. "It won't happen again."

She gave a single nod, then turned back to her notepad, silent.

"Gentlemen," Duncan greeted them. "Have a seat. We have a lot to talk about. Ms. Madeira has agreed to fly the op for us."

Fontana's eyes jerked back to her. She still sat in the chair calmly. "You're a pilot?"

"I am."

"Were you a pilot in the military?" Aiden asked.

"For a while. Till a crash took me down. And, no, I wasn't flying that time," she clarified, crossing her arms beneath her breasts.

In spite of the situation a grin tugged at Fontana's lips. He could read the aggravation in her posture. It was obvious she still harbored resentment for the other pilot that had been on the stick when she was injured.

She held up her small hands with their pretty nails. Scar tissue he hadn't seen before layered both her palms. "The Army considered this enough of a threat to safety that they grounded me, put me in Intelligence for the rest of my tour. But I still fly. My license is current and I do charters in Vail in my free time."

Fontana felt a surge of excitement. If they could get her a chopper in Venezuela they'd be set.

He looked at Aiden, who was in turn looking at the woman. "This is going to be dangerous," Aiden warned.

The woman shrugged, a glint of something flashing in her eyes. "I'm up for it. The Army didn't like my scars but they don't slow me down at all. I can do anything you need me to do and probably more than you expect. I saw combat many times and I never flinched. I'm also good with languages. I speak Spanish and Portuguese fluently, as well as half a dozen derivatives. It was why Intelligence snatched me up when I was injured. I would be an asset to the group."

"It sounds like we have the beginning of a plan," Aiden

said, and Fontana could hear the edge of excitement in his voice. They were all ready to get on this.

Jordyn turned to Duncan. "I don't think he should be in on this," she said firmly.

It took Fontana a moment to realize she meant him. Frustrated fury swept through him and it took every shred of control he had to not blow something up, which was exactly what she was waiting for. Her eyes had widened, as if she could feel the surge of his power. She sat ramrod straight in her chair, but her chin was up, determined.

"In spite of what happened here," Aiden told the woman, instinctively protecting his friend, "Mr. Fontana is a man to have at your back. I've trusted him with my life several times and he's never let me down. He's the one that broke us out of the camp to begin with."

Her gaze swung to Aiden and stayed there. She motioned to the light fixture. "And if he did that inside a helicopter, we could all be dead."

The rest of the group shifted uncomfortably, avoiding his eyes.

Fontana clenched his jaw, but he couldn't even blame her. He wanted to tell her that he'd travelled over a thousand miles, killed at least nine mercenaries, used his mental abilities more in the past forty-eight hours than he had in the past three months, all on about three hours of sleep, but he didn't know if she'd believe him. He looked her in the eye. "I'm tired," he admitted, letting her see it in his face. "More tired than I've been in a long time. I've given more of myself in the past week than I ever have before. But I can't rest knowing there might be men out there being tortured like I was, living in a cage barely big enough for a dog. Now that we have the information we have to move, no matter how tired I am. If you don't take me I'll find a way to get there on my own."

Jordyn could see the absolute weariness in the man's eyes, and she felt herself softening in spite of her determination not to. She didn't owe this man anything, but her heart was suddenly interfering with her mind. When had it started doing that when it came to work?

She stared into his face, trying not to allow him to suffer with desperate hope, but she knew how it could be. When there was something driving you that wouldn't allow you to rest. When that one thing was so important you allowed your health to suffer for it.

That was there in his pretty clover green eyes. Her determination to be a hardass crumbled. The room faded from around them as she focused on his expression.

"You realize that if you do something like that in a helicopter, flying only five hundred feet in the air, we will die. And everyone we might rescue could die."

He nodded once, crossing his arms over his heavy chest. "I am aware of that. It won't happen."

She stared at him for a few more long moments before turning to look at Duncan. Her boss seemed to understand her expression.

"Okay, so we're set," he said. "Brian will be in in a little while to let us know about the money situation. Jordyn, if you can do what you need to do to arrange for the helicopter?"

"You have a chopper?" Fontana breathed.

Jordyn couldn't help the small smile as she glanced at him. "I do. There. Not here. We need to figure out how to connect the dots."

Wulfe stepped forward. "The Terberger corporate plane is waiting for use."

They all looked at each other, wondering at how all the pieces had begun to fall together.

"Jordyn," Duncan said, "while we're finalizing details and collecting materials, why don't you go pack a bag. Prepare for a few days in country. And call whoever it is you need to get the chopper."

Pushing to her feet she gave him a mock salute. "Will do, First Sergeant."

With a final glance at Fontana she left the conference room, her heart racing with excitement. She had a lot to do and little time to do it.

The men settled in to plan. Duncan's experience was invaluable for this aspect. No, he hadn't led anything recently, but he hadn't forgotten anything about when he had. He weighed that experience in with the Dogs of War's more recent altercations with the Collaborative, and their jungle knowledge, and they came up with a plan.

They had to go to Venezuela first for the helicopter. Jordyn had told them it would be a twelve-seater, which was perfect. That would give them room for a six man team, plus gear. It would also give them a bit of room if they needed for sick or injured.

Brian Calvert had set up a trust with the money Dr. Shu had been given by the company. It was a substantial amount, well over fifteen million, and they had plenty of money to finance the operation, which they were now calling Absolution. Fontana would be in charge of Team Alpha.

Everything was coming together.

Duncan put out an all-call to his men looking for volunteers for a high risk, out of the country, armed operation. Within just a couple of hours, Fontana was meeting four men that would be on the team. Duncan briefed him on all of their injuries before they entered the conference room, promising that none of them would impede the op in any way. Fontana would have to see... he didn't mind using former military or disabled vets as long as none of them got him killed.

The first man to walk into the room had the self-assured, confident stride of a man who knew what he could do. Drake Hardwick was a recent hire from the Navy SEALs. Tall and broad-shouldered, he was a badass from his nearly bald head to his cowboy boots. The fact that he had only been retired from the Navy for about six months made him a shoe-in for the op. And Fontana could see the confidence in his expression. More importantly he could *feel* the confidence in the other man. He'd seen shit and lived to tell about it.

Kenneth Bracken was a former Army Ranger, six-four, with night dark skin, massive biceps and a blinding, easy smile. For a moment the easy going personality, plus the Ranger tattoo peeking from beneath his t-shirt, reminded Fontana of TJ, in spite of the vastly different appearance. Big Kenny, or Kenny, as he preferred to be called, had done jungle ops before and had no worries about the prosthetic on his right leg.

"Nah," he chuckled. "This sucker is cutting edge. I run in this, swim in it. It's completely self-contained."

Pulling his pant leg above the knee he knocked on the lower section of the black carbon fiber leg for emphasis. "And the battery that helps power it is recharged by my movement."

"I'm pretty jealous of it, actually," Chad admitted.

Eric Payne was a smaller guy, more compact, his mental shields solid. Everyone was smaller than Zero and Big Kenny, but Payne didn't seem intimidated. There was a confident air to him as he moved into the room, his dark eyes steady, like he'd dealt with looming military before. Kind of made Fontana think of the fiery Jordyn Madeira as she'd rolled into the conference room like she'd owned the place. Payne had been a Marine sergeant years ago, until a sniper in Kandahar had put a bullet through his left shoulder joint, completely obliterating the arm. He wore a cross-chest brace to support the black, full-arm prosthetic he wore, as well as the sidearm he carried, easily accessible in a cross-draw for his right hand.

Shane DeRossett was the youngest of this group, another former Marine, standing with his hands on his hips and chest forward, a smile splitting his handsome face. He had a Texas A&M hat planted on his thick brown hair and reflective wraparounds over his eyes. Duncan had said that Shane was a go-getter but plagued with some vertigo from the loss of his right eye and a percussive concussion in an IED blast just a couple of years ago. Of all of the men that had volunteered, Duncan worried that he would be their weak link, simply because he hadn't been in therapy as long.

The statement had surprised him and impressed him. If the guy was cognizant enough to know that he needed help, hopefully he'd be just as aware on an op.

Fontana appreciated the ballsy attitude, though. He watched the younger man closely but didn't see any hint that DeRossett had any issues. More importantly he didn't feel any anxiety plaguing the younger man.

The volunteers hadn't exactly been crawling out of the woodwork. Most of the people that worked at LNF had gotten used to a slower, less-dangerous way of life, and John had said that many were married now, with young families. Fontana couldn't blame them for not wanting to possibly jump into the jungle from a helicopter and face armed mercenaries.

Fontana knew there was a very real chance of death with this op, but it would kill him not to *know*, for sure, as definitive *fact*, that there were no other servicemen being tortured as he had been. The past two years had been difficult, waiting for something to happen. It was no one's fault, per se, other than the company's, just keeping them on edge and apart for that long.

Now, though, things were happening, and it was hard to rein in his excitement. The men that had volunteered were top-notch and even if the entire operation was a bust, he would enjoy getting back out into the field.

Aiden began explaining to the men exactly what would be required of them, and broached the subject of the enhancements. The men seemed leery at first, then skeptical. Zero's gaze flicked to the trash can, where the pile of glass had been swept away, and the bare fluorescent fixture above their heads. It was obvious something had happened, but Fontana wasn't going to volunteer the information.

"Let's just say that if we get into a pickle we might have a bit of an advantage," he murmured, confident in his own skills.

"Sounds fine to me," Kenny said, reclining back in the office chair as much as he could.

The rest nodded or shrugged, accepting. They would see what he would do in action before judgement.

Jordyn walked into the room to a round of hellos, then rousing excitement when Fontana informed them she would be flying them in. She waved a hand negligently before looking at Aiden and Duncan. "It's a go. She'll be fueled up and ready to go by the time we get there."

Everyone looked back and forth, and they all realized that the entire op was a go, not just pieces of it. Fontana stood. "Let's bug out."

CHAPTER THREE

John handed Fontana and Madeira each a satellite phone. "Just in case your radios cut out. They're already programmed with the numbers. You can drop a pin on each location and we'll be able to follow you, too."

He also handed Madeira a small, handheld gray box. "That has the supposed locations of all three camps, and it's so much more accurate than the sat phones. You should be able to measure in feet rather than miles."

Brian handed Fontana a small zipped men's shower bag. "Grease for palms," he grinned. "If you need more, call me and I'll direct you to one of the banks down there for a pickup."

Then he handed each of the other members of the team separate envelopes with a stack of Venezuelan bolivars inside. Jordyn also got a company card that could be used for fuel.

Duncan watched them get ready and felt himself grow a little envious. It had been a long time since he'd been on the ground and in the heat of battle, but his heartbeat had picked up like he was about to jog into the fray. He looked at John, who had to be feeling the need even sharper. Yep, there it was, that longing in his dark eyes. As if sensing the need, Shannon rested her hand on her husband's shoulder. When John looked up at her, Duncan was so thankful that the two of them had found each other.

Aiden seemed to be struggling with being left behind as well, and Angela wasn't here to distract him. Duncan wasn't sure where the detective was. Probably back at work today, if her bruises from the altercation with the Collaborative's mercenaries had faded enough.

Wulfe, the big German, stood off to the side with his arms crossed over his chest, watching the men gather their gear. His expression was inscrutable. So far he'd been the most remote of the group.

They all had jobs to do. That was what they needed to remember. Yes, Alpha Team was heading into the jungle, but they had plenty to do on their own end. Aiden would be tracking their movements through GPS if they had a signal, and Wulfe would be heading back to Arlington to watch the main players in the company. There had to be some kind of fallout from Priscilla Mattingly's death, and Duncan wanted eyes on it when it happened.

He'd been happy enough running his business and dealing with the day to day issues that popped up, but things had just gotten serious. He looked at Aiden and again, no matter how many times he looked at him, it was shocking to see him cleaned up and engaged with the people around him. There was no doubt that he was, though, and he had both vindication and justice on his mind.

With some final waves, the team clattered onto the elevator, each carrying bulging bags with helmets attached. They were all armed with sidearms and long black cases, which he knew were probably H&K MP5s, or some similar submachine gun. The weapon was sturdy and dependable, and the mags interchangeable if things got hot. Duncan was glad they had something to take with them anyway. It had only been a few months since Preston Harper began updating their armory.

Payne carried a camera bag. It was one of his hobbies and he'd offered to document anything they found. It was an excellent idea, because there was no way they'd be able to transmit video or anything. it was his personal equipment, though, so he'd have to make note to have Preston buy something for future use.

They needed to keep all of the money separate, and legal. If the Collaborative started looking into them for any weakness, Duncan didn't want them to find anything that could be used against LNF.

What kind of hornet's nest was he poking?

Jordyn laughed as Zero knocked into her shoulder. They were sitting in one of the plushest private planes she'd ever been in, and had just taken off, headed toward Venezuela, the country of her heart. They'd have to refuel before they got there, but it would still be easier logistically than trying to fly commercial.

"This is the life, huh?"

She looked around at the cushy accommodations. The seats were recliners, basically, nothing like a regular coach class plane. An attendant was handing out beverages. "It is pretty nice. I wouldn't get used to it, though."

"I know. Sounds like we could be dropping into a shit show. What do you think about all this?"

Jordyn shrugged, her gaze drifting over Fontana at the front of the plane. "Listening to those three, they seem pretty convincing. I think if there's a chance that there are American servicemen being held captive someone needs to do something about it, and why shouldn't it be us?"

Zero nodded, shifting to prop an ankle on the opposite knee. "True. It'll be nice to do something a little more active."

Jordyn chuckled. "I'll remind you that you said that when we're tromping through the jungle in the rain and the mosquitos are eating us alive."

Zero sighed, rubbing a hand over his head. "I know." He grinned. "Izzy wasn't happy with me when I told her what I was doing."

The sweet, slightly eccentric blonde was good for her buddy. He'd changed a lot in the short time she'd known him, and it had to be because of Izzy. "Well, you guys have pretty much been attached at the hip since you retired, right?"

"Yeah, as much as possible working around her shifts at the hospital. It's crazy Jordyn, but I'm not tired of her."

Jordyn chuckled. "Well, that's good to hear."

"I'm serious." He rolled his head to look at her. "I used to be an asshole— cold— I won't lie. I could take a woman then leave her. But Izzy takes everything I give her and spins it around till I'm laughing my fool head off."

Grinning, Jordyn nodded. "The right love will do that for you."

"Have you ever been in love?"

She shook her head. "Nope. Lust, but never love."

"You ought to try it sometime."

She snorted. "Yeah, because there are so many men knocking on my door right now..."

Zero blinked at her. "That sounded a little self-pitying."

Jordyn clenched her jaw, conscious of every single scar on the side of her face. The side next to him. "Not self-pitying. Realistic."

Zero sighed. "I don't think you look as bad as you think. A couple of the guys have asked me if you're attached."

She gave him a skeptical look, appreciating what he was doing.

"That Fontana has been watching you a lot. Do you know him?"

She shook her head, her gaze drifting forward in spite of herself. Fontana's seat was turned as he spoke to one of the other men and she thought he might have just been looking at her, but she couldn't be sure. "No, I don't know him. Just his type."

"Yeah, he seems a little wild, doesn't he?"

"Yeah."

That was the word. Wild. His golden blond hair was wild with curls, and something about his personality seemed wild as well. She couldn't put her finger on exactly why. But seeing him standing at the base of the plane steps had given her a thrill. Fontana was as big as Zero, but seemed more...feral. She knew he had been a Navy SEAL, but it was like his nature had progressed beyond the training, if that made sense. She thought about telling Zero what had happened to her in the conference room, and the subsequent apology, but then closed her mouth. He would see what she had in a while.

CHAPTER FOUR

By the time they touched down at a small airport outside of the capital city of Caracas, their tension had ratcheted up. They were all eager to get moving, but it had taken them an entire day to get here.

Fontana looked at the fading light of the sunset and cursed inside. He had no idea what the woman's skill level was, but he doubted she would be willing to fly a private chopper at night. The chances that it would be equipped with night flying gear were slim; that was a military thing.

He glanced at her. She had come off the plane looking refreshed and eager, but then, she'd been able to sleep on the plane. He hadn't. The big guy with her, Zero, tried to take her packed bag, but she waved him off. Then flipped him the bird. Fontana snorted. The two of them had an interesting relationship.

The woman moved to one of the airport attendants and started speaking, waving one hand toward the lights of the city. She nodded a couple of times and he noticed that she kept the damaged side of her face away from the man as he spoke. With a final nod, she turned back to the men gathered behind her. "There's a decent hotel less than a mile away. He's going to call us a shuttle."

Fontana acknowledged the man with a wave. "Gracias," he said.

That was the smartest move. They could get started early in the morning. Fontana looked at Madeira, glad to have a reason to talk to her. "Do you need to call your contact?"

She shook her head. "I told him it would probably be tomorrow before he saw me."

Fontana gave a nod. "Okay, then. Let's get to the hotel."

The shuttle arrived just a few minutes later and Fontana let Madeira take the lead in dealing with the driver. He knew a bit of Spanish, but it didn't roll off his tongue as fluently as it did hers. She laughed with the driver, hanging over the back of his seat as the group piled on, looking dangerous. Maybe that was why she was being so friendly, to balance out their darkness. The thought made him shake his head.

The six of them *were* dangerous. Whether their weapons could be seen or not, there was an internal switch that had flipped as soon as they'd landed. Yes, most of them were friends and would joke around, but right now it was time to punch in and get down to business.

The driver apparently said something to Madeira that caught her off guard, because she blinked her big eyes. She pressed a hand to her chest as if in question. Fontana didn't hear the words, exactly, but she bowed her head graciously. It was a strange interaction and he wanted to ask her about it, but he didn't have any right to pry. It probably didn't relate to the current operation.

The shuttle pulled into the paved loop of a decent looking hotel. It was several stories tall and well-lit, and seemed to cater to the more affluent. Not the most expensive in the area, but definitely one of the busiest. That suited him fine because it would be easier for them to blend in. The driver unfastened his seatbelt and tried to help them with their luggage, but they waved him away. There were dangerous items in their packs and it was the individual's responsibility to guarantee their safety. A little lost as to what to do, the man turned back to Madeira.

She gave him a smile and pressed a folded bill into his palm, obviously thanking him for the ride. But the driver shook his head adamantly, shoving the money back to her. With a reproachful look at the line of photos of young children taped above the windshield, she pushed the money back into his hand. The man took it with a grateful bow of his head, and a movement from his heart to hers.

Madeira took the blessing with a smile, then headed toward the hotel lobby.

Fontana let her make the arrangements. It was why they'd brought her after all, but it gave him a reason to just watch her. Fontana looked around at the other customers. Several were watching Fontana's team and it put him on edge. A brightly lit sign arched over a doorway to the right. It didn't matter what country you were in or what language the signs were written in, bars were recognizable the world over. He lifted his chin toward the group. "Let's see if they have food in there guys."

They all knew he was just looking to get away from the crowd— they'd eaten on the plane— but they went along with him anyway, just for solidarity. He caught Madeira's gaze as they walked by and she gave him the tiniest nod. She'd picked up the scrutiny of the crowd on them as well. It didn't apply to her because with her coloring and obvious fluency she looked like she belonged there.

He'd worked long and hard to learn to block out external noise, but sometimes it was harder than others, like now. As tired as he was, his shields weren't perfect, and the anxiety in the crowd had begun to get to him.

Venezuela itself seemed... on edge or something. Like one shoe had dropped and they were all waiting for the other one to fall simply because they were used to being beat down.

The curiosity around them had spiked as well. Payne's prosthetic arm and the fact that DeRossett refused to take his glasses off in the hotel had drawn attention, and he didn't want to deal with it.

Fontana chose a fairly dark corner on the far side of the room and moved a couple of the square tables together, enough that they could sit as a group. A harried waitress wandered over when she had a minute, giving the group a wide-eyed look.

"Dos Equiis," Fontana ordered, recognizing the bottle on the wall. He didn't normally drink but it would at least give him something to do with his hands. Hell, it had been years since he'd actually sat down with a group of teammates and just shot the shit. He looked around the men assembled. They joked among themselves like he and his old SEAL team used to. There was a bit of distance between him and them though. He was more than just a *new guy*, he was the unknown element in the group.

"How did you all end up at Lost and Found?" he asked when there was a break in the conversation.

The men all looked at each other. "I think we all applied," Payne said, leaning back in his chair. He wore a black t-shirt, the arm on full display. Even in the bar they still had people watching them. Just not as many. "I heard about the position from a buddy of mine I'd been stationed with."

"Same," Kenny said, tipping back the bottle of Coke he'd asked for.

"My brother told me about it. He lives in Colorado and had seen a newspaper article about the company," DeRossett said, tipping back in his chair. Even in the dimness of the bar he still wore the wraparound shades. "Zero is the only one hired recently that doesn't have an actual disability."

The man in question shrugged, light glinting off his shiny head. "I think I was mentally disabled for staying on the Teams so long when all the young studs moved in."

They all laughed at him, nodding their heads.

DeRossett leaned toward Fontana to stage-whisper conspiratorially. "He doesn't actually shave his head. He's bald as a cue ball."

Fontana grinned, liking the young kid.

"He does that so Izzy can find him in the night. It can be pitch black and that head will shine," Kenny said, grinning and leaning over to pound a fist into Zero's shoulder.

The older man grunted and lifted an eyebrow. "Just wait, Kenny. I don't think you're far off from taking a razor to your head."

"Man," the big man said, running a hand over his thick, short, black hair, "this shit ain't going nowhere. It's thick as it always was."

Zero lifted his beer bottle. "Okay, buddy," he said, but the tone of his voice said he was humoring Kenny.

Kenny ran his hand over his head again, his smile not so sure, and the men laughed even louder.

That was how Madeira found them, laughing and joking with one another. She had a stack of hotel room keycards in her hands. "You boys get to double up. Two queen beds each room. Fontana, you and I both get singles. Suck it up, kids because we'll be in the jungle tomorrow. This will be the most comfortable night you'll have until we get back on the plane headed home."

A couple of them groaned, knowing how right she was. Fontana wondered when she'd last been in the jungle.

"How long since you last visited?"

She glanced at him, her eyes calm. "A couple years. I have family in the area."

"Family with helicopter connections?"

She blinked at him, then turned to ask Zero a question.

Fontana frowned, wondering if she'd just shut him down or what? Well, there was no wondering. She had shut him down. Period. He'd tried to make a joke but apparently it had been too long since he'd tried and he was lame as fuck.

Fontana looked at the bottle in front of him. He'd peeled most of the label off the bottle, but had drank less than an inch of beer. Other things weighed on his mind and he didn't want his brain fogged by alcohol. The group's emotions were pressing on his shields.

No one else seemed to be drinking a lot either.

"So, what kind of things are we going to be dealing with when we go in?" Zero asked, leaning forward on his elbows.

All eyes turned to Fontana, and he sighed. "I hope nothing, but we just had an altercation with the Chief Operations Officer of Silverstone. I'm sure you saw the news articles?"

A couple of them nodded.

"That wasn't how she died, or her men,' he admitted, "but it's how the Collaborative spun it. The fact that they can disappear more than a dozen bodies and no one is the wiser is disturbing. It means they have support from government, probably local, state *and* federal. And definitely more resources than we do."

Fontana looked around the group, appreciating the stalwart acceptance. He'd just told them his team had taken out over a dozen people but they hadn't even blinked. It was nice working for former military like this. They knew what needed done, and it wasn't always pretty. It wasn't always socially acceptable.

"Are you sure there's even going to be a camp?" Payne asked.

Fontana shook his head. "This information we're working from is a couple years old. We're not sure of anything. But we have to check it out just to be sure."

"What did they do to you?"

The softly voiced question slipped in, even through the noise of the bar. He glanced at Madeira before he continued messing with the bottle. "Everything. The drug they were testing, Ayahuasca, was actually having a positive effect on us, but the testing was brutal. Most of the people in my group died within the first few months. Those that survived were tested more and more strenuously. They moved on from illnesses to injuries, sometimes devastating, because they wanted to simulate what might happen in wartime conditions. Broken legs, broken backs. Gunshot wounds. Knife wounds. We recovered from it all."

She lifted a brow, obviously skeptical.

"And when we recovered we were stronger. Mentally stronger. That was the part that they didn't know. Yes, they enhanced our bodies, but they also enhanced our minds."

The group in front of him still didn't shift and he wondered if they understood what he was telling them.

"How strong are you?" Madeira asked.

Fontana gave her a long look. "Strong enough to make you do things you'd never recover from. Strong enough to knock out the power in this room if I wanted to. Maybe even the hotel."

Madeira sat back in her chair, crossing her arms beneath her chest. Finally, he thought, he was getting through to her. "Do you plan on making us do things we prefer not to?"

"No," he said firmly. "I've been at the mercy of men who didn't give a damn about me or my choices, and I would never force another person to deal with what I did. That's why I want to get in and make sure no one is suffering at their hands."

Fontana took a swig of his warm beer, looking away from her penetrating gaze. The guys he could deal with, but there was something about Madeira's eyes that made him want to tell her everything. Right now, he'd given them the surface facts, but there was a reservoir full of secrets he'd never told anyone, not even Aiden or Wulfe. If he had his choice, those details would go to the grave with him.

So, the team's mental security was good with him. He would never intentionally invade anyone's privacy, because it was so precious to him. If possible, he would monitor the people around the team, though. Their safety was his priority.

A young man wandered up to their table, speaking to Madeira in rapid-fire Spanish. Wincing, she turned to the young man and forced a smile. Fontana frowned at the interaction. It was similar to what had happened with the bus driver, but his basic Spanish wasn't allowing him to follow everything said. The kid was excited though, and broadcasting loud enough there was no blocking him out. Then the kid pulled out a cellphone and held it out at arm length. Madeira said no and held up a hand, her anxiety spiking loud enough to hit Fontana, but the kid took the picture anyway.

Fury overwhelmed Fontana and before he could think better of his actions he pulled the kid away from Madeira, sending a zap of power through the cellphone as he pushed him away. The kid took the brush-off good naturedly and returned to his friends, thumbing through the cellphone to show them his prize. When he realized the phone was fried, he gave an outraged cry, turning to look back at their group.

Fontana sat back down, looking at the woman across from him. Her expression had turned guarded, wary.

"Want to tell me what's going on here? Why are these people stalking you like a celebrity?"

She sighed. "Because I kind of am," she admitted. She looked at the group of men she worked with. "My mother was a war hero in Venezuela. She flew the president to safety when there was a violent coup attempt. When the dust had settled, the president knew that she would be seen as a rallying point for bravery and courage. She's very beautiful and well-spoken, and he used her for a long time in his propaganda. Then she fell in love with my father and moved to the States."

She paused for a moment, glancing around the bar and through the door to the lobby. No one seemed to be watching them at that second.

"My mother brought me here many times when I was growing up, proud of our heritage and family. When I was injured in the helicopter crash, they got ahold of the information and considered it courageous, even though I wasn't in *their* Army. My scars are proof that I am as brave as my mother. The last time I came down things got a little wild. My picture was everywhere. Paparazzi stalked me the entire time I was here, taking pictures of my scars and broadcasting them."

She scratched a fingernail over the surface of the table and Fontana knew how difficult that had to have been. Scars were a very personal subject to most military, and to have them glorified like that had to have been hard. He ached for her.

Madeira glanced up, as though she could feel his empathy.

The men were silent for a long moment, before all four broke into laughter. Madeira scowled until Zero clapped a hand on her shoulder. "I've been working with a celebrity and I didn't know it! Fuck!"

"They need to come to Denver," Kenny laughed. "We'll show them courage and an *assload* of scars!"

"So if I show them where my eye used to be, you think I can pick up girls here?"

Madeira shook her head at them. "You guys are such assholes."

But she ended up laughing, her smile broad on her face. Fontana stared, struck with how pretty she looked, with humor filling her face with joy.

Then he shook himself. He didn't need that kind of distraction on this operation.

"I suggest we head to bed and get an early start in the morning."

They all agreed and trouped out of the bar. Zero and Payne took a room, then DeRossett and Kenny. He caught Madeira's gaze, making sure she was as solid as she seemed to be. "I'll see you in the morning."

With a wave, she swiped the keycard and let herself into the darkness.

Jordyn had to drag herself away from the hotel hallway, where Fontana stood watching her. Nothing had been said outright, but something was humming between them. This wasn't the time or place for any kind of attraction to spark, but it seemed to be happening anyway.

There was a way he looked at her, intense and steady, that seemed to be looking into her soul. Hell, if he had mental powers like he said, maybe he was. No, she seemed to trust him instinctively when he said he would not influence them.

She wasn't sure how she felt about the whole mental thing. There was no denying what had happened in the conference room, or his apology later. Duncan and the other two LNF partners believed them, so she was trying to keep an open mind, but it was hard. It seemed so farfetched.

Jordyn wouldn't put it past the government though. During her time in the Army she'd seen some shady shit. The grunts in her platoon had gone on some wild goose chases and lost a lot of men at the whims of some guy in a suit, five thousand miles away. But that was what they'd signed up for.

But what had happened to the kid's cellphone downstairs? She hadn't done anything to it, but she wondered if Fontana hadn't sent a tiny little zing of power through it or something. Like the bulb over her head the other day. The thought that he might have done that for her made her feel appreciative of having someone like him on her six.

She dropped her bag to the bed and moved around the room, checking out the amenities. The window was locked shut, which she didn't like. It was always good to have an escape route.

The bathroom was clean white tile and gray counter. Very nice.

Unzipping her pack, she pulled out her overnight pack. Through the years she'd learned how to pack efficiently and correctly, using every bit of spare room in her bag for essentials like food and water and baby wipes; more ammo for her sidearm.

She glanced at the connecting door between her room and Fontana's, wondering what he was doing right now. Cleaning his weapon? She snorted as her imagination inserted a totally inappropriate image of him stroking himself. It had been a long time since she'd been attracted to a man, and this was entirely the wrong time for it to happen. Digging out her toothbrush and floss, she headed into the bathroom to get ready for bed.

CHAPTER FIVE

They met in the lobby before dawn the next morning. Fontana looked at the team, all clear-eyed and ready to go. Most of them were dressed in some version of black or jungle camo, mostly BDUs and t-shirts. Even Payne's black arm looked tactical. There were no weapons showing but it was very apparent as the early morning workers swirled around them that they were a dangerous crew. Madeira, as diminutive as she was, looked like she could chew nails. Maybe she hadn't slept well last night.

In spite of himself he'd listened for her movements next door. He'd heard her brush her teeth and flush the toilet, then the sound of rustling as she'd climbed into bed. And he'd heard her rustling hours later as he laid upon his own bed waiting for the tiniest sliver of sleep. It had been tempting to knock on the connecting door and see if she wanted to talk. But what did they really have to chat about? She was leery of him, and he couldn't blame her. He probably would have done something inappropriate. Again.

Something about the woman seriously appealed to him though. Yeah, he'd hooked up with a woman when he'd gotten back into the states, but she hadn't been serious. He'd had to fuck her to prove that he could, that *that* hadn't been taken away from him in that damn camp. If it had, he would have offed himself. No hesitation.

Madeira appealed to him as a woman should appeal to him, though, and for the first time in years he felt desire, and need for human touch.

He watched as she turned on her boot heel and headed through the lobby, her lush little ass jiggling a little with her movements. Dragging his gaze away he looked up, straight into Zero's cold eyes. The other man gave him a dangerous look before turning to follow Madeira, effectively blocking Fontana's view.

There was a shuttle waiting to take them where they needed to go. Madeira leaned against the railing, speaking to the driver as the men filed on. Fontana brushed against her but didn't actually mean to. She reacted like she'd touched a live wire, though, jerking toward the windshield to give him more room to pass.

"Sorry," he murmured.

He settled into a seat a few rows back, his gaze falling to her naturally. She gave the driver a smile and nod, then headed to the seat she'd chosen.

The bus trundled out of the hotel turnaround and onto the road. Madeira had said that her uncle's place was several miles outside of the city, so it would take them a while to get there. Fontana watched the city scenery roll by. It was surprisingly heavily populated here in Caracas, with tall white skyscrapers crowding the expansive blocks. There was a lot of homelessness as well, with tent cities here and there. They seemed to be traveling through a fairly destitute area. It didn't smell great either, like the city's septic system was at capacity.

Soon, though, the cityscape gave way to suburbs and then

some farm areas. Even the farming communities seemed to be struggling, though. Trees began filling the area and the vehicles became fewer and farther between.

Eventually the driver turned south and they travelled for about fifty miles, but as the roads degenerated it felt more like five hundred. Finally, they slowed and pulled in through a line of trees. Fontana assumed this was a driveway because it was even rougher than the road. It seemed like they travelled another ten miles before the forest began to clear and several long, white, rust-stained buildings popped up.

Madeira leaned forward, obviously excited. As the shuttle pulled to a stop, an old man came out of one of the buildings, grease-stained blue jeans hanging down on his ass as he sauntered toward them. He was wiping his hands on an even more heavily stained rag, but his dark face split into a bright smile as Madeira walked toward him. With no hesitation she wrapped her arms around the old man, hugging him like she hadn't seen him for years. Which, Fontana supposed, she hadn't.

Fontana tipped the driver and gathered Madeira's bag and weapons case as well as his own, then stepped off into the heat. It was only a bit past midmorning, but the humidity was beginning to boil. He glanced around the compound.

Fontana tried not to be judgmental because he knew it was hard to make a living in Venezuela, but the buildings of the 'airport', if it could be called that, looked to be damn near falling down. There wasn't a single one that appeared to be square. The tin siding was dented and dinged, which in this humid environment, produced rust. There was a lopsided, heavy duty towing truck parked against one wall of the longest building that had to be older than he was, and there appeared to be a car junkyard against the wall of one of the others. There was no way any of those things ran... He hoped the helicopter they would be entrusting their lives with was in better condition.

Madeira was gushing Spanish faster than he'd ever heard anyone speak, and the old man was nodding and reaching down to cup her cheek. Leaning in, he pressed a kiss first to one side, then the other, before looking up at the men behind her.

"Mi Tío Pablo, gentlemen. My uncle. Brother of my mother. Pablo can work on anything that can fly. And even if it doesn't fly, it might by the time he's done with it," she laughed.

Pablo waffled his hand in the air. "If we have luck," he said smiling broadly.

Madeira introduced the men and they all shook hands. Fontana liked the comfortable old man. It didn't seem like anything would shake him.

"Is she ready, Tío?"

He cupped her cheek again. Madeira was obviously a beloved niece. The man nodded and motioned toward the hangar again. "Of course, niña. She has been waiting for you!"

Madeira headed toward the hangar, her steps almost running. It was only as she heard the shuttle toot as it drove away that she apparently remembered her gear. "Oh, no!" she cried, turning toward the retreating vehicle.

Fontana waved the bag and case for her, and she grinned at him. "I thought I was in trouble," she gasped, taking them from him before jogging away. "Thanks, Fontana!"

Suddenly, Fontana found himself entranced with more than her ass. That smile directed at him made heat curl up through his gut, and it wasn't from the jungle.

Following along behind as they headed into the hangar, he wasn't sure what to expect, but it certainly wasn't the spotless, well-lit garage he walked into, or the equally spotless dark gray helicopter sitting on a transport dolly. The windows gleamed and it was obvious that the machine had been well taken care of. It wasn't new, but the bird carried her age well.

"Gentlemen," Madeira breathed, her eyes alight with excitement as she began the introduction. "This is Margarita. She's going to take us wherever we need to go, and she will bring us home safely. Because she loves my uncle as much as I do."

"Dayam…" Shane breathed, lifting his glasses for the barest moment to look at the gleaming machine.

"I think I'm going to love Margarita," Kenny said, sauntering close to look inside. "We got all kinds of room in here."

"This is a Ka-62 medium duty helicopter," Madeira said, her Army green irises lit with pride. "She's used as a Medevac 'copter and for the oil and gas industry, and she has some of the most amazing bells and whistles you've ever seen on a craft."

"How the hell did you get your hands on it?" Payne asked, arms crossed over his chest.

Madeira grinned. "It was actually given to my mother, a gift. Like I said, she's a national hero. She has clearance at every airport. Because, you know, *national hero*."

The men snorted and Zero reached out to rest a hand on her shoulder. "Let's get this bird in the air. We have a long day ahead of us."

Pablo backed the rumbling, lopsided, heavy duty truck back to the dolly and for the first time Fontana noticed the odd hitch. It snapped into the link on the back of the truck. Pablo put the truck in gear and pulled the dolly forward. The tarmac was old but again, in pristine condition. They walked along behind as the old man pulled the gleaming helicopter far enough away from the buildings not to cause too much draft.

Madeira watched the helicopter every second and he could see how much she loved the chunk of metal.

He better love it too, he supposed, because his life was about to depend upon it.

Fontana had been able to think about returning to the camp with a bit of emotional distance in his mind, but as the time drew near to returning where he'd been given so much pain, his anxiety began to ratchet up. They would check the Venezuelan location first, return here to refuel then head to the Brazilian location where the Dogs of War had been created. If there was nothing there, they would find a place to refuel then head to the most remote camp, in Guyana. He'd looked at map after map during prep for this operation, and none of the locations were easy to reach.

Madeira opened a hatch at the back of the chopper. "We can store our gear here until we find a place to land."

The men moved in and threw their bags into the back but unpacked their MP5s and slung the tactical slings over their shoulders. Then they climbed into the cabin of the chopper. Madeira move to the pilot's seat, on the left, and opened the door.

A spate of harsh Spanish flew from her mouth and she raised a fist at her uncle, who sat chuckling in the cab of the truck, waiting for her to lift off. Madeira threw the bright red child's booster seat across the tarmac. "You better burn that, Pablo! No more!"

Fontana found himself grinning as he watched what appeared to be a familiar refrain between family. It was obvious the two of them loved each other very much, even though they didn't get to see one another very often.

Madeira pinned him with a glare. "Don't you go getting ideas! Get in!"

She made a motion to the seat beside her in the cockpit. He hesitated, not sure he wanted to have such a view. He'd ridden in helicopters many times before as a SEAL, but he'd never ridden in front where he could see his death coming that much faster. "I can ride in the cabin with the guys."

"Or you can help me scope out landing sites," she called as she began flipping switches. The rotor began to turn overhead as the engines wound to life.

Growling, he circled the helicopter and twisted open the handle to climb inside. He adjusted the fit on the safety straps, letting them out to fit his frame, and began buckling up. Madeira had already snapped in, as if the belts had already been adjusted to her size. She glanced at him for a moment.

"Do you need help with anything?"

He shook his head, glancing down at the thin blue nylon straps his life depended upon.

Why was he so anxious about this flight? Was it what he might find on the other end of the trek, or did he doubt Madeira's ability? She was such a tiny thing to be controlling this huge machine.

As he watched her though, he could see her competence and familiarity with the helicopter.

It must be the trek itself then. This wasn't something he'd ever wanted to do, come back to the jungle, but it had to be done. Period.

Madeira handed him a helmet. Removing his glasses, he fit the helmet over his head, then slipped the glasses back on. She had already done the same and she turned in her seat to look back at the other four. "You guys good to go?"

Her voice in the headset was deep and firm and the men all gave her a thumbs up. Fontana looked back. They all appeared to be strapped in, but DeRossett seemed anxious. His jaw was clamped and the habitual smirk he had on his lips had disappeared. Fontana caught his eye, pointed at his chest then gave him another thumbs up, this time in question. He was really trying to not read them, but Shane was being pretty obvious.

DeRossett nodded, but Fontana didn't think he was solid. He hadn't seen anything to indicate that the younger man was feeling off-balance, but maybe he'd learned to cover the issue. There was some fear there, right now.

"Don't worry, Shane. This will be the most gentle flight you've ever taken," Madeira told him, her voice calming.

The double engines whined to a fever-pitch and gravity began to pull at Fontana's guts. What Madeira had said proved to be true though. Other than the pressure change he didn't even notice that they were taking off. He caught a glimpse of Pablo's grinning face through the windshield of the truck before they lifted into the brilliant blue sky. Spread out before him was the expansive Venezuelan countryside. There was still a bit of mist hanging over the low areas, as well as several curls of smoke from fires, and a section to the east where it was obviously being deforested. Fontana's head swiveled back and forth, trying to take it all in. Steep faced mountains lined the area and he wondered if they'd ever been climbed.

Madeira gently banked the chopper to the right, heading to the south. "You okay, Shane?"

The younger man still looked a little green around the gills, but Fontana thought he might be doing okay.

"I'm good, Jordyn. You were right. Gentle."

Madeira glanced at him, grinning, and Fontana could almost see the wink through her glasses. The woman was an excellent pilot. He looked at her hands. "I can't believe the Army grounded you for those."

Her smiled turned sad. "Well, I don't have the same range of movement I used to," she held up her free hand and wiggled the fingers. They didn't flex as much they probably had originally, but she seemed to have adapted to the scar tissue.

"If I hadn't already gotten my private license I might have

been more upset. It all worked out in the end. I'm right where I'm supposed to be now."

He looked at her, the insightful words settling into him with a rightness that was a little startling. Yes, they were exactly where they needed to be, and they would do what needed to be done.

Jordyn considered flying her favorite thing in the world to do. It took all of her patience to get the men settled and strapped in. She wanted to snap at them to get the fuck in the bird! But that probably wouldn't have gone over well, she thought with an internal chuckle. Now that she was in the air, all of the anxiety and worry was gone. There was no place for any of it because exhilaration had taken its place.

She truly believed she'd been born to fly. Her mother was the same way. If some engineer or scientist ever figured out how to stay in the air indefinitely they would be the first to volunteer. Everything just drifted away on the wind. All of the worries of the earthbound faded to insignificance.

Today, though, some of that worry persisted. She hated flying blind. They had a general idea of where the supposed research camp was, but until they saw it with their own eyes they wouldn't know for sure. She'd already plugged the GPS location into the instrumentation, but with the way the jungle grew, they may or may not be able to see it.

She also had to worry about where to put Margarita down. She needed a significant clearing to clear the rotor blades. The tail rotor was shrouded, but still needed a clear area, preferably. She'd chopped through some light foliage before, but it wasn't something she liked to do.

"About how long will it take to get there?"

She glanced at Fontana, his eyes inscrutable behind the

mirrored shades. He seemed to have taken to flying well. "I think about a couple hours. The air seems clear here but the closer to the jungle we fly the more tumultuous the air can get."

He nodded like that made sense, then turned back to look through the windshield. "It's beautiful up here," her murmured.

Jordyn almost missed the statement, but she turned to him with a grin. "Yes," she said simply.

CHAPTER SIX

They flew for a couple of hours, just like she'd said. Rain, then shine, then rain again. Nothing seemed to ruffle Jordyn. She handled the helicopter like a pro. He couldn't believe what luck it was that she was as good as she'd said she was.

The helicopter began to climb and she glanced at him. "We're two miles out. I think we need to go high enough we can't be identified and scope out the area." She motioned above his head. "There are binocs there. See what you can see."

Fontana retrieved the binoculars and scanned in the direction they were angled. Again, he admired her skill because she somehow always gave him a good perspective to look down on the area. He scanned everything, his heart pounding.

Then he saw it. In the depths of the green there were clearings, and as he adjusted the aperture on the binoculars, he could see roofs of buildings overgrown with foliage. From right to left he scanned the area, spotting what might have been a trail into the compound as well as the remnants of tall fencing encircling the area. "It doesn't look to be inhabited. Everything appears to be grown over."

Fontana made note of several things he wanted to look at when they got on the ground and sketched out a rough diagram on a notebook Madeira handed him. It looked like a constellation.

Behind him he could hear Payne snapping pictures of the area.

"Okay, let's find a place to put down."

Madeira pulled on the control stick and banked away. "There was a spot about two miles back along a river. We might have to bushwhack a bit."

"That's fine."

He kept the location of the camp in the back of his mind as he watched the terrain below them. It was jungle-like, of course. When they'd started from Pablo's airport, there had been mountains and rocky valleys, but the further south they'd flown, toward the mighty Amazon, the flora grew. Overgrown and thickly lush, it was going to be difficult to get through.

Madeira circled a small clearing next to a lazy river. The rocky beach appeared to be stone, so their footing should be secure, but it would still take skill to land on the narrow area.

"Dropping down, Shane," Madeira murmured into the mic, humor lacing her voice. "There are bags beneath your seat if you need one."

Fontana grimaced. He'd puked on turbulent flights before and it was no fun.

Shane kept his guts where they needed to be, though, and when they set down lighter than a butterfly, he let out a relieved sigh. So did Fontana, but he didn't let the others see it.

"Okay, Alpha Team, let's get the fuck through this jungle."

Madeira completed the post-flight process and the

engines whined down. The rotors still turned lazily, but they would eventually still. He looked at her across the width of the cockpit. "Good job."

"Thank you for not blowing us up," she grinned.

Damn. He hadn't even really thought about keeping a rein on his abilities. He hadn't had a chance to because he'd been so focused on her and the surroundings.

He looked at where they'd set down. The beach appeared to be connected to an old homesite, abandoned long ago. The only reason the grass hadn't invaded here was that it appeared to have a rock walkway, laid decades ago.

The group gathered at the back of the chopper to retrieve their gear. They left their helmets and combat gear, but took their survival bags. Madeira leaned into the depths of the space and dug around. When she pulled out she held three long, well-used machetes. She handed one to Big Kenny, who had the height and width on all of them. The second went to Fontana and she kept the third.

Fontana headed in the direction of the camp. They hadn't seen any roads going in or out, but that didn't mean that nothing was there. With a slow swinging rhythm, he started through the jungle. As his muscles warmed, he sped up, slashing more effectively. Thoughts of the last time he'd been in the jungle nagged at him. Last time he'd done this, he's ended up at the bottom of a muddy ravine with a broken leg and a machete in his ass. Leg aching with remembered pain, he tried to push through the vivid memory.

It wasn't easy.

Forcing his arm to swing harder, he buried the agony in work.

"My turn, boss man," Kenny called a while later.

Fontana eased up, sweat dripping. His t-shirt clung to his chest and body, and he could feel his palm burning from the rub of swinging the machete. He looked at Kenny. "I just started."

"Nah, you been swinging like a mad man for about twenty minutes now. Let some of us have a go before you hurt yourself."

The big man took the machete from his hand and passed it back to Payne, and Madeira stepped forward to push a bottle of water into his hand, cap off. Fontana looked at it blankly for a moment before tipping his head back and drinking it down in one go. It was warm but he didn't care. He hadn't realized he'd lost himself.

Madeira watched him with concern in her expression. She pushed her sunglasses up onto her head so he could see her eyes. "Are you okay?"

Fontana forced a nod. "Last time I was in the jungle it wasn't a pleasant experience."

"Ah, so that's why you were trying to kill it." She smiled gently. "I get it now. Let's let the big man take over for a while, shall we?"

Fontana glanced at Kenny. The huge male swung the machete like he'd done it before, and sweat had already begun to bead on his dark skin, running down his head in glistening tracks. They were all sweating, but that was intensive work.

Fontana also noticed that he'd changed directions a bit. "Was I off?"

Madeira held up her thumb and forefinger a fraction apart. "Just a bit."

Now he felt like an ass. Once again, his emotions had gotten the better of him. He hadn't shattered glass all over her, but she'd still had to deal with the fall out. "Seems like I'm always apologizing to you. Sorry."

She shrugged again as they started to follow the others. "You didn't go off a lot yet, but it would have gotten worse.

No harm done. We're not far away, now. You bulldozed a good chunk of distance," she laughed.

Fontana looked at her, wondering why she'd become so accepting of him. Nothing much seemed to rile her and he appreciated that calmness. Seemed like his brain had been hyperalert and overactive for the past two years.

"Are you okay?"

Fontana looked down into her concerned eyes and it felt like he stepped through a wormhole. He wondered what having a person like Aiden did now would feel like. A significant other who would accept him just the way he was, warts and all. Horrors and all. The thought was so ludicrous that he almost laughed.

"I'm good," he said, turning away. "Just ready to get there."

Jordyn watched the big man close himself off. She could almost see the bricks falling into place around him. It was obvious he'd been disturbed when he'd been hacking at the bush. If he didn't want to talk to her that was fine, she supposed. But he definitely had something going on.

Slipping her glasses back on, she followed the team as they moved through the corridor Kenny had hacked out of the jungle for them. Then, suddenly, he stopped. "I hit something," he called back softly.

Jordyn moved forward with the rest to see what he'd done.

It was chain-link fence under a carpet of green. He'd struck the fence high, a bright silver slash amongst the green. The men reached out and began pulling at the pervasive plants, till they had an area cleared and they could look through the fence and beyond.

Jordyn could see the former camp, now, and it gave her chills. This wasn't the one Fontana and his men had been in, but just the thought of what they'd possibly done here gave her chills, like she'd walked over a gravesite. And it didn't ease as Payne began to cut through the fence and they entered the actual property.

A constellation of plant-laden buildings spread below them. They would have to go to every building just to uncover and see what it was. There were a few clearer areas which might have been trails or parking areas, and they walked along those to get into the main grouping of structures. It was obvious no one had been here in a long time. At least a couple years. Maybe more.

"Did that information you guys stole say how old the camps were?"

Fontana shook his head, looking around thoughtfully. He had the machete out but was using it more to push away limbs and stems than anything. It was hard to tell what they were looking at.

Jordyn bent down and poked at something unnaturally shaped with her knife. The tip of the blade hit metal and she pushed the vegetation away. This was the frame of an old aluminum chair. She moved to another lump, smaller and a little more uniformly shaped. A metal water canteen.

In the jungle, water was plentiful. *If* you knew where to look. For those that didn't know, canteens were a necessity. She couldn't imagine anyone losing their canteen and no one else claiming it. The chair she could understand, but the perfectly good canteen could probably be washed out and used today.

She looked around the area and noticed the poles at the end of one of the buildings. They weren't power poles, they weren't spaced right. But there were three poles spaced about eight feet apart from one another. Ivy of some type had rolled up the pole, shrouding it in green. What was curious, though, were the lumps in the middle of the poles. They looked vaguely familiar; long, thin from the bottom and up about three feet, then thicker, cylindrical, topped with a small sphere shape. She started walking toward them.

Kenny apparently had the same idea. As they stopped at the base he made a cup with his hands for her to step into. Trusting him, knowing that he wouldn't allow anything to happen to her, Jordyn stepped into the grip of his hands, then up onto his shoulders. She reached out to brace herself on the lump, and it swung away from her. Gasping, she ripped at the green.

The ivy fell down in a sheet, and she found herself looking almost eye to eye with a human skull.

In spite of her fear she didn't jerk like she wanted to. She forced herself to look at the skull, and the rest of the bones. The person had been strung up by his or her wrists. There were chains wrapped around the wrists and ankles.

"Do you see any identifying marks," Fontana asked from below.

"No," Jordyn told him, appreciating the calmness of his voice. Her heart was racing from shock and fear. "It doesn't even look like he was clothed. No dogtags. He does seem tall, though. Taller than a native Venezuelan."

She looked at the other poles with similar shapes shrouded in green. Several men had been strung up.

Movement drew her attention, and she thought she caught a glimpse of someone walking through the trees from the direction they'd come. Then they were gone.

Kenny lowered her to the ground, making sure she was secure before letting her go. She forced a smile and a nod before stepping away.

The thought that there were three men strung up on poles was disgusting to her, and seemed to confirm what information the Dogs of War had supplied. There was no way to know for sure how long those skeletons had been hanging there, but it was a pretty good bet that this had been one of the camps they'd been looking for.

She glanced at Fontana. There was a glower on his face, and his hands were planted on his hips as he looked at the poles. Anger seemed to radiate from him.

"What do you want to do?" she asked.

"I want to take them home."

Heart in her throat, she looked around, trying to see beneath all the vegetation. Curves and bumps she now feared were skulls or rib cages. How could they ever know what was under everything?

Movement drew her attention again. There was a lone native man walking toward them, a little stooped with age, holding a staff. He wore a red loincloth and there was a colorful cloth around his forehead. Red paint was swirled on his cheeks, with a line up between his brows and out across his forehead.

Jordyn didn't startle, but Fontana did. Before she could say anything he had his HK to his shoulder, pointed at the man. The other men joined him and there was suddenly a cacophony of sound as Fontana tried to yell at the man to stop where he was. Jordyn held a hand out and pressed down on the muzzle.

"He's indigenous. Just wait. He's not attacking. It's obvious he wants to talk. He might know what happened here."

Fontana lowered his weapon slowly, scowling as the man continued toward them. He hadn't even hesitated.

Jordyn faced the older man and gave him a respectful nod, praying she would understand his language. There were so many variations of the Spanish language, and the natives of the country spoke even more derivations.

He greeted her with a variation that she could understand, though. Jordyn returned it, along with a smile. She didn't reach out to shake his hand. Some of the tribes considered it an offense, especially from a woman to a man, and she didn't want to do that. Fontana had already put them in an awkward position.

The older man propped his hands on his staff and cocked a leg out. Though he moved like a youth, lines tracked his face with age.

"You may call me Grandfather."

"Jordyn Madeira."

"The dead have been undisturbed here for many years," he told her, voice raspy.

"Do you know how many, Grandfather?" Jordyn hoped that the question wouldn't insult the man.

He nodded his head at her and made a motion with his hand. "When the Army men came, they cleared this whole valley with machines. They built stone buildings and killed our game. But," he grinned at her, "Mother has a way of taking back. Within a few seasons you couldn't see the dirt, even though there were many men here. And they had men in cages and on chains like dogs."

Jordyn sighed, knowing that that was what they'd been needing to know. "Where did they go?"

"Most sleep over the hill." He pointed in a direction that they hadn't explored yet. "They should go home."

Tears flooded her eyes. "Can you show us?"

He nodded and walked past her. The older man didn't even look at Fontana as he padded by, sandaled feet finding a quiet path through the foliage.

Jordyn stopped in front of the tense man. "He says the dead have been here many years. They are sleeping over the hill and need to be taken home. He's taking us there now."

Fontana looked down at her, jagged emotion filling his eyes. "They're all dead?"

"It sounds like it. He didn't say how many."

Something vibrated out of Fontana, and Jordyn had to brace herself. He felt angry, and frustrated, and he didn't have any way to expel that emotion. She was glad she didn't have a light over her head again.

Daring to reach out, she rested a hand on his arm, but he pulled away. Without a word, he followed the old man through the jungle.

CHAPTER SEVEN

Fontana dreaded whatever they were about to find, but he had to keep walking. The native didn't have to come out of the jungle to tell them what had been here, but he had, and Fontana appreciated that, but he acknowledged the fear in his heart.

They crested a rise and the trees thinned out a little. He could hear Payne snapping pictures, both forward and backward. Finally, the old man stopped at a tree stump and he looked at Madeira. He spoke quietly to her, then waited as she translated what he said to the men.

"They brought them here. Some were young, not many seasons old, but they were bones. They hadn't been given food for a long time. Some had bruises and other marks on them." She paused as she listened to the old man. "When they passed on, the men in uniforms brought them here. The Grandfather's village is not far away and they tried to watch, because this is Caraño territory."

Fontana looked at the ground, knowing what they were about to find. "Shane, do you have that shovel?"

The young man moved forward, swinging his pack

around, and rummaged on the exterior. He unfastened a couple of strips of Velcro and removed a folded spade. Snapping it open he began to dig.

The men took turns digging. Finally, when the hole was arm-length deep, something white flashed in the dirt. It was an arm bone. From then on they dug with their hands until the dirt was level with the bones of the first body.

Fontana wanted to scream in protest or break something. For the first time in years he wanted to cry, but he refused to let the tears fall. These men had died with honor at the hands of those without any honor, and they deserved to be respected. Pulling the satellite phone from his pack he took a couple of photos and sent them to Aiden.

We need a forensic team, he typed.

Drop a pin on your location and we'll get one there. Somehow.

Fontana wished that Aiden and Wulfe were there. They knew how to calm him, how to direct the impotent anger coursing through him. Looking away from the gravesite, he found Madeira staring at him. She seemed to understand what he was feeling, because she nodded her head. Just that small acknowledgement eased something in him, and he could refocus on what needed done.

"Is this the only gravesite?" He asked her.

She looked at the old man and rattled off some words. He nodded a couple of times, then pointed toward the north.

Madeira turned back to him. "He says that this is the only gravesite that he knows of, and that when the men left they headed toward the north, toward the big cities. There were at least twenty men that left, and a woman with hair as dark as his own, but no color in her skin."

Priscilla Mattingly, he thought with a snarl.

"I am aware that this is his territory. Can he bear with us as we bring more men in to try to find out what happened?"

Madeira turned and talked to the old man. It was obvious

she was trying to explain something scientific to him because he shook his head and motioned for her to continue. It took the two of them several minutes to come to an apparent understanding.

"Grandfather says that is okay, but he will send some of his men to protect you."

"We don't," he started, but Madeira forestalled him.

"I know we don't need protection, but he needs peace of mind that we aren't moving in to take over his territory."

Fontana gave her a single nod. "Tell him within a few days we'll do our very best to be out of here."

The old man didn't seem to like that answer, but eventually nodded. Turning, he walked into the jungle.

They set up camp at the base of one of the buildings. They cleared the foliage away and found enough dry wood to start a fire. They didn't especially need the heat but maybe the smoke from the fire would scatter some of the insects.

Fontana swatted at a mosquito and looked out over the area. They'd gotten the three men down from the poles and had secured them, their bones, rather, in sheets. He didn't know what else to do with them. They'd documented everything they could but he'd known that he couldn't leave the men there until the forensic team arrived. He'd had Payne photograph everything before they'd cut them down. Now he stared out at them, wondering who they'd been. There'd been no dog tags or identifying marks on them that they'd seen, and they weren't even sure why they'd been hung up that way.

Madeira had suggested that it was a warning to the natives, and he tended to believe that. Maybe it had been a warning to everyone. For the five million and thirty-second time, he wished Priscilla Mattingly was still alive so that he could kill her all over again. Or at least have a part in it. Angela Holloway had actually shoved the knife into her heart, but Fontana liked to think that he'd had at least a small part in weakening her to the point that Angela could kill her.

Swatting at a mosquito, he leaned a little heavier against the wall at his back.

Madeira walked toward him through the smoke and squatted down beside him. She held out a green bottle. "This will help with the mosquitos. I'm surprised you can't, like, push them away with your mind."

Fontana cocked a brow at her. "Become my own bug zapper, you mean? I guess I hadn't thought about it. The Jungle Juice might be an easier option. Thank you."

He took the bottle from her hand, making sure not to touch her. The Jungle Juice had a high concentration of Deet and would repel squads of mosquitos. If he'd had more time he would have had a bottle in his own pack, but they'd been a bit rushed to get out of the states.

Fontana spritzed himself, then handed the bottle back to her. "They don't bother me much. If you need it again let me know."

"Thanks."

"You're very welcome." She moved to get up.

Fontana scrambled for something to say. He didn't want her to leave yet. Zero was on patrol, otherwise the two of them would be hanging out together. They were a bit of a pair and getting either one without the other didn't happen often. "Hey, I wanted to thank you, too, for translating with the old man. We would have been lost."

She shrugged, dropping to her bottom beside him against the wall. "That's what I'm here for. I'm just glad he showed himself and told us. He didn't have to."

"No, he didn't. Will your chopper be okay?"

She nodded. "They won't mess with it. It's how Grandfather knew that he needed to come check us out."

"I don't know where Aiden is going to get the forensic team. I hope I spoke correctly when I told him just a few days."

She tipped her head back to look up at the stars. "I think he would understand. The natives know that the dead are important to us."

Her voice drifted off and she sighed. Fontana felt her heat just barely brushing against him and watched as her eyelids lowered. The smooth side of her profile was to him, and he allowed himself to trace her features by the light of the stars. She'd been a beautiful woman. Still was, actually. At least, to him. And he'd seen other men looking at her as well. Zero loomed around her like a protective big brother, though, and probably turned off a lot of guys. Not that she couldn't turn them off herself, he thought with a bit of a smile.

He rolled his head back to look around their makeshift camp. They'd eaten a light dinner of rations then settled around the fire. He'd instructed Zero to take first watch. Shane would relieve him in four hours. Then Kenny. They'd all worked hard today and they needed to catch up. With a final glance at Madeira, Fontana closed his eyes.

CHAPTER EIGHT

Aiden looked at the sat phone in his hand. There was a spinning dial and he could tell there was a picture coming through. He counted breaths as he waited.

When it finally did come though, it was as bad as he'd feared. Without a word, he handed the phone to Wulfe, who cursed, low and vicious. The text message said, *I had hope, Will*.

Yeah, he had too, but they were dashed now. Aiden's mind spun. Duncan was in his office. Pushing up from the table, he headed in that direction.

I might have a forensic team.

Aiden paused to look at Wulfe, curious why he was contacting him telepathically. There was no one around. *Really?*

Wulfe scowled, working his mouth like he'd eaten something sour. *Maybe. Give me some minutes. I need to call Virginia.*

Aiden glanced at the clock on the wall in the office beside him. *How long do you need?*

I will call now. Just need an office for privacy.

Pointing down the hallway to the interview room, Aiden leaned back against the hallway.

"Send me that picture," Wulfe growled.

Punching in a few buttons, Aiden did. Once Wulfe received the picture he headed down the hall to the dark office at the end.

Aiden cooled his heels in the hallway. He sent Angela a text, asking her if she had time to meet for lunch.

Of course I do. For you!

Grinning, Aiden basked in the words. *Thank you, Angel. I love you. And miss you. See you at 12 at your place?*

I'll be there! Love you!

Even as recently as a month ago, he never in his wildest dreams would have expected to receive a text like that, from anyone. A lot had changed recently.

He glanced down the hallway at the office on the left. That was his brother's office. Again, a string of words he never even considered using before. Brother. Abandoned at a church when John was no more than four or five, the same way he'd been. The chances of them both being scattered to the winds, then finding each other again were so minuscule that he doubted anyone could figure it.

His life had changed drastically in the past month, and he would fight to protect his new normal. When they'd fought Priscilla and her mercenaries a few days ago, he'd known that the shit was about to hit the fan. So far, though, it had been quiet. The company appeared to be regrouping, deciding what to do. Priscilla had been an integral part of their daily operations. Her funeral, as well as several others for the more minor employees were scheduled over the next few days. Aiden, Fontana and Wulfe had a limited amount of time to work before the Collaborative would move.

His eyes drifted to the door. Wulfe needed to hurry up.

"Good morning, Officer Rose."

The other man didn't respond for several long seconds. "How the hell did you get this number?"

Wulfe could almost see the foul expression on Operations Officer Rose's face. "No matter. I have a gift for you."

Rose was silent on the other end of the line, as Wulfe expected him to be. They hadn't met under the best of circumstances, and Rose would always hold that against him.

Wulfe let the silence draw out, but Rose was good. He didn't rush to fill it.

"No? Not interested?" Wulfe taunted. "I'll have to call one of my other CIA contacts then. Tell them about the violations we've uncovered in South America by members of your government."

The officer sighed heavily. "What violations? I don't have time to play these games. I actually have a job to do."

"Hm. Yes. What is Damon Wilkes doing right now?"

The silence stretched again, a little sharper this time. "He appears to be grieving a lost employee."

"How soon can you have a forensic team in the air to South America?"

"A couple hours. Why?"

"I thought you might want to investigate the mass grave part of my team just found."

"Why would I want to do that?" Rose asked. "It's not my country."

"No, but some of the men in it are American servicemen who had taken part in a shared government testing program with the Silverstone Collaborative."

Wulfe let that sink in.

"Are you being legit with me?" Officer Rose's voice lowered to a growl. "If I dispatch a team to another country, I damn well better have proof. How do you know that it's American servicemen in there?"

"Because I have a roster of names that were sent there, and even what branch. Some will be from other countries, yes, but there will be American bones there."

"I can't do this without some kind of proof. What 'team' are you working with?"

"Doesn't matter. I will send you a picture."

"This better be legit, Wulfe, or you can just lose my number forever. You get me?"

"I get you, Officer Rose. But there are conditions to this gift."

"What conditions. What are you talking about?"

"This needs investigation, but you need to sit on the information until I tell you. If you do, I will give you two more locations."

"You know for a fact there are three locations?"

Wulfe grimaced and hoped the bluff worked. "Yes. Maybe more. We have boots on the ground confirming now."

Wulfe let Rose think, not saying anything. If the officer didn't take the bait they were stuck. No other options.

"Send me the picture."

And he hung up. Wulfe sent the photo to the same number and waited. He could see when the text was read. Exactly one minute later the phone rang in his hand and he answered it.

"Okay. Send me the location and how to get there. I will sit on what we find as long as possible. But I have to answer for the forensic team to my boss."

"The longer you wait," Wulfe responded, "the more information you will have to convict Wilkes. You've been investigating him for months. Another week or three will not make much of a difference."

"Who the hell are you, Wulfe? What Agency are you with?"

Wulfe chuckled at the frustration he could hear in the other man's voice. In the process of surveilling Wilkes, he'd realized that he wasn't the only interested party. "No agency, Rose. But we call ourselves the Dogs of War. If you stick with this to the end you'll understand why."

"Did you have a part in the death of Priscilla Mattingly?"

"Get that team in the air, Rose. We'll be talking."

Wulfe hung up on the other man and sent him the coordinates that Fontana had supplied, then called Fontana on his satellite phone. "I have a CIA forensic team coming in. You should vacate the area within the next two hours."

"I can do that, assuming the weather breaks. It's raining like a bitch right now."

Wulfe could hear the crack of thunder in the background. "If you don't leave, CIA might take you in."

"Understood. We'll bug out."

"Call tomorrow."

Fontana sighed on the other end of the line, and Wulfe could hear the anxiety. Tomorrow he would be heading to the camp where they had been held. "Roger."

Aiden stood where he'd left him, leaning against the wall in the hallway. "It's done. CIA is sending a team down now. I called Fontana and he's getting out of there."

Aiden's mouth hung open. "CIA? What the hell have you been doing out there in Virginia, Wulfe?"

He grinned, glad that he could still shock his buddies. "Making connections."

Maybe it was time he told Aiden what he'd been up to for the past two years.

Fontana stashed the phone in a breast pocket of his vest, within easy reach, then swiped the rain from his face. He stepped under the tarp roof they'd erected and looked at Madeira. "Can you fly?"

She glanced out at the pounding rain. A flash of lightning split the sky, making it seem darker outside than it actually was. "I prefer not to fly in lightning. If it eases up I can, of course."

He nodded and looked at the rest of the men. "We need to wrap up camp. Leaving within the hour."

They started moving. It wouldn't take them nearly that long to pack their gear, but it was always better to have more time.

"I'm going to see if I can spot our lookout," Madeira said, "to let Grandfather know what's going on."

"And I'll leave a sign even the CIA should be able to read," he told her, flashing her a grin.

Then he sobered. For a moment he'd forgotten what lay just over the hill, where the sign would be pointing. And what lay just a few feet away from their own camp.

Fontana started gathering trash and left items, and lining it up into an arrow, pointed over the hill to the grave. It didn't seem respectful enough, but he didn't have time for anything else.

They *would* find those men justice.

CHAPTER NINE

Madeira stepped out into the rain, her emotions reeling. When Fontana had grinned at her, she'd been gobsmacked. As if the man weren't handsome enough with his curly dark blond hair and bright green eyes. He had a smile to freaking die for and the dimples in his cheeks made him look younger than she ever would have expected.

Then it was like he'd realized that he shouldn't be grinning in such a solemn spot, and his expression, his entire demeanor, had dimmed. She'd wanted to force that smile back, somehow. She'd wanted to bring the light back into his eyes, because his sadness was wrecking her.

Turning away, she headed toward where she'd last seen Grandfather walk into the forest. A young man met her at the tree line just outside where they'd cut the fence to enter. She told him that they would be leaving, and a new team coming in to carry the dead home. He seemed to understand, bowing to her.

By the time she returned to camp, most of it had been stowed in their bags. When they got back to Pablo's airport they would have to spread everything in the hangar to get it to dry. She packed up her own small items, then stood looking out at the rain. She counted the rumbles of thunder and timed the lightning. Fontana moved up beside her. "I think it's moving away," she told him. "We can go."

They trouped back the way they'd came, through the fence and the path they'd cut into the jungle. They'd only been here a long day, but already the foliage was leaning back in to fill the gap. Big Kenny took the lead, swinging the machete, and within a few minutes they were back at the chopper. Stowing her gear, Jordyn moved around the machine, looking for any sign that it had been damaged in the storm. Nothing. She ran through her preflight check as the men stowed their own gear and loaded up. Fontana climbed in beside her and she glanced at him. She couldn't read anything in his closed down face.

"Are you tight?" she asked him.

With a sigh, he glanced at her. "Yes. I'm good. Let's get the fuck out of here."

Didn't have to tell her twice.

The flight back was uneventful and the weather cooperated, which was a little surprising. She'd thought that the storms were settling in to stay, but it was so hard to tell here. They were on the leading edge of the rainforest and things could change, literally, minute to minute. As they flew north toward the airport the land began to dry, until Jordyn was fighting to see through red swirling dust as she landed Margarita on the trailer for her uncle to back into the hangar.

Such a drastic change.

Hugging her uncle, they moved around Margarita, checking her. Payne and the rest of the men spread their equipment out in the sun to dry.

"Take the men up to the house," Pablo told her. "They are probably hungry. There is meat in the pan on the stove. I've already eaten, so the rest is yours."

"Thank you, Uncle."

It wasn't hard to entice the men to eat. Men could always eat. Especially men who weren't always sure where their next meal would be coming from. Besides, most anything was better than rations. Fontana had disappeared though.

She scooped out some meat onto a couple of tortillas the neighbor lady made for her tío, and some crumbled cheese. Then she poured some of her mother's homemade hot sauce over the meat. She was actually a little surprised that Pablo was giving up some of his precious sauce. Every few months Jordyn's mother would send a care package to her brother. Sometimes it made it here, other times it didn't, probably stolen during the trek. Mail delivery in rural Venezuela could be hit and miss sometimes, especially packages. Pablo had learned that it was more secure and definitely worth the expense to have a drop box in Caracas. Whenever he went in for parts or groceries he checked it.

She also grabbed a beer from the fridge.

"I think he's out back talking to the dogs," Zero murmured, not looking up from his food.

Jordyn smiled, loving the gruff man. He knew she was wondering where Fontana had gone.

Letting herself out onto the back patio, she scanned the yard for Fontana. There he was, sitting with little Humberto beneath the Araguaney tree. Lalo, the fluffy white dog, sat a few feet away, chewing on something he probably wasn't supposed to have. The dogs were more scavengers than pets, anymore. Tío Pablo did what he could but Tía Emely had been the one to dote on the dogs, and when she'd passed a few years ago none of them had been the same.

She held the plate out to Fontana. He looked up in surprise. "I don't expect you to serve me," he said huskily. "Or feed me for that matter."

"I know but if I didn't dip some out for you, Kenny and

Zero were going to fight over it. My uncle has turned into a great cook."

He snorted, taking the plate from her hand. Humberto sniffed hopefully but Fontana shooed him away. "Sorry, dog. Not getting any."

"He likes you," she murmured, sitting beneath the tree as well. She made sure to keep space between them.

"He's desperate," Fontana said, shoving a huge bite of taco into his mouth.

Jordyn watched him chew, looking for a flash of those dimples again, but she didn't see them. "He was my aunt's favorite."

"Where is she?" He asked, taking another bite.

"She died about four years ago. Cervical cancer."

His chewing paused and he looked up. "I'm sorry."

Jordyn sighed, missing her aunt. "She was a remarkable woman. Lived through a lot of craziness but didn't let it get her down. And she lived life the way she wanted to. Pablo never knew she was sick until the very end, when it was too late to do anything about it."

"She sounds like a remarkable woman."

Jordyn smiled softly. "Yes, she was. I can only hope to be as strong."

"Well, I didn't know the woman personally, but I think you've got her beat. It seems like you've lived through your own craziness and survived."

Automatically, her chin tipped up, as if she could feel someone—him— looking at her damage, even though he was sitting on her good side. "Yes. I survived mine, and have the scars to prove it," she grinned.

If there were anything other than acceptance from him, she would move on. She'd decided long ago that the scars on her hands and face were a part of her now, and she would live with them the rest of her life. As long as they didn't interfere with her breathing or fine motor skills, she saw no need to get them 'fixed'.

"How did it happen?" he asked.

Jordyn was surprised. He'd seemed pretty... closed off. She hadn't thought that he would even ask her such a personal question. She'd taken his distance as disinterest, but maybe she'd been wrong. "I had just returned from leave and I was being flown out to my Forward Operating Base. It was supposed to be a super quick shuttle ride, but the pilot was young and thought he would take a bit of a detour through a pass. There were Afghans in that pass, watching the FOB," she chuckled. "Both parties were surprised. They started firing at us and the pilot banked away, but we'd been hit. I will say, he put us down right outside the main gates of the FOB, so when we crashed we had help there almost immediately. I was secured in the fuselage, but the chopper had fallen over onto the door. Fuel leaked down on me for almost half an hour while they struggled to get me out of the chopper *and* fought off the Afghan scout party. Just as they reached me, the whole thing torched, probably from a stray round or metal shrapnel."

She sighed, remembering the feel of the corrosive fuel on her skin, then the mind-numbing pain of the fire. All she remembered was screaming, until she thought her lungs were going to pop. Then she quit screaming when she realized she needed that oxygen she was expelling. "It took about forty minutes to cut me out, and the last three I was burning. By the time they got the flames on me smothered and headed into the base, I'd been out there about fifty minutes, soaked in fuel."

"Damn," Fontana breathed. "I've been burnt before, and it is a feeling like no other."

"Yes," she agreed. "I still feel the pain sometimes. If I'm blow-drying my hair on too warm of a setting or something, sometimes one of my nerves kicks in, screaming. Those overhead radiant heaters in some store doorways? Yeah, makes my skin scream. But, I've gotten used to it."

Fontana took the last bite of his second taco and set the plate aside. She didn't miss the fact that he'd left a scrap of meat there for Humberto, or that the little dog snuck in and grabbed it as soon as possible.

Distracted by watching the dog, she was startled when Fontana reached out and turned her chin toward him. Then, with his other hand, he reached out and brushed her hair away from the right side of her face.

Jordyn caught her breath, shocked that he'd reached out this way. He looked at all of the scarring on her head and around her ear, then looked down at her hands. When he looked up at her, his eyes had warmed. "Like I said, you've got her beat. These were extensive injuries."

His thumb traced circles on her right hand. When Jordyn looked down, she could see him making the motion, but mostly felt only pressure. Then the circles shifted to the top of her hand and she could feel every delicious stroke.

"I see no reason for you to change anything about yourself."

The strength in his voice was her undoing. It was one thing to tell yourself that, or have your mother tell you the same, but for some reason it was very different when a man said it. No, it was very different when this particular man said it.

"Thank you, Fontana," she whispered. "That's a very nice thing for you to say."

"It's the truth," he said simply.

"Where is your burn," she asked.

Fontana stiffened and pulled away, letting her hand fall. What had she done? "I'm sorry. I shouldn't have asked."

He sighed, looking out over the dusty ground. "No, it's okay. It's just... I have no scars."

Jordyn was confused. "I thought you said..."

"I did, but the scar is gone. When we were going through testing, we were being given regular doses of the serum. They burned me, but you can't tell where anymore."

She stared, shocked at what he was telling her. How could it leave no mark?

"I don't understand," she whispered.

Fontana held out his right forearm. "They used a blowtorch from elbow to wrist until the skin blackened and peeled away."

She held his wrist in her hand and traced fingers over the tan skin. Not a single mark.

"Then when that didn't keep me down long enough, they used a flame thrower."

He'd stripped down to his black t-shirt to accommodate the heat, and now he lifted the front of it up under his chin. Jordyn's gaze drifted down, over his rounded pectorals and mounded abs. The man was lean, little wrinkles of skin bunching around his belly button. Golden hair furred his chest and narrowed to a strip down the center of his abs. If she could have swallowed right then, she would have, but her mouth was suddenly parched. The man was absolutely delicious.

There were no scars, though. At least none that looked like burns. She reached out and traced a line down his right side. The skin shivered from her touch.

"That was from an injury when I was a SEAL. Before the testing program. Everything received during the program healed."

His words were clipped, and she looked up into his eyes. There was a struggle going on there. The physical scars may have healed, but the mental scars were still there. "But you still felt the pain."

"Oh, yes, we felt the pain. Pain killers would have interfered with our response, we were told. We were never given pain control."

Jordyn thought of the hours and hours it had taken her to heal. Not having prescription drugs would have been unbearable. It had damn near been unbearable *with* drugs, every single second of her recovery had been agony.

"I'm so sorry," she told him. Jordyn doubted that he would accept a full hug from her, but maybe... scooting her butt around, she leaned into his shoulder, lacing her arm through his own. He didn't move for a long minute, then he leaned a little of his weight into her. Jordyn didn't think about the time passing. She just leaned into him and hoped he felt her understanding.

Eventually, not wanting to crowd him, she pulled away. "Tomorrow is going to be hard for you, isn't it?"

They were traveling to the camp where he'd been held captive, Taraza.

Fontana sighed, looking out over the fading skyline. "Yes. Good thing we'll be in the jungle. No lightbulbs."

Jordyn jerked back and looked up at him. There it was. The dimple in his right cheek appeared as he gave her a lopsided smile, the green of his eyes glittering.

Jordyn laughed. "It's a damn good thing. You freaked me out when that happened."

"I know. I apologize, again. When my emotions run high my control gets a little frazzled."

"Hm. Must make it hard to be in a relationship then."

The words hung in the air awkwardly. She snapped her mouth shut and looked out into the distance, praying that her skin didn't color. Times like these she was appreciative of her Venezuelan heritage. Why the heck had she said that?

Because she wanted to let him know she was open to a relationship without actually saying the words.

"Mmm..." he said, but he didn't make eye contact with her.

Jordyn put some space between them, suddenly realizing that she had no idea if he was attached to anyone or not. They hadn't exactly talked about it. The fact that he was ready to go around the world at a moment's notice kind of made her think that he didn't have anyone to be accountable to, but that was kind of a big thing to get wrong.

Maybe it was best to get away now.

"I think I'll go in and sort out where the boys will sleep."

Hoping that he would tell her stay, she paused for a moment, but he stayed silent.

Pushing to her feet, she fought not to look at him again, humiliation snapping at her. She'd been practically laying against the man and he must be taken. The silence had felt like agreement. Okay, she'd been a little bowled over by him touching her face and his apparent acceptance. Obviously she'd read too much into the action.

No more.

Fontana gritted his teeth and watched Madeira leave out of his peripheral vision. Arousal throbbed in his veins. She'd leaned into him and he'd been struck dumb for a minute, relishing the feel of her breast against his elbow, as ridiculous as it sounded. The woman was tiny, but voluptuous. And it had been such a long time.

Aiden and Wulfe thought he was a player and he'd never disabused them of that notion, when in fact he was quite the opposite. Just because he looked like he could have any woman in the sack he wanted didn't mean he did.

When she'd said something about a relationship, he'd literally locked up. The thought of opening himself up to anyone with his deepest and darkest secrets held no appeal. He'd been through torture and didn't want to do it again. He thought sex might be nice again someday, but it would have to be with the right person.

Madeira leaning against his arm had been nice though. She'd been trying to console him. He got that. He just couldn't let himself feel that, though. Especially now, the night before he had to walk back into his own private hell.

The possibility that anyone would be there was slim. The Collaborative had to have realized that the camp was compromised after they broke out. Mattingly probably had people out of there within few hours.

Or she'd had everyone killed like in the camp they saw today.

For a moment he allowed himself to think about the men they'd left behind. There hadn't been a lot of men, but definitely a few. Had she killed them all to clean up her mess? What had happened to Smoke, the Brazilian guard who had been one of their main jailers?

If he was still around, Fontana would like to kill him. Slowly.

Humberto wandered over, as if he could feel how messed up Fontana's head was. The little dog stepped over his thigh, then curled up between his legs. Fontana let himself absorb the dog's comfort.

Tío Pablo's house was big enough to accommodate all the men. There were two cots out on the back patio he kept for pilots who had to sleep over, as well as a guest bedroom for passengers and a pullout sofa. Pablo himself usually slept in his recliner out in the hangar. A few years ago, he'd had a problem with thieves and he'd gotten used to sleeping out there.

Fontana was still outside. When he came in, she would give him the guest room.

Jordyn had her own bedroom. Or what she'd always considered hers. It was the room where she and her mother slept together when they came down to visit during her childhood. The walls were a pale green, with an old wrought iron bed that squeaked when you lay on the mattress. Her aunt had decorated it with satin roses and a series of pictures of them all together.

Jordyn's mother had treated their biennial trips as adventures, and it was one of the favorite things she'd ever done with her mother. At night they'd lay in the bed and look up at the stars they could see through the window and her mother would tell her about growing up as a girl there on the farm and getting into trouble with her older brother.

They'd laughed and laughed.

Jordyn checked the kitchen, but the men had already cleaned up after themselves. Good. She was tired. Miracle of miracles, the bathroom was also free. Grabbing a black sports bra from her pack and a pair of black boy shorts, she headed in. Not the most fashionable, but it would keep her cooler when she slept. For a few blissful minutes, she allowed herself to bask in the hot water of the shower. She scrubbed the sweat from her head and wondered when her next shower would be. Tomorrow when they flew in, they were going to have to play it by ear. They had to scope the area out, but they couldn't fly directly over it, just in case there was someone there.

She rinsed the soap from her body and stepped out of the stall. The towel she used was faded with age, but clean. Apparently the once-a-week housekeeper her mother had hired was still working. Pablo surely wouldn't have washed them.

Jordyn patted herself dry and slipped her clothes on. After wearing her fatigues, her safety vest and the thirty-pound pack on her back, a bra and shorts felt naked. Hanging her towel on the rod she padded toward her room.

The back slider door opened and closed. Pausing, she waited to see who would come around the corner. Fontana stepped inside, big and broad and tentative. He glanced up and spotted her in the hallway. He went completely still, then he cleared his throat. "Kenny said my place is in here?"

Jordyn couldn't move, caught as Fontana looked at her. Even from this distance she saw him glance downward, over her body. His jaw flexed and tightened, and he looked away.

Jordyn waved a hand toward the guest room beside hers. "Make yourself at home. There are fresh towels in the bathroom."

Then, with a final, lingering glance at his profile she slipped inside her door.

———

Fontana knew that the vision of Madeira standing in the hallway in the bra thing and minuscule shorts would be burned into his brain forever. Those fucking curves... she was going to kill him. They weren't technically in a military structure so there was nothing that said that they had to stay apart, but he didn't know if he wanted to open himself up to what she could do to him.

Power raged in his mind and he had to look away to clamp it down. That was another thing. Normally, he had a pretty decent grip on himself, but something about her riled him up. Weakened his walls, or something.

Just before she disappeared into her room he glanced at

her ass. Fuck, it was luscious. Thoughts of gripping those voluptuous hips in his hands he entered her from behind... God... he slammed the doors shut on his brain. There was no way that was happening. He wasn't in a position to even *consider* a relationship. There was too much danger swirling around them right now.

The guest room was plain but spotlessly clean. Fontana dropped his pack to the floor and sank to the bed. He would grab a quick shower then try to get some sleep. His eyes were gritty from being awake for so long. When had he last slept deeply? It had to have been days. Maybe when he first got to Aiden's and he knew he was secure in the warehouse with physical backup and alarms. Since then he'd catnapped when he could.

Fontana hated feeling vulnerable, and sleep was the most vulnerable time for him. His defenses fell and sometimes his power leaked. He wished that the bulb exploding over Madeira's head had been the only time that had happened, but it wasn't. There were a handful of times when he'd woken to find that every bulb in his hotel room was shattered. And it didn't matter what kind of bulb it was. He'd overloaded LED lights till they snapped, he'd even overloaded the amber halogen lights in parking lots. Those took concentration, though. Wall outlets had burned up, as well as chargers. When he fell asleep and his defenses came down, it was like the electricity that he normally controlled ran wild.

Digging through his pack he found the plastic bag with his chargers in it. He selected the MP3 charger and plugged it into the wall, then plugged the device in. For some reason when he slept with music playing in his ears, he could control the power a little better while he slept. It was like a tiny part of his brain monitored and controlled the music, which somehow controlled the rest of the energy flowing through him.

It was a bit of a balancing act, though. He didn't like to use the player all the time because it put him at a security disadvantage. With the buds in his ears he couldn't hear shit. Sometimes, though, he could *feel* someone walking toward him. Like he was reading their electrical signature.

It had been two years since he'd had an Ayahuasca injection, but his powers continued to grow. As well as the dangers.

Digging through his pack again he pulled out a clean pair of underwear and his shower bag. Stripping off his outer vest and weapons, he kicked his boots in line beside the bed, ready when he got up. Then, palming his sidearm, he let himself out of the bedroom and into the bathroom. His limp was more pronounced now than it had been all day. He was absolutely dog tired.

Cranking the hot water, he let it pour over him. Leaning against the tile wall, he let his body relax.

The thought of Madeira's fine ass popped into his brain and he was instantly hard. He ran a hand over himself, first scrubbing with soap, then just because he wanted to. Madeira was so damn sexy. He didn't think she had any idea how sexy. The scars on her face had probably shaken her confidence.

Fontana closed his eyes, thinking about the light shining on her face earlier. Personally, he thought she was one of the most beautiful women he'd ever seen.

Had she been waiting there for him to notice her when he'd walked in? No, that seemed a little calculated. It had looked like she'd just gotten out of the shower. Plus, her hair had been wet.

The thought of her in this shower stall, with no clothes on, lathering her plump breasts with the soap he had in his hand plunged him toward orgasm. It only took a few tight-fisted strokes to finish himself off.

It took the edge off, but still left him wanting her.

Later that night he was still rock hard. Every time she moved in that damn bed, the springs squeaking, he envisioned being there with her, making those bed springs scream as he rocked into the cradle of her hips.

Why the fuck was he hooked on this woman? It had to be the exhaustion plaguing him. He was so tired.

Finally, he put the earbuds into his ears and cranked the music. His men were outside so he wasn't going to be attacked in the night.

Closing his eyes, he prayed for sleep.

CHAPTER TEN

Anton Scofield straightened the blue tie, hating that he had to show up for this ridiculous thing. Fuck Priscilla Mattingly. She'd been a bitch in life and she was still screwing him over. He had better things to do than to attend her fucking funeral.

He glanced at the clock on the wall. The car would be waiting for him downstairs, and Damon wanted to talk before they headed to the cemetery. Probably wanted to bitch at him again for something else he didn't know about. Anton was the face of the company. He wasn't supposed to be the one doing the dirty work. Priscilla had had her tasks and Anton his own. If they'd crossed at all it was because he was covering up one of her fuck-ups.

The woman had been evil, but she'd made the company a lot of money. It would be damn near impossible to replace her. Hence Damon's attempt to fit Anton into Priscilla's heels, so to speak.

Positioning the colorful pocket square, he turned from the mirror and headed for the door.

"Michelle," he called out toward the kitchen. "Or whatever the fuck your name is."

The gray-haired woman stepped from the kitchen, wiping her hands on a towel. She frowned at his muttered words. "Yes, Mr. Scofield?"

"Whatever it is you're cooking stinks. I want Italian tonight. With a 2015 Paul Dolan Cabernet Sauvignon. I'll be back at seven."

The woman tilted her chin up and he could see the fury in her eyes. "Yes, Mr. Scofield."

Laughing, he called the private elevator. He would have to watch the kitchen cameras tonight and make sure she didn't spit in his food.

The elevator arrived and he stepped inside, then turned to watch through the glass as it went down. As soon as he'd seen the atrium in the center of the exclusive high-rise, he'd known he'd wanted to live here. The atrium reminded him of his days in the country as a boy, and the manicured gardens all around his home. They'd been pristine, of course, his mother a nagging, vengeful harpy if they weren't.

The elevator hit the bottom and the doors slid apart silently. Striding from the box he passed the security desk and the manager's station.

"Your car is waiting, Mr. Scofield."

He rolled his eyes to the security guard, then back to the car parked directly in front of the building, and its glass doors. The stupidity astounded him. How the hell did people make it through the day? "Obviously."

William, one of his personal guards, had the door open and waiting as soon as he stepped toward the vehicle. Samuel, his regular driver, pulled away from the curb smoothly. The rest of his security team followed along behind, pretending to be useful.

"We're going to the office first, Samuel."

"Yes, sir."

Anton pulled his phone from his pocket and began responding to emails, which seemed to be never ending, now that Priscilla's were being forwarded to him. Even with his assistants wading through the bulk of them, he still had more than he could manage. And there were some that the assistants were never supposed to see. They were all working on a bit of a learning curve.

There was no way Anton could be expected to go through all those emails himself, though. Damon would just have to accept that.

There were a lot of things that Damon was going to have to get used to in the coming months. He might actually have to do some of the dirty work himself.

For years, Priscilla had been happy enough to do the dirty work, along with the brilliant Dr. Edgar Shu. The man had been a true, off-the-charts genius, as well as a sociopath. When he'd been in the States he saved babies from some of the most deadly diseases with his remarkable cutting edge therapies. But when he'd began devoting his time to the Spartan project there'd been a marked change in his personality. Anton had been shocked at some of the things Shu had done, shocked and impressed. He had devoted his attention to creating a super-soldier, at any expense. Too bad the man had died in the jungle. The company had yet to recover and Anton secretly believe it might never recover.

And Priscilla had been right there encouraging the doctor. The research camps had been her babies and she'd developed an unhealthy fascination with some of the captives. There'd been several men that hadn't done well in the program so she'd made them her security detail.

A few of them would be buried this week as well.

They pulled up in front of the Silverstone Collaborative, one of the tallest and longest buildings in downtown Arlington. It took up a lot of prime real estate. The taller part of the building was the corporate tower, and the longer, lower building to the south was the research division. His new albatross.

Anton liked being the face of the company at parties and government shindigs. He loved the wheeling and dealing that went along with his position, and he felt like he'd been an asset for the company for many years. When opportunities presented themselves, he tried to take advantage of them. Why not?

Samuel pulled the car to a stop and William hopped out to open the door for him. Stepping from the vehicle, Anton buttoned the front of his suit jacket together and strode into the lobby. Clean and pristine, it tried to be the benign embodiment of what a good company should be. If the public ever figured out what was behind the curtain, so to speak, they would all be in the deepest shit imaginable.

It was all about appearances.

He punched the button for the thirtieth floor then shoved his hands in his pockets. Damon had been walking a dangerous edge this week. Maybe his fuck-buddy Priscilla had meant more to him than he let on.

When he walked into the office Damon was staring out the window. He'd done that a lot recently.

Dustin Truckle, Priscilla's Head of Security for the Silverstone Campus, sat in a chair in front of Damon's desk. Anton was taken aback for a moment but didn't let his distaste show in any way. He wasn't sure why Damon had decided to include the other man.

Damon looked up when Anton walked in and scowled. "The press is already at the cemetery waiting."

"Well, of course they are," Anton laughed. "I let a contact know we'd be heading there."

Damon rounded on him. "Why the fuck would you do that?"

Anton looked at his boss closely, seeing the real weariness in his eyes. Had the man actually considered the bitch more than an occasional lay? "Because we need the press, Damon. You have to appear to be torn up about losing your Chief Operating Officer. And if you have to give a statement I think you know what you need to say. She was a devoted employee for so many years, she helped complete so many projects, blah, blah, blah. But you need to appear to be the business owner who just lost a valued employee, not a grieving lover." He moved a hand at Damon's look. "You can't go out looking like this. Is that suit even clean? And when did you last shave?"

Damon looked down at himself and seemed taken aback. He scraped a hand back through his hair. "I've been here all night."

"You have a change of clothes in your bathroom. Go take a quick shower and get cleaned up."

Damon turned, as if to do as Anton said, then swung back. "Mr. Truckle is taking over the research division. It seems to be more than what you can handle."

Alarm coursed through Anton. "What do you mean he's taking over? I've been in charge less than a week. I'm learning. It wasn't like Priscilla and I were having lunch together and exchanging blow by blow accounts about our days."

"Exactly." Damon's cold eyes turned frosty as he took the dig and he drew himself up, leaning into Anton's personal space. "You've been in charge for a week and haven't done shit to figure out who killed her. Or done anything to get the damned information back. Those little five dollar memory drives that Shu deemed more reliable than our million-dollar company servers have the information we need to get the Spartan project back on track again. Right now we're fumbling around in the dark, trying to guess at what he did. And it's not turning out well. Not to mention recruitment is down," Damon gave him an even more pointed look.

Anton clenched his jaw. "When the participating countries don't see results, they don't want to throw their best military men away."

Damon folded his arms. "Well, we're in a catch-22, then, aren't we?"

"If you would just allow me to raise the bounty..." Anton started.

"You've already done that! Twice!" Damon poked him in the chest. "Right now I'm wondering what the hell you're doing for all the money I'm paying you."

Anton glared at Damon's back as he walked to the bathroom in the corner of the office and slammed the door. Truckle stood up, a smug look on his angular face as he stroked a hand down his thick brown beard. "Sucks to be replaced, huh, Anton? I'm sure you did the best you could." Crossing his arms over his muscular chest, he looked Anton up and down. "I'll take care of everything from here on out. No need to worry your pretty little head."

Truckle tapped his cheek condescendingly and turned away.

Anton gritted his teeth and remained where he was. He'd been bullied before. If he gave Truckle any kind of indication that he was rattled, the security guard would continue his abuse. Just before he exited the office, Anton called his name. "Sucks that she had to die before he made the effort to remember your name."

Truckle gave him a toothy, predatory smile before slipping through the door.

Once he was alone in the office, Anton relaxed a little. Truckle, a slow-talking good ol' boy from the south, rubbed him the wrong way as soon as he'd met him. He was disgusting. There was no recognition of authority in that coal-black gaze, just sardonic rebellion. He had no idea what Priscilla had seen in the man. He'd only been here a few years. If Damon thought Truckle was going to do any better than he had...

That needed not to happen. How did he prove to Damon that he had the company's best interests at heart? Well, obviously, either get more test subjects or find the drives. Maybe even both. He reached for his phone to start jotting notes.

Heart thudding in her chest, the woman eased back into the darkness of the office. She didn't touch the door, very aware of the tiny little squeak it had developed recently. It had almost given her away last week.

Her mind reeled with everything she'd heard. Anton, condescending slime that he was, had confirmed what she'd observed herself. Damon Wilkes was behaving like he'd lost a girlfriend rather than an employee. It was obvious they'd been sleeping together for years but he wasn't one for emotional attachments. That was why she hadn't been sure about his behavior.

Some secret little part of her was glad that he was in pain. After all the years of abuse she'd taken from him, it was good to see something finally put a chink in his armor.

CHAPTER ELEVEN

When they got up the next morning, Jordyn's gaze immediately went to Fontana as she'd entered the kitchen. She'd dreamt about him last night. The feel of his fingers on her chin, the heat of his gaze as he looked at her had all conspired to leave her restless. It was easy to imagine that he was burning with need for her and that was why he'd looked like that last night, but in reality she knew he wasn't. The man was remote, only speaking as much as he needed to. He probably thought she would welcome any attention she could get.

No, that wasn't fair to him. He seemed like a decent guy, just... a little out of place.

Sometimes it was hard fitting into a new team, and even harder taking the lead. All of the LNF people knew each other. Fontana was the outsider. They didn't necessarily mean to exclude him but when they talked there were things that he just couldn't relate to. He didn't know anything about Duncan's new baby and the bossman's resulting new outlook on life, or how bad the twins were being for John and Shannon. They tried to bring him into the conversation, but it was hard playing catch-up like that. He did laugh, though, when they explained about John's love of the word *fuck*, and how he'd recently undertaken a campaign to cut the word from his vocabulary so that the twins didn't learn it. John and Shannon tried to use other words, but they slipped occasionally, and it was probably only a matter of time before the twins picked it up. They were just ornery like that.

"I actually caught John singing the theme from Frozen," Shane told them, grinning. "Last time he brought the twins in."

They all shook their heads, bemoaning the utter domestication of a true hardass.

There was an odd look in Fontana's eyes, like he didn't understand what they were talking about, and she wondered again about his background before he'd been in the camp.

As she hugged her uncle goodbye, she thanked her lucky stars for the family that she had.

"I will call you as soon as I can," she promised.

Cupping her face like he always did, he pressed a kiss to her forehead. "Fly safe."

Fontana wore his sunglasses, but she'd seen his bloodshot eyes before he'd covered them in the house. The poor guy looked like he'd been pepper sprayed or something. As the men packed their bags into Margarita's hold, she angled to catch his attention. "Are you tight?"

He nodded grimly. "Yeah. I'm good." He glanced at the helicopter, as if considering something. "I honestly don't know how I'll react to being there. If I start to unravel, put a bullet in me."

Her mouth dropped open in shock. "What?" she gasped.

His jaw hardened. "Put a bullet in me. Don't let me get those men killed." He tipped his chin toward the team. "Or you."

Even through the sunglasses she could feel him staring at her as if trying to convey something to her.

"I don't think I can shoot you," she admitted.

"You have to," he murmured. "Shoot me in the thigh. It won't kill me but hopefully it will get me out of whatever loop my brain falls into. I know I'm okay right now, but I can't promise you that I'll stay that way once we get there. Swear it to me, Jordyn."

The shock of the request was just as startling as hearing her first name on his lips. For a long moment she just stared, then she nodded her head reluctantly. "If you get out of hand I'll do what I have to do, but you need to make me a promise. I want you to try to talk to me first. Look for me. Grab me, do something to get my attention."

He nodded and reached out, stoking a finger down her cheek. "Don't let me hurt you, Madeira."

She gave him an arch look. "You called me Jordyn before."

A slight smile tipped up the corner of his mouth and the dimple made a brief appearance. "Slip of the tongue."

"You're allowed to slip. I'll let you."

The dimple deepened with his smile. "I appreciate that. Thank you."

Then something occurred to her. "I've only ever called you Fontana. Do you have a first name?"

"Yes."

Turning, he walked toward the helicopter. She sputtered with laughter. "Seriously? You're not going to tell me?"

He ignored her, climbing into the secondary cockpit seat, but there was a slight smile on his face.

Madeira— Jordyn— knew that he was anxious about flying to the camp today. She glanced at him more often the closer they got. Her looks should have felt intrusive, but instead he kind of appreciated her concern.

They'd been flying for almost four hours. The weather had cooperated for the most part but again, the deeper they got into the jungle the more erratic the weather became. Just like Venezuela, Brazil was going to test their mettle with gusts that made the chopper shudder and rain to slow them down.

As they neared the location, Madeira took the helicopter high, then pivoted on a wide imaginary axis to let Fontana scope out the camp below. They wouldn't be seen by anyone below, probably, but it would give him the opportunity to try to decide where to land. As he lifted the binoculars to his eyes, he tried to prepare himself for what he might see.

It was a bit of a letdown when he finally saw it. Shades of green upon shades of green, with a few angular contraptions thrown in. There was a beat up truck on one side of a building, and he thought he saw a person under one of the overhangs. "Contact!"

When he recognized the shaped of the cinder block medical building, the rest of the landscape began to look familiar to him. "There used to be a hole they cut into the jungle for her to land, there," he pointed, "but it's gone now. We'll have to range further out."

Madeira nodded and swung the bird back to the northwest, from the direction they'd come. "There was a cleared field back here."

They flew for almost half an hour over lush jungle canopy before they finally circled a long, cleared field. Fontana hated that they were so far away, but there had literally been no other place to land the large helicopter. They'd seen the track of a single road winding into the camp, but it was more of a path. Certainly not big enough to land.

"Going down, Shane," Madeira called out in friendly warning.

"Roger!"

Madeira circled the field once to look for the most accommodating spot. An old man came out of a hut at the edge of the field, waving what looked to be a homemade hoe at them. When he realized they were going to land on his crops, his hands went to his head in dismay and he dropped the tool. Fontana felt a twinge of regret as the wheels settled into the soft dirt of the field. He wasn't sure what was growing there, but the wheels would probably crush at least a few of the plants. It couldn't be helped, though.

"Let's try not to damage this guy's property any more than we already have," he called out.

As soon as she powered everything down Madeira hopped down out of the cockpit and circled around to the old man. He was looking at his field sadly. The rotor wash had compressed a large swath of the field, but Fontana thought it would rebound in a day or two. And he was amazed to see that Madeira hadn't crushed any of the plants with her wheels. Was she really that good? Or was it just luck that she'd missed them? He thought she was that good.

Madeira started calming the man, explaining that they weren't here to intentionally damage anything and that they would pay for what they had destroyed. The man's gaze flickered at the mention of money, and Fontana knew that they had his cooperation. Funny how well cash worked all the way around the world.

Madeira gave the stooped old man a handful of cash, promising double if they returned and her chopper was fine. The farmer looked at her consideringly, then nodded his head, promising to have his son watch it for them.

Fontana thought they were done, but Madeira asked him a couple of questions. Normally, he was a lot better at listening to Portuguese than speaking it, but Madeira was using words he'd never heard before. Her voice was lyrical, moving up and down in tonality. The farmer didn't appear to mind talking to her now, and he answered her at length. At one point he pointed into the jungle in the direction of the camp. By the time Madeira finally said her goodbyes, they'd been standing there in the heat and humidity for the better part of fifteen minutes.

Gathering her pack from the back of the helicopter, she kept a smile on her face as she turned toward the direction of the research camp.

"What did he say?" Fontana whispered.

Waving a hand at the man a final time, Madeira turned and led the team through the lines of plants and into the jungle. "I'll tell you in a minute," she hissed. "Let's get out of this clearing."

All of the men moved silently into the brush behind Madeira, following her lead. She'd been hiking for about twenty minutes before she finally turned. The men circled around.

"That was Señor Gata. He bitched and complained about my landing on his six plants, which, I didn't actually. But he understood when I explained that his field was the closest to our destination for many miles. He said he understood that, and that at least I had offered to pay for the damage, more than the other group had a few days ago. They pushed him down and threatened him and his family with guns."

"Did he describe them?" Payne asked, scowl on his normally easy going face.

"He said they were a military team like we appeared to be, but there was no soul in their eyes, no humanity. They landed their big machine and disappeared for three days. When they came back, there were more than they had come with, and three of the men seemed to be tied."

Ice ran down Fontana's spine, and he shifted his stance,

grip tightening on the MP5 in his arms. "There were hostages here?"

Madeira removed her glasses so that he could see her olive-green eyes. "Sounds like it."

Spinning away, Fontana tried to control the anger coursing through him. After all the time they'd spent in the states dodging the Collaborative, there had still been men here. Nausea turned his stomach at the thought of what they'd possibly gone through. Fuck! All this time later and there'd still been prisoners. He turned back to Madeira. "When?"

"He couldn't say exactly. Just several days ago."

Sadness and guilt began to replace the anger, but he pushed it away. He needed to keep the anger. It would serve him better for what they had to do. He could wallow in his own guilt later.

"Anything else," he snapped.

Madeira didn't seem to take it personally. She shook her head and put the sunglasses back on. "Nothing concrete. He did mention that some of the people in the area believe the old camp to the south was haunted, but they couldn't say exactly why, just things they heard and items that had disappeared."

Hm. If someone had broken out of the camp…

"Okay, men, let's get the fuck out of here," Fontana growled. "I want to get as far south as we possibly can before we lose the light."

They started in with a slow jog. The foliage here wasn't as thick and a few times they ran along bare dirt paths. Fontana made sure to stay cognizant of the direction they were heading, and adjusted accordingly when the paths veered away. The men kept up well, but he found himself glancing back to check on Madeira. The woman puffed along without complaint and looked like she could go for a long time. Determination drove his feet, but the old injury in his leg was beginning to ache big time. After a couple miles of jogging, he slowed down. They were having to duck and dodge more trees anyway.

"Don't brush against that," Madeira warned, pointing at a tall tree bristling with sharp thorns. "You will want to rip your skin off."

The group veered wide. Several times, she warned them of unknown hazards; they'd all done jungle deployments but it was nice to be reminded about the dangerous things by someone who knew them more intimately. Eventually, Fontana just let her take point. She kept up a grueling pace, only slowing down when they started to have to hack their way through the fading light. They slowed to a walk as Kenny took the lead, hacking away with his machete.

When the land began to slope down toward a river, Fontana had a bit of a flashback about the last time he'd gone down terrain like this. Rather forcefully. His right ass cheek and leg twinged as he remembered the pain. Actually, he realized, they probably weren't far away from where the accident had actually happened.

At the bottom of the slope the foliage thinned to a slight rocky beach. A muddy creek about twenty feet across, not quite a river, flowed strongly in a southeasterly direction, drawn toward the mighty Amazon. Fish glinted in the stream, and Fontana knew there was a decent chance that they were piranha.

Without hesitation he waded into the stream and across, feeling things brush against his legs as he did. If they crossed quickly, they could avoid any nastiness.

Fontana gasped as the water line moved up over his thighs. It was a lot deeper than he'd expected. And the current was a lot stronger.

"Wanna piggyback, Madeira?" Zero asked her, pausing at the edge of the river.

Laughing, she shook her head at him. "Not even. I think you'd dunk me just for the hell of it, then I'd have to tattle on you to Izzy."

They all grinned and Zero waved Madeira ahead of him. She removed her pack and rifle and held both above her head as she waded into the water. Fontana waited on the other side, breath held, for her to meet him. She gasped as the water level got above her crotch, then up to her waist, and she seemed to be struggling against the current a bit, bouncing on her tip toes. Fontana dropped his pack to the ground, ready to jump in if she needed assistance. When she got to him she allowed him to take her pack and rifle as she clambered up onto the bank.

Behind her there was a splash. They turned to see Shane DeRossett flailing in the water. Fontana frowned as the man's pack went under and he hoped he'd sealed up the top correctly to make it waterproof, otherwise it was going to take on water and pull him down. The young man kept his weapon up out of the water, even though he was gasping for air. Dropping Madeira's shit, Fontana took off down the short beach, hoping to catch the man before he really got into trouble.

Shane struggled, obviously unable to right himself.

"Lose the pack!" Madeira cried.

Shane either didn't hear her or didn't want to do it, because he continued to struggle. Fontana got to the end of the beach and leapt into the water, mere feet from the flailing young soldier. He got a glimpse of Shane's single brown eye, wide with fear, just before he went under completely.

Before he could grab him, Fontana hit a submerged tree, bashing his bad leg. Gasping in pain, he prayed he hadn't broken it again. Disentangling himself, he shoved himself over the tree with his good leg. Shane was a few feet away. He'd resurfaced again and it looked like he'd finally shoved off the pack. The man's weapon was long gone, but they could worry about that later. Surging forward, arms slamming through the water, Fontana grabbed the other man's vest and righted him.

Shane seemed disoriented and Fontana allowed himself to peek at the man's emotions. He was scared, but it didn't feel like it had a deeper cause than being tumbled in the river. Fontana had worried that the guy was having a PTSD flashback or something, but he wasn't reading that.

Fontana planted his legs down, praying that the river was no deeper than it had been and that his bad leg would hold. Someone upstairs must have been listening because he was able to catch his footing and stay vertical. He held onto Shane's camo safety vest and looked around.

They were at least a quarter mile from where they'd crossed.

"Are you okay?" Madeira called out.

Fontana glanced to the left and the steep bank where she stood. It was obvious she'd run here, and she appeared to be ready to jump into the river with them if she didn't get an answer. "We're okay."

"It looks like there's another beach a little further down," she pointed. "Might be easier to get him out there than try to go back up against the current."

Fontana agreed so he nodded, letting the current carry them along. He saw the beach and angled for it.

Madeira beat him there and helped drag Shane up onto the rocky stretch. The younger man was groaning slightly and holding his head. She went to her knees beside him as they stopped, calling his name.

"I'm okay, I'm okay. I just...," his voice drifted away. He kept one hand up over his eyes, obviously aware his glasses were lost.

Madeira pulled his hand down. "Hey, I've seen you

without them before. I think we all have. Don't worry about it."

Shane let his hand fall to the beach as he tried to catch his breath. He blinked up at the sky for several long seconds before he sat up. Even then he swayed a bit, so Madeira put a bracing hand on his shoulder, but he appeared to be gaining strength. Finally, he looked up at Fontana, who stood blocking the sun from his face. "I can't thank you enough for dragging me out of there."

"What happened?" Fontana growled.

Shane looked out at the river. "As soon as I stepped into the water and it started to swirl around me, vertigo hit me. I couldn't figure out which way was up or down, and then my pack started to pull me under. I'll be honest, sir, I panicked."

Yeah, that's what he'd thought.

Shane looked down at the ground around himself. "Did I lose everything?"

"Looks like it."

Cursing, he struggled to his feet, swaying slightly. Madeira curled a fist into the fabric of his vest, holding him vertical.

Now that the adrenaline was ebbing off, Fontana could tell that he'd bashed his leg pretty good. It was throbbing with pain. He looked down to see if he could see what he'd done, but the leg of his BDUs covered it.

"Are you okay?" Madeira asked, reaching out to touch his shoulder.

He glanced at her. "I'm fine. Take care of him."

Within a few minutes the rest of the team joined them. Big Kenny and Zero each carried an extra pack— Fontana's and Madeira's— in addition to their own.

"Payne headed downstream to see if he could catch your pack," Zero told Shane.

The other man grimaced and Fontana felt a little bad for

him. It was such a rookie move, losing your pack. Obviously, though, the vertigo had gotten him.

"I'm sorry guys. One minute I was hoping I didn't step onto a freshwater stingray and the next my head was reeling. I felt I'd just downed a bottle of Grey Goose and I couldn't keep my feet." He looked at Madeira in exasperation. "I can fucking fly in a helicopter but I can't wade through a stream."

She grinned and shrugged, her glasses perched on top of her head. "We all have our issues."

Wasn't that the truth?

"We've only got about an hour before dark," Kenny rumbled. "What say we set up camp and let you guys try to dry off. In this humidity that might be asking a lot. And that'll give Payne time to find us."

They all looked at Fontana and he nodded. Personally, he couldn't wait to get the fuck off his leg.

CHAPTER TWELVE

Jordyn knew Fontana was in pain, and she worried. Normally, he walked with a bit of a limp but right now it was more pronounced. He gathered several armloads of firewood before he moved down the rocky beach to settle on a stretch alone, with his leg propped up on a log and an arm over his eyes. There were lines of pain around his mouth and his eyes had been shuttered, like he was hiding how bad it was.

If he had his leg propped up, she wondered if it was swollen. Digging in her pack she found the first aid kit and took out one of the cold packs.

Shane had recovered. He was steady first on his ass and then on his feet, and had helped to clear the beach for their camp. Payne came back an hour later dragging Shane's sodden pack. He looked worn out and dropped down to the log they were using as a bench, setting his own pack aside. Immediately he started unfastening the Velcro across his chest that held his prosthetic in place.

"You okay," she asked.

Nodding, he made a face at her. "I got wetter than I expected. Had to wade in and then swim to it."

Shane looked apologetic. "I'm sorry guys. If I had any idea I was going to keel over, I'd have let Zero carry me."

"Fuck that," Zero snapped, shaking his head at the younger man.

"What? You'll carry Madeira but not me?"

"She's *half* your fucking size," Zero laughed. "And she made it just fine."

They laughed as he started going through the pack. It was saturated of course. They spent a long time laying everything out on tree limbs and rocks in an effort to get things dry. She didn't know if anything would work in this humidity and Shane's weapon was a lost cause. There was no finding it in the murky river.

Jordyn walked over to Fontana, making noise so that she wouldn't startle him in case he'd dozed off. She needn't have worried. He stared at her the entire time from beneath his arm. "I wanted to check on your leg."

"It's fine," he said, voice clipped.

She gave him a lopsided smile. "I'd like to check to make sure. Even a minor scrape can develop into something bad if not taken care of."

His silence seemed to be agreement, so she reached out to untie his lace-up boot. The pant leg was tucked into the top of it. When she tugged on a knot and he gasped, she realized how much pain he was really in. "Sorry, Fontana. I'll try to be more careful."

Unlacing the boot she spread the sides, then unlaced it even further down so that she could slip the boot off without tension. His black sock was damp, so she peeled it off as well, then began to pull up the pant leg.

Jordyn had seen a lot of catastrophic injuries in her life,

and she knew this had been a devastating break. There was a deep divot and scar tissue on the outside of his swollen calf, and right now it was angry and red. "How did you hurt it?"

"Which time," he laughed, grim. "When I jumped into the river I slammed into a submerged tree. Thought I broke it again for a minute."

Standing, she moved to the bottom of his foot and looked up his length. "I don't think it's broken, but it could be cracked. How did you injure it originally?"

"Escaping from the camp two years ago. Fell down an embankment in heavy rain and slammed it against a tree, I think. Compound fracture treated in the field. We had a few basic supplies, but it just didn't heal the same way every other broken bone the Collaborative gave me had."

Watching him thoughtfully, she reached for the ice pack, activating the little packet inside. Shaking it vigorously, she leaned over his foot and the tree to place it on his lower leg. He gasped and leaned up to look at what she was doing, then went still.

When she looked up at his face, she realized she was bent over in front of him and he had a perfect view down into her breasts. Fontana blinked and looked away quickly, toward his leg, but it looked like it had been a struggle. Jordyn felt a little embarrassed. She hadn't leaned over him like that intentionally, but it was good to know he was affected.

"Leave this on for twenty minutes, then take it off. Maybe it'll help with the pain right there at the old break. Will you take some ibuprofen?"

"Yeah. I will, thanks."

Damn. She bet that was a concession to how much pain he was in too. Jordyn moved back to her pack and drew out the white bottle, shaking several into her hand. She also grabbed him a small bottle of water from her pack and returned, handing the items to him. He sat up completely to take the pills and turned around to lean his back against the tree he'd had his leg propped on. He downed the pills and the water in one continuous swallow, then handed her the bottle back.

Repositioning the ice pack on his leg, he sank back against the tree. "DeRossett okay?" His voice was low so that the others wouldn't overhear.

"Yeah," she said softly. "He's fine. Embarrassed. Pissed. Frustrated with himself. You know how it goes."

He snorted. "All the kids that have recently been rolled out get like that. How long has he been out of the Marines?"

"Mm, maybe two years. He's still pretty wet behind the ears."

"Literally."

Jordyn tipped her head back and laughed, then clapped a hand over her mouth. She held a fist out and he bumped knuckles, grinning as she sat down beside him.

"So, are you still wet behind the ears?" she asked, deadpan.

He sighed. "Yeah," he admitted. "And everywhere else."

She chuckled, nodding her head. "Your sock was wet. You better deal with that."

"I will. I just wanted to sit here and bask in the pain for a minute."

"No jungle rot on this op."

Even the thought of it made him cringe. He'd seen the effects of moisture on uncared for feet. Leaning over he untied his other boot and pulled it off. Then his sock. Damp but not soaking wet. They would be fine by morning. He glanced at Jordyn's feet, then had to take a second look. She'd obviously taken her own advice because her tiny feet were bare, and she had little pale purple toe nails. "Purple, huh?"

"Hey," she said defensively. "There's only so much black

and camo a girl can take, you know? I like pretty underthings and pretty nails. What can I say?"

He held up his hands in a placating gesture. "Hey, I'm not saying anything. I like pretty underwear too."

She gasped, realizing he meant her own. She pointed a finger at him and narrowed her eyes in warning.

Fontana smiled, liking the fiery woman. There was an easygoing humor to her that he really enjoyed. They were joking around, but there was a buzz of attraction there too. And why couldn't attraction be fun?

"Is your underwear purple?" he asked curiously, unable to help himself.

Shaking her head, she gave him an exasperated, arch look. "Nope. Is yours?"

Fontana looked at her oddly, then laughed. "No. Why would you ask that?"

She waved a hand. "You just said you liked pretty underwear."

He laughed again, shaking his head. She'd totally turned that around on him. Avoidance at its best. Now he would be wondering. Constantly. The tiny glimpse he'd gotten had maybe been navy or black then if it wasn't purple.

"You won't even tell me your first name," she groused.

Fontana shrugged. "Maybe someday."

They went quiet, content to just sit, but the mood was lighter than when she'd first come over. They'd had an active couple of hours and they needed the rest, and for the first time in a long time he felt like he might be able to sleep. Or maybe he was just hitting his wall.

Reaching into her left BDU pants pocket, she pulled out a couple of protein bars. She held one out to him and he took it, stomach rumbling. They munched through them without comment.

"Are there natives here?"

She gave a short laugh. "Oh, I'm sure. You just may or may not see them."

He nodded thoughtfully. Once he was done with his protein bar he stuffed the wrapper in his pocket and rolled to his back, head resting against the tree. Tiredness suddenly overwhelmed him and it was all he could do to keep his eyes open.

"I might take a catnap," he said softly.

"That's fine." She pulled out sleek black smartphone. "I have bubbles to pop."

Fontana snorted. He would never understand women and their games. Aiden's girlfriend Angela loved them as well. "Can't believe you brought your phone."

"Waterproof up to a hundred meters and shatterproof with this case on."

"Hm," he murmured, slipping away.

———

Jordyn watched him fall asleep and didn't feel put out. The poor guy was sleep deprived enough, and then to add on heavy activity it was a lot for him to take. Would he admit that? No, of course not, but then, he was male. They didn't usually admit much of anything.

Jordyn played games for a good while, losing herself in the mindlessness of it, but she listened to Fontana sleep. His respirations were fairly rapid, but after about half an hour they slowed down, getting deeper and fuller; then she could tell that he was deeply asleep.

The other men talked a bit around the fire, but they weren't especially loud. Pulling up the camera on her phone she snapped a picture of the campsite. It looked a little ridiculous because Payne's arm prosthetic and Kenny's leg prosthetic were hanging from a tree to air dry, as well as all of

Shane's wet clothing. Not exactly what you expected to see in the jungle. Then, because she had it out, she turned the phone to snap a picture of Fontana. The man was incredibly good looking, especially with that intense glower gone. She could almost see where his dimples hid.

As night fell, Fontana slept on. Jordyn was afraid to move because she didn't want to wake him, but she needed to rest too. Lowering herself quietly, she curled up on her side beside him, propping her head on her arm.

Howler monkeys woke them before dawn the next morning. It was a relief when Fontana finally heard the others start moving around. In the wee hours of the morning, with the fire burning low, he'd woken. For a moment he'd been disoriented, because he wasn't hearing the music he normally had to listen to in order to fall asleep. Instead he was listening to quiet breathing beside him.

Opening his eyes he'd rocked his head to see Jordyn sleeping like an angel. She was curled up facing him, one arm folded beneath her head and her knees pulled to her chest. It was a humid night, but she slept like she was chilled.

Well, neither one of them had changed their clothes after wading through the river.

The most amazing thing, though, was that his left hand was resting on her drawn up knees.

He sat up carefully and lifted his hand away, making sure not to bump her. He was a little shocked at himself. He didn't normally reach out to people like that, especially not in his sleep. What had made him do that?

Shaking his head at himself, vowing to think about it later, he looked down at his leg. It wasn't as swollen as it had been, and definitely not as painful. It was like the enhanced healing from the serum would work up to a certain point, then no further. If they went at it hard today it would hurt again, but at least he'd gotten some decent sleep last night.

Then that thought sunk in. He *had* gotten decent sleep last night. He glanced at the watch on his wrist. After two a.m. They'd settled down late afternoon, and he'd gone to sleep within a couple of hours of that. So, he'd had at least four, maybe closer to *five* solid hours of shut-eye. Damn.

He knew by the energy in his blood that he wasn't going to be able to go back to sleep so he'd headed out into the darkness to take his turn at watch.

And now, as he walked into camp after several hours on watch, the sensation of the heat of her beside him last night came rushing back. His skin prickled with awareness. She looked up from stoking the fire and gave him a smile.

The awareness turned into arousal.

"Want some?"

It took him a second to realize she meant coffee. He blinked and swallowed, looking at the pot of hot water. He nodded and she poured him a cup, then held it out to him.

Fontana moved forward to take it from her hands and he gave her a nod. "Thanks."

The other men were beginning to rouse, drawn by the scent of coffee. Even if you weren't a drinker, it was a staple in the military. And even though it was just barely dawn, they'd be ready to go in a few minutes.

Circling the fire, Fontana moved to his pack. What he was wearing was mostly dry, but he needed to change. He glanced at Madeira. It looked like she'd changed as well. Maybe she'd gotten cold in the night after he'd left. Where had she gone to change her clothes, he wondered. He'd been up.

Dragging his attention back to his gear, he shook his

head. They had serious shit to do today and he needed to keep his mind focused.

"Let's go, Team Alpha. Full battle rattle. We roll out in ten."

It was distracting as hell trying to put out a fire, pack your bag, suit up for combat and watch a guy change his clothes all at once.

Jordyn forced her head down to look at her bag. She'd rolled her damp clothes up and put them in the waterproof side pocket on the bag. They wouldn't smell great by the time she got back to her uncle's place, but at least they wouldn't get moisture in everything else. Everything else in her bag was surprisingly dry.

Fontana did some kind of shimmy and dragged a fresh pair of BDUs up over his ass. He was wearing tight athletic undershorts beneath, but for a second she had a nice view of his grey-clad butt. Not purple, she thought with an internal chuckle, but mouthwatering, none the less.

She was totally breaking the code though. When a woman was in a combat environment with men, it was paramount that she be as sexless as the other guys. The men needed to know that they could depend upon her as well as anyone else, without the worry that she was trying to hook up with one of them. Off duty was one thing, but in a hostile environment like this it was the most important thing. Of course, being seen as sexless or "one of the guys" was in the best interest of the women in combat and some protection from unwanted attention or sexual assault.

So, she turned her body away from Fontana's lean lusciousness. When it sounded like he was about done, she glanced back at him. "How's the leg?"

Frowning, he adjusted a strap on his vest. "It's ok. Better than yesterday, definitely. I've got a pretty good bone bruise."

She winced. Sometimes those hurt as bad as actually breaking the bone.

Neither one of them said anything about sleeping next to one another the night before.

They started into the jungle just a couple of minutes later. Big Kenny took the lead plowing through the brush. Apparently, his prosthetic had dried perfectly because there was no noticeable hitch in his gate, and the terrain was difficult. It wasn't level by any means, but he cruised along at a good speed, hacking through everything.

Jordyn pulled out the small gray box to check their GPS position. They were less than a half mile from the position of the camp.

She held the device out to Fontana, showing him where they were.

"Kenny, I think we're going to have to go quiet."

The other man nodded and stowed the machete, then pulled his MP5 around. It was suspended on a nylon strap over his shoulder and swung around easily.

Jordyn fastened her helmet to her head and made sure nothing jingled. She checked the goggles on top of her helmet. When they pulled them down there was a tiny switch where the night vision could be turned on. The equipment was invaluable in a place like this.

They went into stealth mode, moving quickly and as quietly as they could through the thick brush. It was dim in the early hours before dawn, and she used the NVGs to see her way. In less than two hours the sun would be coming up, but right now it was a little misty and dewy. She took point, with Fontana almost directly behind her. It took almost thirty minutes to get through the last mile and they were all tired by the time they got there, but hyper-aware.

Jordyn stopped and sniffed. She smelled smoke.

She glanced at Fontana and he nodded. He'd smelled it as well.

She crept forward, hoping that they were close. Within ten minutes they reached the remnants of a chain-link fence. It was grown over and leaning in. Jordyn had a feeling they probably could have walked over it, but she looked at Fontana.

There was a dark, intense look on his face, like there was an internal monologue running through his brain. Jordyn knew she needed to keep an eye on him.

Fontana looked at the team. "Kenny, DeRossett and Zero head east. You're Team Bravo. We'll head west. No contact unless unavoidable. Recon only."

Everyone 'roger'ed into their mics and they took off. Fontana took the lead in their group, then Jordyn, with Payne at her back. She scanned everything she could see in the dim light of pre-dawn. It was still really early, so they didn't see any immediate movement inside the fence, but they did smell smoke.

They hiked another fifty yards before Fontana found a break in the fence. It didn't look like it had been used by anyone else, but they scanned the area carefully, looking for trip wires or cameras. They crossed through the fence and crouched, looking around again. Jordyn didn't see anything obvious, but Fontana seemed to be heading in a specific direction. She glanced at Payne, but he shrugged. His weapon was held at the ready. The camera was strapped high on his chest to keep it from banging around and being damaged.

Fontana crept around the corner of a building and paused, staring. "This is the old cafeteria," he whispered over their headsets. He crept forward, then lowered beneath a window. Using his taut thighs, he lifted up to glance through the glass. "Contact."

Jordyn breathed the tension out through her nose.

"Two local women cooking, one washing dishes."

Jordyn could hear the woman banging dishes now. She hadn't noticed it until he'd mentioned it. The entire camp was shrouded in misty darkness, broken only by a few weak bare-bulb lights. Now that they were closer she thought she could hear a generator somewhere close, but she couldn't pinpoint where.

There were no other sounds of activity in the camp, and no visible movement. If the women were making breakfast for a crowd, they could be here any time.

Fontana moved away from the cafeteria building and moved toward a path to the left. Then he stepped off into the brush and followed along parallel to the trail. That was pretty smart. If they happened upon someone they wouldn't automatically see the team.

They passed several small huts that looked to be unoccupied. One had a light burning inside through the window, and they crept around it carefully. They'd just cleared the corner when someone jogged down the front steps and onto the path. They let the person's sounds completely disappear before they started to move again.

Then, suddenly, Fontana went still. Jordyn almost ran into his back but she caught herself, then peered around his side.

There was a cage in front of them. It had to be eight feet tall and probably ten wide. The entire front was a wall of iron bars. There was no one inside the cage and the door stood open. But it gave her chills. Was *this* where the men had been kept when they'd been here?

From Fontana's reaction she would say yes.

Glancing around she checked to make sure they were still

hidden, then she touched Fontana's back. He jerked, though she'd barely touched him, and tossed her a glance. With a nod, he started forward again, circling the cage. Then he stilled again. Ten feet away there was another cage, and this time there was a body inside.

CHAPTER THIRTEEN

The body wasn't moving.

Fontana stared hard into the early morning, trying to see the body breathe, but his own heart was thudding so hard he couldn't tell. He thought he might have seen something but he couldn't be sure it wasn't his own heartbeat until he got closer.

Madeira was at his back and he took comfort in that. She didn't push or rush him, but he knew if he needed anything she would be there. He took a step forward, and she stayed damn near glued to his ass. Payne brought up the rear, and Fontana had seen the man move enough that he knew that the man would die to protect them if needed. The prosthetic hadn't hindered this op in any way.

The body inside the cage moved.

A million thoughts raced through Fontana's brain. This had started out as a recon run, but now that they'd seen a captive their plan needed to shift. If they went up to the cage and the captive didn't speak English or Spanish they could be fucked if he drew attention to them. The prisoners had been from many different countries. If the person did speak a language they understood, he could give them insight into what was going on.

Fontana knew he could get the cage open. That was easy. It had been one of the first things he'd ever done to break the Dogs of War out of the camp. But if the captive was too weak to escape they could be putting their entire team in danger. Trying to escape at dawn, just before potentially a lot of people came on duty, was not smart. Rescue needed to be done at night when he could destroy the lights.

He opened his senses toward the person, but felt nothing.

"Team Alpha, do you read?" Zero's voice was barely a breath.

"Go ahead," he whispered.

"We have multiple contacts, both friendly and hostile."

"Affirm." Fontana clenched his jaw, hating what he had to say. "Pull back. I repeat, pull back."

"Roger."

Fontana hated to do it, but they'd been a little ill-prepared for what they'd found. He'd expected indigenous people to have moved to the buildings. He hadn't actually expected anyone to be here from the Collaborative.

There was a chance that the man in the cage was there for another reason, but he seriously doubted it. They would pull back, scope out the area today and make a plan to get the prisoners out tonight.

As they began to withdraw Fontana glanced at the cage again.

The man had rolled his head over and was staring right at them.

Immediately he put his finger to his lips to keep him silent. The man gave the tiniest of nods. Taking a chance, Fontana pointed at the upper corner of the cage, where the cameras used to be. The man gave another minuscule nod. Brushing his left hand down his right forearm in an old Navy

SEAL sign, Fontana asked how many enemies. His eyes began to tear because he refused to blink as he watched the man tap the bar of his cell four times. Fontana gave him an 'ok' signal, then made the motion of a watch on his wrist, then the sun going down. The man seemed to understand everything Fontana was telling him, because he gave a slow nod and closed his eyes. It was obvious to him that the man appeared injured, and he hated leaving him behind.

It took everything he had to back away from the captive, but they had to go. The sky was getting too light and they would be spotted if they didn't retreat, either by a person or a camera. The result would be the same. Their asses would be fried.

———

Getting out was a lot easier than getting in. Jordyn didn't relax until they were outside the battered chain-link fence and back on the path they'd cut earlier. They'd didn't speak until they were at least a half a mile away from the compound. Taking cover at the buttressed base of a giant ceiba tree, they hunkered down to compare notes.

"Report," Fontana said.

"There are at least two men in cages, both Caucasian," Zero told them, sweat rolling down the sides of his face, "as well as a long bunkhouse. We peeked in the windows and we could see a few soldiers. Can't tell if they're organized, or not. They do have weapons, but they're not uniform. They seem to be a hodgepodge of whatever they could throw together. There was a lookout, smoking a cigarette, so we had to shift."

Fontana nodded. "We saw a captive as well, and he spotted us. It think he understood when I started using hand signals. There are at least four guards. I told him we'd be back after sundown."

"Do you think that was smart?" Shane asked. "What if he tells them?"

Fontana shook his head. "I don't think so."

"There were at least two other cages behind the one with the captive," Jordyn told him.

Fontana glanced at her. "Really?"

She nodded, shifting her weapon. "I couldn't tell if they had men inside them or not."

Fontana grabbed a stick and started scraping away tree leaves to get to the loamy dirt beneath. He started sketching out the position of the buildings and what he'd seen. Then Zero took the stick and added his side of the camp.

"So, all told, we have a minimum of three male captives, six guards, three kitchen workers. Did we see any kind of supervisor?"

They all shook their heads. "Guy that left the hut?" Jordyn asked.

"Probably."

They all looked at the map for a while before Fontana went down onto his knees. That position probably hurt his leg, but he was too hard-headed to not do it. He pointed at one of the shapes in the dirt. "This used to be the medical building. We set fire to it before we left."

"It looks to be in use," Zero told him. "You can see where it was burnt, but there was a light on the exterior. And a beaten path to the door."

He blinked, and Jordyn thought he was going to say something, but he bowed his head and pinched the bridge of his nose for several long seconds. When he finally looked up his eyes had chilled. "We'll take rotation surveilling the camp today. Watch inbound and outbound traffic, as well as prisoner movements, if there are any. Then when night falls we'll go in and get them out. I hate to waste the day, but I'd rather be safe than sorry."

"Agreed," Kenny said. "How do we get those cages open?"

Fontana waved a hand. "Don't worry about the cages. I can get those. And I'll take care of the cameras if there are any. It's actually getting the captives back to the chopper that worries me."

"Did anyone see a usable road?"

"I saw vehicles," Payne inserted, "so there has to be a road somewhere. Or a path. Something."

"That's one of the things we'll look for today. Two man shifts, four hours each. We'll insert at zero two hundred."

They all agreed. After shedding some of their gear, she and Kenny left for the first shift. "There's a bit of a hill in the direction we went earlier. We can see a good bit of the camp."

His words were proven true as the sun burned off the fog. They could see damn near everything. But there were no exterior guards. Did they really feel that safe there?

About seven a.m. local time things started moving. But not like they'd expected. There was no plan to anything going on. The men in uniform got up and headed to breakfast, and there were a few people in plain clothes moving around. They appeared to be Caucasian rather than Brazilian, but she could be wrong.

At eight-thirty most of the people in plain clothes headed toward the cinderblock building. Not long after, two of the guards escorted one of the prisoners into the building. The captive was in there for the better part of their shift. Jordyn waited nervously for him to return. Shane and Payne had just gotten there to relieve them when they saw the man being escorted back to a cage. This time, though, they were dragging him back.

Jordyn fumed, wanting to run down there and get the man out. She felt terrible that they'd stood by as he was injured. She wasn't sure if he was American or not, but it didn't really matter. He was not there of his own free will. This is what

Fontana had gone through for months. As well as the other two men that had come to LNF.

They passed on information to Shane and Payne, then they returned to their day camp at the tree. Kenny rested a heavy hand on her shoulder. "Patience, little sister. We'll get them out."

Yes, they would.

Fontana listened to Kenny's report as dispassionately as he could, but it was hard not to react when he heard about the man being dragged back to his cage. He glanced at Madeira. Her face was closed down and her sunglasses on, so he couldn't see her eyes. Anger radiated off of her though. Enough that she didn't speak a word until Kenny had finished.

"We need to kill those fuckers," she hissed, careful not to raise her voice. They were a good ways away from the camp, but they were being careful. "If they're forcing men to live in cages, they need to die. Maybe we'll just leave them in the cages and let them suffer like these men have."

Fontana was all for that. Actually, he'd prefer to kill them. It was no less than they deserved.

"Did you see who was in charge?"

"No, not really. But there was one man that had keys to what you called the medical building. Older man, glasses," she positioned her hand a little above her own head. "'Bout this tall. He could have been a janitor for all we know, though."

She paced a bit. Fontana watched her but didn't say anything. She was realizing the situation in minutes, when he'd had years to deal with it.

"I'm sorry, Fontana," she said, pausing before him. "I

didn't *not* believe you, but I don't think I understood and absorbed exactly what you'd gone through."

Fontana appreciated that. Because for a long time he'd thought that they were crazy. Surely their own government couldn't have turned on them so completely. Who would believe them if they did go public? It wasn't until they'd cracked the encryption on the drives last week that he'd felt a bit of hope. They would document this camp just like the last one, and they would scream bloody murder until they were heard. The men in the cages couldn't speak, but *they* could.

"Sit down and relax." He moved to the side of the tree and scraped away some leaves for her, then positioned her pack against it so that she could either recline back against it or lay her head back.

She smiled slightly at his lame attempt to make her comfortable. "Thanks."

Jordyn sat on her butt then leaned back against her pack. She pushed her sunglasses up on her head and crossed her arms beneath her breasts.

Fontana hadn't been *aware* of her until now, but the position did taunting things. She crossed her muscular thighs and leaned forward, looking up at him. "Who else is involved?"

Fontana debated the wisdom of telling her, but decided that if she was in it this far, risking her life, she needed to know. So, sitting down beside, he went through the list of people that had been listed in the information. Her mouth dropped open and she could only shake her head in disbelief.

"Congressman Albright is the one that fights for veteran's affairs!" she cried.

Fontana dipped his chin. "And three of the others are veterans themselves."

Tears filled her eyes suddenly and she looked away. Swiping her fingers across her cheeks she huffed out a breath.

"I'm so *pissed* right now. I want to hang them up by their tiny balls."

Fontana smiled slightly, appreciating that she was as emotional about it now as he was. "Thank you for being mad."

She looked at him again, her expression determined. "You have my support in anything you feel you need to do here. Or back in the States. I'll back you on it."

She held out her fist and he grinned, bumping knuckles. "Thanks, Jordyn."

Her eyes softened at the use of her first name and she turned her face away, giving him the smooth side. Using thumb and forefinger, he turned her chin toward him. "Don't hide from me."

Her cheeks flushed, kind of like she was embarrassed, but not. No, she felt the same awareness he did, and if there weren't two other men not very far away, he'd be tempted to taste her, and tease her. She could be brave if she *chose* to, but he didn't want it to have to be a choice for her. She deserved to be secure and know that she was wanted, and loved.

His mind screeched to a halt and he drew his hand back. Love had no bearing on what he felt for her. He wanted her, but he didn't love her, didn't know if he *could* love.

Forcing a smile, he pushed to his feet. "I'm going to go look at the camp."

CHAPTER FOURTEEN

"I'm heading out," Wulfe told Aiden. "We need to know if anything is going on. I've texted my informant but get silence. I need to be there to see what's going on."

Aiden nodded, pausing in the middle of the hallway. "Take care of yourself, damn it. We just got back together and now we're separating again. I don't like it."

Wulfe gave him a shrug. "Have to be flexible if we're going to take them down."

"I know." Reaching out, he clasped Wulfe's arm in his own. *Seriously, dude, you need to cover your ass. You'll have no back-up.*

I am aware. I promise I will take the utmost care.

They stared at each other for a long moment before they pulled away. The satellite phone in Aiden's pocket chirped with an incoming call. He answered it as quickly as he could, anxious to hear any kind of news. "What's going on?"

Fontana sighed on the other end of the line. "We have an active camp. Good guys and bad guys. We're scoping things out today and going in tonight. We have survivors."

Aiden let that sink in for a moment. "How many?" he breathed.

"We think just three, but we'll know more by tonight."

"I don't care what time it is I want you to call me when you get out."

"Will do."

"Are you doing okay?"

There was silence for a moment. "I'd be lying if I said I was unaffected. Being here and seeing the cages... yeah, I won't be sleeping tonight. Or for the next week probably. It's exactly the same, Will. Just greener where the jungle has started to swallow everything. And there are fewer people. It's not bustling like it used to be."

"Can you tell if it's still Collaborative?"

"There's nothing with their name on it, of course, but I feel like it is. They've moved back into the med center. Madeira saw them taking a man in there, then dragging him out hours later. Same MO as they used to do with us."

"Fuck," Aiden breathed. "But there are only three prisoners?"

"That's all we see. There could be more stashed somewhere."

Aiden huffed out a breath. "Okay. Wulfe is leaving now, heading back to watch Silverstone corporate. They're all attending the Bitch in Blue's funeral in a bit. I'll send a satellite phone with him. Is there anything you need us to do?"

"Not right now. I'd take a caramel macchiato if you had one available."

"Noted. Stay safe, Fontana. Team working well?"

"Yes, they are. More able than I ever could have expected."

"Good. Remember to call me."

"I will."

Aiden hung up, looking at the phone thoughtfully. The

GPS coordinates of the call scrolled past. The team was a long way from home. He really hoped they all returned safe.

Fontana had to see the camp in the daylight. Madeira offered to lead him out to the viewpoint where Shane and Payne were on duty for their shift, and he nodded. Taking up their MP5s, they took off. Zero and Kenny were chilling between the knees of the massive tree, trying to keep from being eaten by all the bugs. The problem was, there were bugs on the ground as well, and the Jungle Juice didn't repel them the way it did their airborne cousins.

The two of them were silent as they walked. Madeira wove through the trees like she'd been born in the jungle, and he really appreciated that he'd brought her along with them. Or maybe it was vice versa. If she hadn't agreed to put her life on the line to bring them none of them would be here right now.

Cresting a small rise, they crouched down to maneuver behind a clump of thick bushes. Payne gave them a chin nod, gun held across his knees as he knelt behind the bush. Shane lowered the binoculars to look at them. He gave a nod of his head as well and held the binoculars out to Fontana.

Fontana didn't like the gnawing feeling in his gut. It had been two years since they'd broken out, but he could remember every pain-filled second of being there. He could remember the feel of the textured floor of the cage, the inability to get away from being under scrutiny. They'd been watched for everything. It was only later when they'd began to build their mental ability that they'd finally gotten some relief, because they'd been able to direct the guards' attention elsewhere.

His body spasmed with remembered pain from the cattle

prod. They'd used it all the time, for every minor or major infraction. It had been their favorite torture device to use on him.

Hands trembling the tiniest bit, he lifted the binoculars to his eyes.

In a way, it looked the same. The cages were spaced about twenty yards apart, but some kind of green ivy hung over the sides. Same with the med center to the left. There were marks where the building had burned, but he could also see where they'd tried to paint over all of the damage. He wondered what it looked like inside. They would have to check before they left. It was going to be like breaking out all over again. He wondered if they still stored information here. Surely, they couldn't be that stupid.

Well, they still held prisoners here in a compromised location. Any average person would have closed the camp down and gotten rid of the evidence like the first camp they'd investigated. Right?

It was exactly a week today since Priscilla Mattingly had died. Anton Scofield had taken over from her, but so far it didn't seem like anything had changed. Was he even aware of what she'd done for the company?

Fontana sank down on his ass and propped his elbows on his knees, continuing to look through the binoculars. "Have any of the vehicles moved?"

"No."

He looked and tried to guess which cage had been his. Aiden had been in the one closest to the med center, then Wulfe. There had been a couple of cages between Fontana and Wulfe. His had been pretty distant. Panning to the right, he paused. That was it. He recognized the hut almost directly across from his cell door. There had been a woman living there, one of the nurses, with the coldest eyes he'd ever seen on a woman. She'd watched the guards abuse him and several times he'd caught her grinning, enjoying his pain. Then, the night the abuse had changed to molestation, she'd actually sat at her window and watched.

He'd hated that woman with the power of the sun.

Something blocked his vision, but Fontana had already lowered the binoculars, not wanting to see his cage anymore. Emotion and a remnant of fear, as well as disgust, quaked through his body. His heart was racing and his teeth were literally gritted. He became aware that there was a hand on each of his arms, and someone was leaning into him from the front. Madeira's short dark hair brushed his cheek on one side, and she held them pressed together with her rough hands. The scars on her palms weren't usually noticeable, but he could feel them against his skin now.

Shifting, he pulled back to look at her.

Those pretty Army green irises were wide in her face and she seemed a little fearful. "You weren't responding to us, and we thought you were going to lunge up out of here. You tensed like you saw someone you wanted to fight."

He blinked and shook his head. "Just ghosts. Thanks guys. I'm good."

Gently, he pulled away from her— their— comfort and stalked back down the hill.

Jordyn wanted to follow Fontana. She really did. But she knew the man had to rebuild his defenses.

When he'd drawn in a breath like he was about to shout something, she'd leaned around to get a better look in his face. There had been anger there, and fury, as well as terror. Even with his eyes pressed to the reticles of the binoculars, he'd looked like he was about to beat the shit out of someone. She wasn't sure what he'd seen, but it had to have been bad.

Shane had grabbed his left arm first and Payne had maneuvered around to hold his right, while Jordyn had blocked his view and pulled him in tight from the front. For a long moment he'd just shaken in her arms before he'd pulled back and looked at her.

Jordyn had seen torture before, and every bit of that memory was still in his eyes. Fontana had pulled back like she'd looked into his soul and found him lacking. She really hoped he didn't think that.

And for a moment—just a moment—she'd thought the jungle had shaken with his terror as well.

"Did you feel that?" she asked Payne, hoping she was crazy.

He'd nodded grimly, his mouth clamped tight. Oh, hell.

CHAPTER FIFTEEN

Anton stared at his assistant, wondering if the young man had finally gone off his rocker.

Lukas Evans was every man's fantasy. Tight ass, sleekly styled hair, perfectly groomed outfit. Anton had found him in a Starbucks, running the store damn near single-handed. There had been a sharp cunning in his big blue eyes, and he hadn't put up with anyone's shit. When Anton had asked him if he'd like a job, the first question out of his mouth had been, "Do I have to fuck you to get it?"

Anton had smiled. "Only if you want to."

They'd been working together for the better part of a year now, and Lukas had grown into one of the most competent assistants he'd ever had.

Which made his statement all the more ridiculous. "Why the fuck would I want to go to Guyana?"

Lukas shook his head. "You're not going because you want to. You're going because you want to get a grip on the scope of what Priscilla did. Guyana is one of the last Collaborative research properties. You would have to go at some time anyway, so why not go now— sooner— and get a grip on what's going on before the bearded dickhead moves in and takes all the credit."

Lukas' words had merit, but Anton had no desire to fly halfway around the world.

Damon had been dismissive the day of Priscilla's funeral, and Anton didn't want to piss him off so badly that he'd fire him in a fit of rage. Every day there were employee emails and messages rolling in asking him for guidance. And he could admit to himself that he was damn near clueless.

Maybe it would be smart to go to Guyana. If he showed up in person, surely they would recognize his authority. And maybe he would spot some things that could be modified or changed. Lord knew he needed to impress Damon with something.

"Fine," Anton sighed. "See if the company plane is free. There's no way I'm flying there commercial."

Lukas nodded, looking smug. "I knew you'd make the right choice."

"Oh, don't be too excited. While I'm gone you get to run herd on dickweed. I want you to watch everything he does."

Lucas snorted. "Which dickweed are we talking about?"

"Both of them, actually." Anton laughed.

Lukas typed into his tablet furiously.

Anton watched the boy, enjoying the play of muscles in his back as he turned toward the window. "It occurs to me that I may be gone for a while."

Lukas looked up and caught his gaze. "Yes, you will," he said slowly, a grin tugging at his full lips. "Maybe we should lock the door and have a more in-depth meeting."

"You read my mind," Anton said, watching the young man walk toward him, ever so deliberately.

Fontana stalked into the jungle to get a grip on his emotions. Two years after the fact, he hadn't recovered from what had been done to him. He wanted immediate vengeance, but in reality, it was a long, drawn out process.

He came to a smaller Brazil nut tree, the base of this one only stretching about twenty feet. Scraping his boot through the loose litter in the lee of one of the knees, he made sure it was safe before sitting down and leaning back against it. Cupping his head in his hands he exhaled, trying to recenter himself.

What had been done to them had been horrific, but they had survived. And they'd recovered physically at least, still working on everything else. Yes, it had been hard at first, but things were falling together the way they were supposed to. Tonight, they'd infiltrate the camp and steal back the men trapped inside. If anyone interfered, he had no problem taking them out. Maybe, if he did both of those things, the pressure in his head and mind would dissipate.

He'd been dealing with the repercussions of being in the camp for two years. It was time he dealt with the ghosts.

When he returned to the other tree, Jordyn and Payne were talking softly. Fontana wandered over and sat down, looking between the two of them. "I appreciate what you did for me up there."

Payne shrugged. "We all have triggers. We knew we'd have to watch you when we came to this location. What you were feeling was completely natural. I still break into a panic attack if a jet screams over my head. I know it's highly unlikely that it will drop a bomb right in front of me like in Kandahar, but it's training that you received, and your brain has learned to take steps to protect you."

Fontana appreciated the former Marine's words. No one had actually ever talked to him about it before.

"I can't let anyone fly me anymore," Jordyn admitted.

"Not in a chopper anyway. Not even my mother. Pisses her off to no end." She shrugged her shoulders, and Fontana noticed that she'd taken her bulletproof vest off. Her t-shirt beneath was marked with sweat in the armpits and down her chest.

For the first time he noticed how damp he was himself. Too many other things on his mind to even notice the heat. He reached for the water nozzle on his pack and drank. Warm and stale, but it quenched his thirst.

Jordyn held a meat stick out to him. "Fresh from the wrapper."

He snorted and took it from her, and as soon as he bit into the meat he realized how hungry he was. She seemed to sense it too because she handed him another one.

Fontana chewed mindlessly, intent on getting it in his stomach. This entire trip had been stressful for him and he hadn't been taking care of himself.

"Is there anything we need to watch for when we go down there?"

Fontana looked at Payne. "The med center is where they do the experiments. We started a fire in the building when we evacuated two years ago, but apparently it didn't burn well enough. Before we get these prisoners out we'll have to check the building again. If they're stupid enough to use a compromised location, they may be stupid enough to continue storing the data here. If we can find more information on the Collaborative, I'm all for it."

Payne nodded. "I think that's smart."

"How many people were here when you were in residence?"

He looked at Jordyn. "We started with twenty men in our group. And there were almost fifty guards here. That included both hired guards and Brazilian Army. There were at least thirty medical staff."

"We didn't see anywhere near those numbers," she

frowned. "In fact, I don't think there are thirty people total in the camp right now."

"It seems to be running with a skeleton crew," he agreed.

Jordyn looked at him, and he could see the worry in her eyes. "We can deal with it. Those men need to be rescued. Did you recognize the one that spotted you?"

He shook his head. "No. I seriously doubt it's any of the men from the original group. There's no way they could have survived this long."

"What time are we going in?"

Fontana looked at the watch on his wrist. "About zero two hundred. Most everyone will be asleep and the lookouts, if there are any, will be drowsy."

Payne nodded. "I'm going to crash for a couple of hours then."

"Me too," Jordyn said. "If those men are not able to run or even walk, we're going to have to carry them back to Margarita. It would be easiest if they're ambulatory, but if not, we need to make sure we aren't pursued."

Fontana looked at her and gave her a grin. "Oh, don't worry. We'll take care of anyone that might even think of pursuing us."

The thought sent a thrill through him, and apparently her as well, because she grinned back at him. It was so wrong that the thought of getting vengeance on some of the evil in the world made them so happy.

Madeira reached into her pocket, then held her fist out to him. He tried to bump her knuckles, but she shook her head. She held her fist out again and he figured she was handing him something. Opening his hand but leery, he held it out.

She left a handful of multi-colored Swedish fish on his palm. Fontana's mouth watered at the sight of the candy. "Oh, no way," he breathed. He popped a classic red into his mouth and let his eyes fall shut as he chewed. The repetitive chewing, and the sugar, relaxed him like nothing else. With a grin, he gave her a thumbs-up as she crossed to her pack.

It took forever for two a.m. to swing around.

Jordyn tightened one of the Velcro straps along the side of her combat vest. It had to be perfect when they inserted, because there was no fixing it there. They were going to be too busy. Everyone else was geared up as well, and they were all basically dancing in place.

"Paramount is the safety of the team and the prisoners," Fontana told them. "We're going to stay together as a group as much as possible. At some point I'm going to peel off to check the med center. Zero, you'll be my backup. Let's roll out."

Zero nodded. It was just barely visible in the light of the flashlight Fontana held. They all had night vision goggles on their helmets, but they hadn't flipped them on yet. They needed to go as far as possible without using them so that the batteries that powered them stayed fresh.

The night was black as pitch and the trees swayed above them, like it was going to blow up a storm. Jordyn prayed it at least waited until they had gotten out safely before Mother Nature let loose on them.

They fell into step behind Fontana, pulling the NVGs down over their eyes. Everything turned brilliant green as they hiked through the jungle toward the camp. They went over the same section of downed fenced that they had the previous night, but he angled in a different direction. It seemed like he was going to the farthest cage and would work his way back.

"Madeira," he said over the com. "I'll open the cage and

take care of the cameras, but I want you to be the first contact. Try to be non-threatening."

She snorted softly. "Roger."

That made sense. She spoke more languages than the others, plus she was female. As long as her scars didn't scare the men to death, they might be okay.

There was a lone guard traveling along the main path between the med center and the cafeteria. Everything else branched off of that path, including all of the prisoner cells. Fontana made a motion for them to hunker down behind a hut, so they did. Then he padded out behind the guard and snapped his neck. In a flowing motion, Fontana caught the guard as he fell and dragged him into the brush.

Madeira began keeping a running count of bodies in her head. Later they would probably want to reconstruct what had happened.

Fontana led them to the first cell. There was a man on the floor, curled on his side. Bones poked up out of his hips and he appeared to be unconscious. Reaching out, Fontana touched the cell door lock. Madeira heard a click and a squeak as the door popped open. Then she heard a pop from the upper corner of the cell. That must have been the camera.

The bony man was suddenly spinning around, hands out to try to fend off attack. He didn't have the energy, though, and he fell weakly against the bars. There was a giant swath of something dark on the front of his abdomen. Madeira was afraid to know what it was.

Jordyn jumped up into the cage, swiping the helmet off her head. She positioned the helmet so that the shine from the NVG goggles illuminated her face. "My name is Jordyn Madeira, former US Army. Do you speak English?"

The man licked his cracked lips. "L-little."

"What country are you from?"

"Denmark."

Ok, that was one language she knew nothing about. "Do you know how many prisoners are here in the camp right now?"

He held out a spread hand, all four fingers and the thumb. Five. "One," he pointed at the med center.

"Would you like to leave this program?"

The man's eyes glistened in the weak green light and he nodded vigorously. "Please."

They removed the man from the cage. Shane took his arm as he sagged, and Jordyn had a feeling they were going to have to carry him out of there eventually.

"What's your name?" she asked the man.

"Aksel."

"Aksel, do you know how many guards?"

He shook his head. "Not many. Just two, night time."

Well, damn. That meant there was another guard wandering the property. Fontana looked around.

The next cage was much the same, but this time the prisoner was American. He wept as Jordyn moved in toward him and wrapped his arms around her when she spoke to him. Normally, she wouldn't have let him near her with all the weapons she was carrying, but her heart was breaking for the man. For a moment she held him tight, letting him feed off her strength if that was possible before she pulled back. "We have to rescue the others. What's your name?"

"Hughes. Brandon Hughes. Marine Corps."

"Come on, Brandon. Let's get the fuck out of here, Marine."

He was a little more mobile than Aksel and looked around the group expectantly. They didn't have any spare goggles to give him, but Kenny kept a strong hand on his wrist to lead him.

The next man they rescued barely even opened his eyes

when she entered the cell. This was the man she and Fontana had been spotted by last night. Jordyn told him they were here to rescue him, but there was no response. She crept closer. The man was burning up with fever. Getting around behind him she positioned her arms beneath his armpits and pulled him to the door. It should have been harder than it actually was. The man groaned but didn't rouse. He would have to be carried out of the camp. Hell, she could probably carry him.

Fontana shook his head. "You guys stay here with him for a minute. Madeira and I will go check the remaining cages and get the last prisoner."

Jordyn was good with that. Their group was getting bigger and less stealthy. They needed to make sure they didn't draw attention in any way.

She followed Fontana down the dirt path. They passed several huts too close for comfort and they looked for the last prisoner. They checked three more cages, all empty. Then they heard a sound.

Jordyn wasn't sure what exactly it was other than rustling. And grunting. Fontana went low, crouching down as he peered around a final hut.

A blast of icy cold hit her as Jordyn observed what was going on in the final cage in the farthest reach of the camp. Was that feeling from Fontana? Rage consumed her, and terror. Fontana started to lunge forward, but she grabbed him by the arm. "Wait," she hissed.

The cage door was open and inside one body rutted over another. The body beneath was still, as if afraid to move. Jordyn thought she might have seen a glint of a blade in the aggressor's hand.

There was a harsh exhalation as the man orgasmed, arching harshly into the body beneath.

Fontana vibrated with fury, but he held still as the guard

pushed away from the body and exited the cage. Chuckling, he made a kissing sound to the prisoner, but the man on the floor didn't move. Buttoning his pants up, the guard put the knife away in the belt sheath and adjusted himself. Then he shut the cage door, turned and casually walked away.

Fontana moved before she could stop him. Faster than her eyes could track, he was across the space between them, tackling the man to the ground. She winced as the guard huffed out a breath. People would hear that. Then Fontana was driving his fists into the man's body.

Jordyn raced after them, not sure she wanted to get between Fontana and the guard. They scrapped and rolled until they were almost underneath the weak pole light. Suddenly, the smaller man rallied, swinging punches. Fontana's helmet was knocked from his head and fell to the ground, rolling into the brush. Then they faced off, and Fontana went still.

"Well, well," the guard said in heavily-accented English. "Look who came back. Pretty Boy Fontana."

The knife appeared in the guard's hand, waving almost delicately in the air. He crept closer to Fontana, who hadn't moved. Jordyn swept her NVGs off and circled wide, trying to get behind the guard, but he danced away.

"Mr. Fontana and I are old friends, aren't we?"

Jordyn looked into Fontana's face and felt terror go down her spine. There was a slack nothingness there, like he didn't care what happened to him. He stared into the guard's face as if he were looking at a viper, entranced with his movement.

Jordyn glanced around. So far, they hadn't been exposed, but people would hear if she tried to shoot the man. Making her weapon safe, she pushed it behind her shoulder on the nylon strap and drew out her belt knife. Crouching low, balancing on the balls of her feet, she moved closer.

The guard only had eyes for Fontana. "Yeah, you broke

out of the camp and suddenly we're the ones being blamed. It wasn't pleasant here for a very long time."

Fontana's lack of response was terrifying. Jordyn wasn't sure what was going on, but he had shut down completely. Would she actually have to shoot his ass to get him to move? It was up to her.

The guard looked at her finally, his face curling into a menacing mask. "And what did you bring me? Oh, isn't she a curvy piece of ass. Even under all that gear I can tell she'll be delicious."

The guard lunged.

CHAPTER SIXTEEN

Fontana heard Miguel's words, but he couldn't make himself move. Remembered pain and terror kept him immobile, and scenes flashed back through his mind on blast. Blood and pain, the spine cracking torture of the cattle prod shoved into his ribs, men slamming him face down into the textured floor, cuffing his hands and feet to the bars of his cell. Usually, it had been right after the med center experiment, when he was at his weakest, when the group had come after him.

It had started with Miguel. The man had always been insecure, and he'd taken that insecurity out on the prisoners, more harshly on Fontana. Maybe because he'd been everything Miguel wasn't; tall, good-looking, fair-haired. Then Miguel had brought friends, other guards as evil as he was. When Fontana had scanned one of their minds, he'd learned that the guards had applied to be a part of the research group and had been denied. So, they all carried a heavy dose of resentment.

Miguel had been the spark to incite the rest of the group.

DESTRUCTION

The first time it had happened, Fontana had been out of his mind with pain from the experiment. He hadn't even been conscious enough to realize what had happened, until he'd woken up with pain not associated with what the Collaborative had done. One look at Miguel's smirking face as he'd walked by the cage had told him what had happened.

The next time the experiment hadn't been as harsh, and he'd been aware when they'd come to him in the night, rushing through the cell door to overwhelm him. He'd fought that night, and the men had not had an easy time of abusing him. It had still happened though.

The humiliation had been staggering. And he had vowed that it would never happen again.

It had been soon after that that he'd realized he could push on their minds. *Finesse* them. Make them reconsider their actions. The next time the group had come after him in the night, Fontana had planted a crippling sense of dread that they weren't going to make it out of the cage alive. He'd stood there, fists clenched, pouring every bit of his energy into that push as he waited for them, ready to target the dread on whoever stepped forward.

It had been Miguel of course, and Fontana had made him fear exposure and discovery by his family. He made him hear the thundering footsteps of the Captain coming up the path, and the wild roar of the jaguar in the night. Fearfully, the guard had backed away from the cage and taken off. The rest of the men had scattered like mice. And they'd left him alone for a while.

It was almost two weeks later when the Collaborative doctors had almost killed him. They'd given him a cocktail of scorpion venom and the effect on him was almost immediate. His heart had stopped several times and the doctor had kept him in the med center for an entire day before finally letting him return to the cage. Miguel had escorted him, and he'd seen how weak Fontana had been. As they'd shoved him into the cage, Miguel had squeezed his ass cheek, and Fontana knew they would be coming for him that night.

He'd rested as much as he could, feeling the occasional arrhythmia in his heartbeat. He still wasn't completely healed, but he would have to fight. The last time Miguel had run away in fear. This time he would have to prove to his men that he wasn't a chicken shit.

When they'd appeared out of the night and stepped into the light from the pole, Fontana had attacked. No hesitation. The guard with the weakest, simplest mind was only about twenty. Slamming power into him, he'd convinced the boy that Miguel and the others were there to attack him, and that he needed to protect himself. The boy had ripped his knife out of the sheath on his belt and started swinging. He'd taken out two guards before Miguel had planted a knife in his chest.

Swinging his attention from the fight, Fontana had sent power into the alarm system. Immediately, the sirens began to wail. The Army came running, but Miguel had disappeared into the darkness.

And now, two years later, he was threatening again.

Blinking, Fontana gasped in a breath. His mind caught up with what was going on. Madeira, several inches shorter than the guard, had just nailed Miguel with a roundhouse punch that sent the man staggering. Fontana sent a blast of concentrated power into Miguel's consciousness. He'd been arching down with a vicious knife attack toward Jordyn, but Fontana wouldn't let him get away with molesting anyone else. Running forward, he tackled Miguel again, slamming him to the ground. Fontana felt the slice of the blade across his lower belly, but he didn't pause. Reaching for his own blade, he slammed it into the smaller man's side. Then again. Miguel looked up at him, wide-eyed, as if he couldn't believe that Fontana had turned on him.

Fontana watched every second of the man's death. Maybe if he watched it closely enough he would feel better about what had happened to him. He wasn't naïve; he knew abuse like that happened, especially during war time, but it had been so abhorrent to him.

Now, though, he was getting the satisfaction he'd dreamed about. Hot blood washed over his hand, making his grip on the knife slick. He tightened his fingers, drew the knife out and slammed it in again. Miguel sighed out his last breath, clutching weakly at Fontana's vest.

"I think he's dead," Jordyn whispered.

It took him a long minute to respond to her words. Moving back off the body, Fontana looked down at what he'd done. And he felt no remorse. Only satisfaction.

Reaching out he swiped his bloody hand in the grass. He didn't want any part of Miguel on him ever again.

Fontana pushed to his feet, his legs trembling. He felt sapped of energy, but vindicated. Miguel had been like a plague in his mind for years. Maybe now he could have some peace.

He met Jordyn's eyes. Even in the dim light he could see the slight smile on her lips. At least she didn't seem to be disgusted with what he'd done. He hated to even think about what she read in his actions.

"I'm sorry," he whispered. "I never expected…I thought he was dead."

He waved a hand at the body on the ground.

"I could tell you had some pent-up emotion there."

He nodded, then seemed at a loss what to do. Jordyn reached out and cupped his face in her hands, looking him in the eyes. "Let's get these prisoners out of here."

He appreciated her touch right then more than he ever could have expressed. Turning his head, he pressed a kiss to her rough palm. "Yes."

The man that Miguel had been abusing was... a woman. Jordyn looked at Fontana, shocked, as she crouched near the slight body inside the cage. "I didn't think there were women in the program?"

"There weren't, that I know of."

Fontana stepped inside and crouched down as well. It was obvious the woman had been abused, but she was also out cold. "Think he knocked her out?" Jordyn asked.

Fontana shook his head, feeling for a pulse. "She's a little feverish. I think she's fighting something off."

There wasn't a lot of light that reached inside the cage, but they could see that the woman was not very old, and her hair looked like it had been shaved and was just growing in. She was naked, and it was obvious that she hadn't been eating well. Or they hadn't been feeding her.

Jordyn tried to think of anything she had on her that could be used as clothing, but she didn't have anything. Her pack was back at the makeshift camp.

"I'll be back in a minute," Fontana told her.

He disappeared into the night. When he appeared again he had his helmet on with his night goggles and held an armful of cloth.

"I remembered seeing a clothes line behind the cafeteria," he whispered to her, then he disappeared again.

There was a long linen shirt that would be perfect. Jordyn sat the woman up in her arms and popped the shirt over her head, then manipulated the arms through the holes. There were deep purple bruises on her body Jordyn could see even in the dim light. Scrambling in her belt pack, she grabbed a package of Wet Wipes and tried to clean the remnants of the assault from her flesh. Fontana had found a pair of shorts as well, so she pulled those up the woman's battered, bruised legs. Jordyn kept expecting her to wake because this contact was so personal, but she didn't. By the time she'd gotten the woman dressed Fontana had returned, carrying her helmet. He handed it to her, then made a motion at the pole light. It went out immediately, plunging them into darkness.

Jordyn fastened her helmet on and dropped the goggles over her eyes. This was much better.

They carried the woman out of the cage, then Fontana took her into his arms. That left Jordyn as security. With a final look at the body of the raping bastard Fontana had killed, they took off back toward the team.

Jordyn was amazed at Fontana's power. Everything electrical around him seemed to die, but only when he wanted it to, and when it was convenient for them to pass undetected. And when he'd killed the guard, she was sure she'd felt the ground shake beneath her.

They met the other team at the previous cage. The prisoner there still hadn't roused so he would have to be carried out. The woman hadn't woken either, so that was two. Fontana whispered into the mic and explained about the woman. Every helmet turned to look at the body draped in his arms.

"There's one more in the med center, Aksel says. Hughes, can you confirm that?"

The man blinked wide eyes into the dark as he nodded at Fontana's question. "Yes. Jackson. He didn't come back last night when he should have."

Fontana looked at Zero. "Change of plans. You need to carry. Madeira and I are going into the med center. I want you to take these prisoners and get them out of here. As long as everything goes quietly, we'll meet back at the tree."

Zero nodded and took the woman from Fontana. The team helped get the unconscious man draped over Big Kenny's shoulder, an easier way to travel that would allow him to keep his weapon in his hands. Shane and Payne would run security and lead them out of the camp.

It was not ideal, but Jordyn knew there was no way on earth that Fontana would leave anyone behind. And she was okay with that. They'd go in, get Jackson and get moving.

"Is there a security guard on duty inside?" she asked Hughes.

"I'm not sure. There might be a nurse sitting with Jackson, but I'm not sure if someone is on duty there all the time or not."

Well, damn.

The team broke up and she prayed that they would make it out safely. No one in the camp had stirred yet, which she thought was amazing. Fontana and the guard had made a lot of noise while they were fighting, crushing plants and skittering in the gravel, but it had been at the farthest edge of the camp. Maybe that was *why* the cage was all the way out there. And maybe the people in the huts had gotten used to strange nighttime sounds in the jungle.

She thought that someone would notice the quaking of the land, though. Obviously, they hadn't, because it was still quiet.

She followed Fontana in a crouched jog as they headed toward the brick building. There was no one on the outside, and when they'd watched movements the day before, there hadn't been a lot of guards going in or out here. That didn't mean that there weren't a few inside though.

Fontana led her right up to the building. There was only one exterior light here, and he'd knocked it out as soon as they'd gotten within fifty feet. Now, crouching down beside the door, he reached out to the lever handle. It wasn't electronic, but she still heard a click before he pushed it open and squeezed through. Inside, the hallway was lit with little lights down along the floor, making the NVGs flare with brightness. Jordyn stretched the goggles up onto the helmet. The bright overhead fluorescent lights were off, but they had plenty to see by. Fontana made a motion to the left and they headed in that direction.

They checked every room they came to, but most of them were dark. Then they came to one room that had a light on beneath the door. Very lightly, Fontana rested his palm against the gray metal surface. Jordyn watched him close his eyes. He seemed to be concentrating on something inside. When he opened his eyes, he gave her a quick, cautioning glance. That was when she heard the footsteps approaching.

A Brazilian Army soldier opened the door and looked at Fontana. He nodded his head. "Here you go, sir."

The soldier opened the room and let them inside. He didn't look to be very old, but there was a little experience there. He was Brazilian, but young enough that English was easy. Jordyn was stunned, because she hadn't expected Fontana to have this kind of control. The soldier smiled at them and she realized he had a sidearm on, but he'd made no move to reach for it. It was as if Fontana was an old friend of his.

"Are you the only guard in the med center?"

"Yes, sir. There's a nurse on the other side monitoring the patient. He didn't react well to whatever they gave him today."

"Do you record everything in the camp?" Fontana asked, voice casual.

"Oh, no, we don't have the set up for that. A couple years ago men broke out of the camp and destroyed a lot of the equipment. Now we just monitor the prisoner cells, mostly."

He waved at the wall to the left. "You can see where the old camera monitoring equipment burned."

Yes, the wall was still singed at the top, and most of the wrecked equipment had been moved out, but it looked like they'd tried to salvage one of the old wheeled carts. Now there were just two recorders on it.

Fontana planted his feet, weapon held loosely in his arms, but Jordyn thought she could see lines of tension around his mouth. Maybe this wasn't as easy for him as it appeared.

"Is there another camp like this?"

The man nodded, frowning. "Yes, somewhere in Guyana, but I think they're closing it down for some reason."

"Did this one ever get shut down?" he asked.

The man shook his head. "No. They stopped bringing new test subjects in for a while, but it never actually shut down."

Fontana's face looked pissed, and she realized why. Their escape hadn't worried the company at all. Men had been here, being tested upon, the entire time.

"I thought you had more people here."

"We did, but something happened last week and we have new orders."

"What are those orders?"

Fontana stared at the man hard, and Jordyn wondered if she dared reach out to him. It looked like he was about to collapse.

"We're transferring the prisoners out to Guyana, then they're going somewhere else. I'm not sure where."

"When did you transfer people out?" she asked.

The man blinked and looked at her, then his gaze sharpened, and she realized she'd fucked up. Shit! She should have let Fontana ask the questions.

"Hey," the soldier said, backing up, "you're…"

Fontana didn't let him finish. With a rifle butt to the jaw

he knocked the soldier out cold. And probably shattered his jaw.

"Sorry," Jordyn hissed.

Fontana staggered and Jordyn reached out to prop his shoulder before he fell. "Are you okay?"

He nodded, his arm heavy around her shoulders. "Yes. Controlling people like that takes a massive amount of power."

Jordyn maneuvered him to the office chair in front of two monitors. Most of the screens on the monitor were snowy. Those must be the cameras Fontana had knocked out. "Why don't you deal with this? Figure out what needs destroyed. See if they recorded anything. I'll find the prisoner."

Fontana nodded, looking at the screens, then pointed. "There."

The man was stretched out on a table, looking lifeless. A woman was leaning over him, doing something.

"That must be the nurse. Be careful. They were as cold as the guards when I was here." Fontana told her.

Jordyn left him sitting in the chair looking for evidence on an old computer. Before she left she put a zip tie around the guard's wrists. Hopefully when he roused it would take him a while to alert the others in the camp.

Lifting her weapon in her arms, she headed down the hallway, back the way they'd come. Then she went into the other hallway that branched off. She crept along, trying not to make any noise. Then she came to a room with an observation window from the hallway. Standing, she peered inside very carefully.

The light-skinned black man on the gurney was emaciated, his belly concave between his rib cage and hip bones. The nurse stood at the man's side, and she was cupping his cheek. Jordyn blinked, wondering if she was seeing correctly.

The man on the gurney was awake and looking up at the nurse, and there was a slight smile on his lips.

Jordyn rocked back to the wall, then peered through the glass again. The dark-haired nurse was stroking her thumb across the man's cheekbone now and whispering to him. She turned away from him to reach for something on the rolling metal table beside her, and the man's head rocked to track her.

Jordyn took the chance to get close to the open door, trying to hear what was being said.

"I'm sorry this is going to hurt."

Jordyn stepped through the doorway, furious, weapon trained on the woman. "You're not fucking hurting them anymore."

The woman stilled, a syringe of clear fluid in her hand. Her blue eyes widened with fear, and her mouth fell open. "I'm not," she started, but Jordyn cut her off.

"Are you the only one in here?"

The woman blinked. "There's a security guard on the other side. Are you American?" she asked incredulously.

"Doesn't matter. Unfasten him."

The man on the gurney held a hand out to Jordyn. "Don't hurt her, please."

Jordyn was confused. The man wasn't restrained in any way. What the hell was going on?

"What's in the syringe?" she demanded.

"A vitamin shot. The food that they feed them is not enough to maintain his body. He's losing weight faster than it can be replaced."

Shaking her head at the craziness, Jordyn looked between the two of them, then back at the nurse. "Do you work for the Silverstone Collaborative?"

The woman's mouth tightened. "Technically, yes. But I don't agree with what they're doing here."

"She's been helping us," the man on the gurney said. He caught Jordyn's eyes. "She's not an enemy."

Something about his earnest gaze swayed her, but she was still cautious. "You trust her to inject you with whatever is in there?"

He nodded, his eyes tired. "I do. It will help me. She's only ever helped us."

She looked into the man's earnest expression and wondered if the woman was such a good liar that she'd convinced him. The woman's hands were shaking.

Jordyn nodded to her. "Go ahead. Then put your hands above your head and back up to me."

The woman gave the man the shot, then did exactly as Jordyn told her to do. Without any wasted motion she zip tied the woman's hands in front of her. Jordyn pushed her to face the wall where she could watch her as she moved to the man on the gurney. "Are you Jackson?"

The man nodded and tried to sit up, but it was hard for him to do. Jordyn pushed on his back to support him. "Are you mobile?"

"Some."

"We're getting you out of here if you don't mind."

"Fuck, yes," he breathed. "Did you get the others?"

"Yes. Do you know how many were left?"

"There were just five of us left. You got them all?"

She nodded, holding out a hand as he lowered himself from the table. He stayed vertical as his feet hit the floor, but she thought it was a near thing.

"We need to take Kelle," the man said. "None of us would be alive if she hadn't been here."

Jordyn looked at the woman against the wall. She'd turned her head and there was hope in her expression. Tears filled her eyes and threatened to fall.

Fontana stepped into the doorway.

"Did you hear?" Jordyn asked him.

He nodded. "Turn around," he told the nurse. "What's your name and what do you do here?"

"Kelle Mattox. I'm the night nurse. If anyone has to stay in the med center I stay here with them."

Fontana stared at her hard for several long seconds, frowned, and met Jordyn's eyes before flashing back to the nurse. "You know what the Collaborative does."

"Yes," she admitted, tears filling her eyes. "But I was afraid if I tried to leave, the men would be worse off than with me here. I'm the only one that has done anything to try to save them."

"It's the truth," Jackson said.

Jordyn wanted to believe the woman. She wanted to believe that they'd had some kind of comfort here. Apparently, Fontana did as well, because he nodded his head. "Fine. We'll take you with us but be warned. If I have one issue with you or think you're playing dirty, I'll blow your head off and leave you in the jungle for the cats to eat. No hesitation. We're leaving now."

Kelle nodded at everything he said, looking scared. Jackson moved toward her and stumbled, and she caught him, even with her wrists bound. Jackson slung an arm around her shoulders and she braced him up.

Fontana took the lead, followed by the prisoner and nurse, then Jordyn as they headed toward the door of the med center. Fontana checked to make sure no one was outside, then led them through. Jordyn dropped her night vision goggles down over her eyes and followed them out.

They left the camp as quickly as possible, but it was hard with Jackson. He and the nurse fell twice. Fontana cut the zip tie from the woman's wrists and they stayed vertical as Fontana led them over the downed chain-link fence and into the jungle. Within half an hour they were at the tree, and the prisoners that were conscious welcomed Kelle and Jackson openly. That made Jordyn feel better about bringing the nurse.

The woman they'd rescued from the last cage was still unconscious, so Jordyn had Kelle check on her. They turned on a flashlight to let her see.

"I was off-shift when Becca came in yesterday, so I have no idea what the experiment they conducted on her. She should have woken up by now, though."

Jordyn caught her eye. "She was also sexually assaulted."

Anger flashed in Kelle's expression. "There's one guard that..."

"...won't be an issue anymore. Fontana killed him."

"Good. Lousy son of a bitch."

Kelle cleaned the woman up but admitted she didn't know what else to do for her. She had no equipment or medicine. She made her comfortable then moved to the male prisoners. One male had a swath of exposed muscle across his stomach, where they'd removed a large chunk of skin. Kelley bandaged it but admitted that they would need to do a lot more to it later.

Jordyn thought Kelle was on the up and up, and Fontana apparently did as well because he left her unrestrained. Sitting down beside Fontana against one of the tree roots, Jordyn leaned into him just a bit.

"You doing okay?" she asked. "I thought you were going to go down trying to control that guard."

He gave her a slight smile. "I thought I was too, honestly. I've never controlled someone that hard before."

Jordyn glanced at the watch on her wrist and pressed the button to illuminate it. "Just after three-thirty. We were only in there an hour," she breathed. "It felt like days."

Fontana chuckled, tiredly. "Felt like years for me."

"We need to get back to Margarita and get the fuck out of here."

"You'll get no argument from me."

Jordyn climbed to her feet, then held a hand down to Fontana. She loved that he didn't wave her off, just gripped her wrist and let her pull him up. Then he surprised her even more by dropping a kiss to the top of her head before turning away.

CHAPTER SEVENTEEN

Fontana was bone-deep tired. He'd never understood why using his mental abilities sapped his strength more than anything physical he might do, but it did. And it was making him do irrational things. Like kiss Jordyn on the head.

"We need to get out of here, Team Alpha. Dawn is less than three hours away and the missing prisoners will be noticed. Two of the wounded need to be carried. We'll take turns doing that. Right now, we need to get as far away from this place as possible. Let's go."

It was slower going than what he wanted, and he was partially responsible. The prisoners hadn't been out of their cages or done any exercise in months, and he hadn't had a chance to regenerate any power. He needed food and sleep. And the ground was treacherous. They'd cut through the brush, but it was difficult going, even when Fontana allowed them to turn on the flashlights. Zero continued to carry the unconscious woman, and Kenny carried the man. He roused at one point and struggled to be put down, but as soon as he took his own weight he passed out again. Kenny just caught him and hoisted him over the opposite shoulder.

They took a break when they got to the beach camp at the edge of the river. Shane handed out protein bars to everyone, as well as bottles of water.

"I suggest we move a little downstream before we cross," Payne suggested. "There was a spot that's only a few feet wide."

They got up and followed Payne to the spot. Jordyn was beginning to get nervous because the sky was lightening, and they still had a pretty good distance to go. When they came to the crossing, Kenny and Zero made sure the prisoners got across safely, then Kenny turned to Shane and held out his arms.

"What the hell are you doing?" Shane snapped.

"I'm carrying you across, Marine. I almost broke my good leg chasing you down the river."

Even in the dim light Jordyn could see Shane flush, but she was kind of in agreement for Kenny's offer. "Just do it Shane and we'll get back to Margarita."

"Fuck that. Just let me hold onto your belt loops or something."

"So that you can pull me in the water when you fall? No way."

Shane looked at the flowing water and just that made him sway.

"Shane!" Jordyn snapped.

He looked at her, but even he knew he was fucked. "Fine."

Big Kenny swung the man up into his arms, and it attested to how massive Kenny was that he didn't even stagger. Shane was lean, but he wasn't small.

"Look at me, Shane." Jordyn pointed two fingers at her eyes. "Don't look at the water."

Shane did exactly as she told him, looking over Kenny's shoulder and into her eyes, and they were across the water in seconds. Kenny set him down safely, then Fontana crossed with his pack and set it at his feet. Jordyn shifted her own pack off and waded into the water. It was chilly this morning but refreshing. Luckily it didn't get any higher than her thighs. The current was strong, but she made it across okay.

Now to get back to Margarita.

"Is this active enough for you, Zero," she called.

Her buddy chuckled and glanced at her over his shoulder. "Oh, yeah."

It was another arduous four hours to get back to the helicopter. Surely by now the men had been discovered missing. She strained her ears, listening for any kind of pursuit. If the guards made it into the woods, they would see the path they'd taken to get out. They'd cut it into the damn jungle. Maybe they should have left some neon signs pointing the way...

Eventually they made it to the edge of the jungle. Jordyn had been checking her GPS coordinates the entire time, and the old man's field was less than half a mile away. Fontana held up a fist, indicating he wanted them to stop, then he scouted ahead, his limp more pronounced than she'd seen it. Jordyn crept forward as well, scanning the entire area she could see.

Margarita looked fine, gleaming in the early morning light. There was a young man about a quarter mile away at the edge of the field. It was obvious this was the farmer's son.

"It appears to be fine," Fontana said, voice low. "Let's pay the man and get out of here."

They hustled the prisoners—survivors— to the helicopter and found them seats. The two who were still unconscious were laid out on the floor on blankets. The rest moved into seats. Team Alpha stowed their gear and began strapping themselves in. The farmer's son ran to them and promised that he had been watching Margarita very carefully. Jordyn handed him a wad of money. "This is for your papa." She handed him a second wad of cash. "And this is for you. Thank you for taking care of her."

The young man grinned and waved as he backed away.

Jordyn did a quick inspection as the men loaded the survivors up, but the skin on her neck was prickling. They needed to get in the air and get out of here.

Margarita hummed in her hands as the rotor built speed and lifted into the air easily, even though she was at her cargo capacity. They had planned on finding another airport if this camp had been empty, but now she needed to get back to her Uncle's.

Fontana drew out his satellite phone and called Aiden. Even though he had to yell over the sound of the rotors, it was important enough that it needed done. He advised that if the CIA wanted several material witnesses, including a current Silverstone employee, they should have a team at Pedro's airport by the time they got there, or soon after. Fontana also advised him that they needed a medical team because they had wounded survivors. He agreed with something Aiden said, then hung up.

Fontana gave her a thumbs up and slipped the phone away.

Jordyn flew high and fast and knew she would be close to exhausting her fuel getting back to her uncle's airport so far away, but there was no way she was stopping. She also wanted to get Fontana back to the house. It was obvious he was staying awake for her, but she didn't need him to.

"Take a nap," she suggested, switching to the private channel. "There's no way I'll nod off right now."

He shook his head. "If I fall asleep now my control might slip. I won't be responsible for us crashing."

Ah, yes, that was a very good reason to stay awake.

"Well, talk to me then. It's just you and me right now."

He looked at her for several long moments, then out the

window. Jordyn left the channel open. When he didn't break the silence, she did. "Do you feel like you completed the mission?"

"Partly," he admitted. "We never expected there to be men at the same camp where we'd been. It's ridiculously stupid, but it's ballsy. The woman that had been in charge, Priscilla Mattingly, she was like that. It tells me that they had enough of a hold on the area that they weren't worried about the authorities shutting them down."

"Well, you know they had at least partial Army support."

"Yes."

"If the CIA is involved, are you going to have to testify?"

He sighed. "Possibly. It was kind of a matter of time before we had to bring them in. This is bigger than all of us together and we knew we would need help to take them down."

"Are they going to stop us from going to Guyana?"

"Fuck, no!" He turned to glare at her, but she grinned.

"I didn't think so," she told him, and he realized she'd been teasing him.

"I never expected there to be people there," he breathed. "I mean, locals maybe, but definitely not the Collaborative. And I certainly didn't expect them to still be testing on our military."

"That's the disgusting part. It's been two years."

"Yes."

She could hear the weight of guilt in his voice and it worried her. It wasn't anyone's fault that those men were there other than the company's. "Do you think they've had success? That's why they're still doing it?"

He shook his head. "I don't think so. Before we killed her, Priscilla intimated that they needed the original formula, which only we have. Everything else they've come up with is guesswork on the part of the medical personnel that had been helping Dr. Shu with our group two years ago."

"That's crazy." They were silent for a while.

There was something else she wanted to mention, but she didn't want to piss him off or humiliate him. Maybe she would wait until they were on the ground.

Fontana had always considered the Central Intelligence Agency a bit of a misnomer, but Chief Operations Officer Kevin Rose was proving to be a competent man.

He'd brought a dozen men and women with him, and they all seemed to be just as competent.

By the time they got to Pablo's airport, the CIA team had landed and set up a triage for the wounded. There was not a bit of confusion, and for that Fontana was appreciative. Stepping off to the side of the ordered chaos, he called Aiden, like he'd promised earlier.

"So, what am I supposed to tell the head fucking spook?" he asked when Aiden came on the line. "Because he's already looking at me, waiting for his chance to pounce."

"Tell him the truth, I guess. Don't incriminate yourself in anything. Wulfe said he already asked about what happened to the Bitch in Blue."

"That may be easier said than done. We left a bit of a mess back there."

"Was it bad?"

Fontana sighed, beginning to pace down the tarmac as he talked. He thought about his old abuser. "Yes, but it was good too. I got some closure I didn't expect to get."

There was silence for a moment on the other end. "That sounds very self-analytical of you."

He snorted. "I don't know about all that, but I think I

definitely gained some perspective. And I'm getting a broader feel for the situation in general. We need help to do this and I guess the CIA will have to be it."

"Wulfe says Rose is a decent guy."

Fontana glanced up the tarmac at the man still staring at him. He wasn't in a suit or anything, but the khakis and button up shirt spoke to some kind of department affiliation. No one else in his group wore anything identifying them as CIA either. Smart.

"Well, it's a good thing I trust Wulfe because I'm going to have to take his word on that."

Aiden snorted. "We both are. Make decisions we can live with."

"I'll do my best," he said softly.

The thought of exposing themselves and perhaps being put back into another cage, or another testing program, made his balls shrink. And that's exactly what the government would want to do with them. They would want to try out the super soldiers. "How do we keep ourselves out of their clutches?"

Aiden sighed over the line. "I'm not sure exactly. I guess the only advice I can give you is to try not to admit to anything you don't have to."

"Yeah, okay. I'll try not. Later, Will." Laughing, he hung up the sat phone and glanced around at the rest of the people milling about. Madeira was doing something underneath the helicopter, her uncle leaning in beside her. He wanted to go over and see what she was doing. Not that he knew anything about helicopters; he just wanted to hang with her. He had a feeling that as soon as he headed in that direction Rose would intercept him.

Might as well bite the bullet and get it over with.

Fontana headed toward the triage area. Pablo had opened one of the big hangar bays, the massive door slid to the side.

A red and white plane that had been there was now parked on the tarmac, and inside the shaded space several people were working on the survivors they'd brought in. Fontana started walking toward the hangar, he wanted to check on everyone and make sure they'd gotten them out in time.

Officer Rose intercepted him as soon as he cleared the doorway. "Mr. Fontana."

He paused, knowing that he had to talk to the man. And he had to try not to piss him off. They were going to be relying on him for help. "Officer Rose."

The well-kept, dark-haired man grinned at him, looking a little disheveled. It's wouldn't be obvious to most people, but Fontana could tell that this was not what the man had planned to do today. The clothes he wore were a little too corporate office wear, or something. They weren't necessarily jungle or adventure clothes. It was like he had a 'go' bag, but it wasn't exactly what he'd needed.

Rose reached out a hand and Fontana took it reluctantly. The tight, competent grip surprised him.

"When Wulfe called me and offered me this mess on a golden plate, I didn't believe him. Were you the 'boots on the ground' that found the compound here?"

"Yes."

"I have a team still working on excavating the mass grave, but we're already found American identification. We'll need to debrief you at some point. As well as your team."

Fontana sighed inwardly, knowing that they would have to have some kind of documentation when— or if— they went public. "Fine. Might have to be in a few days."

He moved to step around Rose, but the officer held out a hand. "Wulfe said there were three locations."

He paused. "That we know of."

"And you just came from the second?"

"Yes," Fontana said.

"Where's the third one?"

"Guyana, supposedly."

Fontana didn't want to supply any more information than he had to before he had to.

"I want to send a team in with you when you go."

There was an excited gleam in the officer's eyes. Not necessarily avaricious, but he'd seen the expression before. Officer Rose was a man working his way up the food chain. If he had any idea who all was involved in this mess, he would be all over Fontana. It didn't appear that Wulfe had given him a lot of details yet.

"I'll give you the location of the camp we just left. There are still Brazilian Army and hired guns there, as well as a med center where they were testing on the men. And woman, it looks like."

"I would appreciate that," Rose said, "But even more than that I want to go into the last camp with you."

Fontana glanced around the hangar, his eyes spotting the men from LNF. They were heading toward the house, and Madeira was across the way now working on some piece of equipment. "The six of us work well as a team. If we need backup or cleanup, we'll call you."

Anger flashed in the other man's eyes, but it was gone quickly. "I don't think you have any idea of the assistance we could give you. If you find more prisoners like these ones, you're going to need help. Medical, tactical."

"And you expect me to put my life, and that of my team, in the hands of a team I know nothing about? Yeah, not happening."

Rose planted his hands on his hips. "We're not novices. This is exactly what my team was built for."

"I'm not risking my people. Period."

"It wouldn't be a risk. We have to be better than that." Rose waved a dismissive hand over to where Madeira now had her head lowered over Payne's prosthetic arm, and he was motioning to something in the elbow. Even as they watched Madeira reached behind her for a tiny little screwdriver to adjust something in the joint, and the scarred side of her head was exposed.

Fontana fought the anger which surged in his gut and looked the officer up and down dismissively. "You have no idea what you're talking about. I would take both of them, or either one of them, over you and your team in a heartbeat. You're beating a dead horse, Rose, and beginning to piss me off."

Fontana skirted around him and headed toward the hangar where Payne was now flexing his prosthetic and nodding at Madeira. She looked up at Fontana and grinned, her glance flicking quickly past his shoulder to the officer, then back. "Is he supposed to be that purple?"

"Probably not. We just had to get a few details straight."

Her eyes danced with humor and he wanted to lean down and drop a kiss to her lips, but he held himself in check. It had to be because he was so tired.

Jordyn reached out and touched his arm. "The guys headed inside to get something to eat and catch some sleep. Payne is going to stay out here with Pablo and keep watch on everything. They've already been questioning my uncle, but he doesn't have any information to wheedle out."

"But they've tried, huh?"

She nodded.

Fontana looked at Payne, assessing the other man's alertness. His dark eyes were narrowed against the bright sunlight and he had a fairly heavy dark beard coming in, but he seemed fine. "If they do anything noteworthy, can you come get me?"

Payne nodded. "They might be flying the prisoners out."

"That's fine. If they can provide the medical care needed, I want them to."

"Did you get all the information you needed from Aksel?" Jordyn asked him. "Did he know how many men had been taken to the next camp?"

Fontana shook his head, feeling drained. "Let's go talk to him."

Aksel was drinking what appeared to be chicken broth from a cup, both hands wrapped around the heat, even though it was heading toward eighty degrees in the shade of the hangar. He looked up when they stopped in front of him, and his eyes filled with emotion. He set the cup aside and struggled to stand, the line of an IV trailing from one hand.

Fontana helped him stand but didn't understand why he needed to until Aksel wrapped his arms around his shoulders. Fontana was surprised at how tall the man was. He hadn't seemed that tall when they'd been in the camp.

"I'm sorry," Aksel told him, pulling away. There were tears in his eyes as he looked between Fontana and Madeira. "I had given up hope. We were there so long."

Jordyn reached out a hand to rest on his arm. "It's okay. You don't have to thank us."

"You don't understand," the survivor shook his head, sorrow lining his face. "We were forgotten."

"You weren't forgotten," Fontana said firmly. "And I do understand. I was there two years ago."

Aksel stared at him, blinking. "You were in the camp?"

"Yes. I was there for eight months before we broke out."

Aksel's watery hazel eyes widened. "You were the ones? The ones that changed everything?"

Fontana shrugged. "Maybe. Don't tell Officer Rose."

Glancing around, Aksel nodded. "I will not."

"What do you mean we were the ones that changed everything?"

The survivor wavered and they urged him to sit down again. Fontana knelt in front of the man's cot and Jordyn came down beside him.

"I wasn't there when you broke out," Aksel said, "but two men were. They said you had taken a chance to get out and it worked. At the time, they weren't able to go with you and they didn't blame you for leaving them behind."

"Are they still alive?"

Aksel shook his head. "Don't know. They got moved."

Fontana looked down at the concrete floor. It had been one of the hardest things to do; walk away from the camp knowing there were other men there. When they'd left, though, he honestly hadn't believed that they would survive very long, and they hadn't been able to communicate with them.

"How long have you been at the camp?" Jordyn asked.

"I'm not even sure," Aksel told her. "I think three, four months. Not very long."

"And how many different men have you seen go through the camp?"

Aksel was quiet for a long time, and he looked down at his hands, obviously naming people off in his head. "*Drieëntwintig*. Um, twenty and three."

Twenty-three men. "And the woman?"

Looking over at the unconscious woman on the cot, he shook his head sadly. "Not military. But they tested on her same."

Anger surged in Fontana's gut. It had been hard enough to be tested on when you were trained for it. He couldn't imagine a civilian going through what they had. He looked down at his hands, remembering all the broken bones and needle pricks and nausea from things they'd given him or done to him.

A rough hand covered his own and he looked at Jordyn.

There was a look in her eyes like she understood what he was thinking. He appreciated that she tried. If he told her everything, she'd probably run for the hills, even with her military experience.

Aksel was lost in his own thoughts. He had lain down on the cot, and Fontana could see the weariness in his posture. "Thank you for answering my questions. I think the team is going to fly you out and they will get you back to your country and family if they can."

Tears filled the man's eyes and he buried his face in his hands, weeping softly. Fontana squeezed the man's shoulder, then pushed to his feet. Jordyn leaned down and pressed a kiss to the side of Aksel's face, murmuring softly to him. Fontana saw him nod, but he kept his face covered.

After the man made it home, he would be sure to check on him.

Weariness pulled at Fontana, making his feet heavy. His bad leg was throbbing again. Probably because he'd been using and abusing it. It would heal. He just needed some rest.

Jordyn moved to one of the women caring for the dark-haired survivor and started talking. There were several nods passed back and forth, and the woman made a note on a portable tablet with a stylus. She smiled at Jordyn and took her hand. Fontana thought she might be promising to take care of the woman, but he couldn't be sure until he talked to Jordyn.

Kelle Mattox, the dark-haired Collaborative nurse was sitting beside one of the men, holding his hand even though he didn't appear to be conscious. She was dozing off. Fontana thought they'd made the right decision in bringing her back with them. If she had the kind of information in her brain he thought she did, she was worth her weight in gold to the CIA. Jordyn had been right about that when she'd convinced him to bring her.

Fontana found himself waiting for the compact woman. Though he was tired and dying for food and a bed, he wanted more time with her as well, but she had to be just as tired. It had been hell getting out of the jungle. Then she'd had to have the concentration to fly them home. Most of the men in the back of the chopper had nodded off.

He watched as she moved from bed to bed checking on the survivors they'd gotten out of the camp. Eventually, she returned to him. "Are you ready for some rest?"

He nodded, almost too tired to walk back to the house. When she moved close and wrapped her arm around his waist to walk toward the shaded back patio, he didn't pull away. Instead, he pulled her tight against him.

CHAPTER EIGHTEEN

Jordyn knew Fontana was about to crash. His eyes had been alert when he was talking to Aksel and gathering information. Now they seemed dull. He'd reached his wall.

As they walked through the kitchen she grabbed a bottle of water and twisted off the cap. "Drink this."

He guzzled it down, like she expected him to, then handed her the empty bottle. "I'm going to go hop in the shower," she told him. "Why don't you grab a sandwich or something?"

He nodded and moved toward the fridge.

Jordyn felt bad leaving him there, but she seriously needed to get some trail dirt off of herself. Digging through her pack she threw her damp clothes into the washer. She'd check later with the rest of the men and see if they had things to wash. Then she drew out a pair of shorts and a t-shirt.

The hot water felt amazing as it streamed over her body. She hoped that the people that they'd rescued would be okay. Aksel would be fine eventually, but he would need the care of his family and a lot of understanding. The unconscious woman was a different story; recovering from rape and torture like that would take a strong heart and iron determination. Jordyn knew that for a fact.

Hopefully the medical staff would take care of her appropriately and they would figure out who she was. So far, the woman hadn't regained consciousness, and they couldn't pinpoint exactly why she wasn't waking. They would be flying her to their base later today, wherever the hell that was. The woman Jordyn was speaking to had been very cagey about where the team had come from, as well as where they were returning.

Rinsing her hair with cool water, Jordyn left the shower stall and toweled off. The bathroom was steamy, and it was a little hard getting her clothes on, but it would feel good when she stepped out into the cool of the house. When the blinds were drawn like her uncle liked to keep them, the sunlight couldn't overheat the interior. Then, the fans were on high all the time, keeping the air moving.

When she left the bathroom, she took her dirty BDUs and t-shirt to the washer. Once Fontana was done with his shower she would start a load of wash.

Jordyn peeked into the bedroom, but he wasn't there yet. Moving back out to the kitchen, she stopped in surprise. Fontana had finally stopped moving and the tiredness had caught him. There was a half-eaten sandwich in his hand resting on his thigh. Fontana's head drooped over his chest, his hand lax. He was sound asleep.

Jordyn didn't think she'd made any noise but he jerked his head up, his gaze latching onto her immediately. She held her hands out in front of her. "Hey, just me. Why don't you go clean up?"

Fontana stuffed the rest of the peanut butter and jelly into his mouth and nodded, pushing up from the chair. He wavered on his feet and Jordyn reached out to grab his arm. "Maybe you can wash up later."

"No. I can't lie in a bed until I clean up."

"I'll go start your shower. Why don't you start getting your gear off?" She motioned to his weapons and the safety vest with the bullet-proof inserts. Nodding, he moved to the bedroom and started removing his gear. She could hear the heavy-duty Velcro ripping a room away. Adjusting the temperature on the spigot, she pulled the lever to start the shower then backed through the curtain. When she turned to leave the bathroom, Fontana stood right behind her, wearing the same gray underwear she had peeked at the night before. And nothing else.

Jordyn looked at his broad, strong body blocking her way and had to curl her fingers into her fists, otherwise she would have reached out to stroke him. That fuzz of golden-brown chest hair called to her, and she wanted to run her fingers through it, but she forced her arms to stay at their sides. Instead, he reached out to her, cupping the smooth side of her face in his palm. She looked up at him, stunned as his thumb ran back and forth over her cheekbone. "You're so beautiful."

Once upon a time she would have believed that, but now? No, she was nowhere near beautiful. Yeah, she had a pretty nice body, but the wrapping was torn and patched and nowhere as neat as it once had been. She had no illusion about that fact.

Jordyn glanced away and tried to step back, but he cupped her shoulders in his hands. "I can see in your eyes that you think I'm lying to you, but I'm not. I love looking at you and imagining what your mouth tastes like."

That thumb brushed over her lower lip, catching on the moist skin just inside. Jordyn looked up at him, but his gaze was on her lips. Before she could think better of it she flicked her tongue out to moisten them.

Fontana sighed out a groan and cupped the back of her neck. "You're killing me woman. I need to kiss you, because I have to. Please. I have to know what you taste like."

Jordyn's heart tripped into overtime as she lifted her head in invitation. Without hesitation he lowered his head to her mouth, resting his lips on her own. For a second, they just breathed each other in, as if they were tasting the essence of the other person. It was intimate in a way she hadn't expected, and when he actually took her lips in a kiss, she gasped into his mouth. Fontana sealed his mouth over her own, and a shudder rocked through her. The man was hot, and he knew how to kiss, though there was a hesitancy to his movements that she hadn't expected. He seemed like this big, handsome guy that got things done, but he wasn't kissing her the same way.

Jordyn appreciated— and hated— the restraint. They were literally in a situation where lives were in the balance. This wasn't the best time to try to invest in romance. But on the other hand, she'd never met a man like Fontana. He made her forget her reasons to be cautious and more importantly, he made her feel like the woman she used to be.

Reaching up, Jordyn cupped his face with her right hand, her left resting on his chest. She angled her mouth and tasted his lips, stretching on the tips of her toes to be close. There was a hint of peanut butter there, and an earthiness that appealed to her. One of his hands covered her own on his chest and she realized she could feel his heart pounding beneath their fingers. Had she really caused that reaction in him, or would any woman do?

A little dazed, she pulled back, very aware that her body had responded to him. She tugged at her t-shirt, praying that he didn't look down at her hard nipples. But then she looked down, and realized she wasn't the only one affected. The slick fabric of his athletic underwear left nothing to the imagination. Suddenly she was worried about things other than her hard nipples.

"We shouldn't do this," she started, then gasped as he brushed a knuckle over one of her nipples pressing against the soft cotton of the t-shirt. When she glared up at him, he grinned at her.

"I haven't had anyone respond for me like that for a long time."

Jordyn's stance softened. "Well, you're sexy. What can I say?"

He grinned even wider, all the tiredness from minutes ago gone from his expression. "Thank you for that."

She shook her head and skirted around him in the tiny space. She needed distance, both physical and metaphorical. "Too bad I don't sleep with men I don't know. Maybe someday you'll tell me your name." She paused in the doorway and without turning around, said, "You need to take your shower."

The last thing she heard was Fontana's low chuckle, then his startled cry. Jordyn giggled. He should have checked the temperature before he stepped into the stall.

The dream started with guards slamming him to his back. They fastened him to the metal medical table, then they put these paddle things on like they did in the movies and shocked the shit out of him. He arched up off the table, power flowing through his veins in a painful dance of light. Usually, he was the one controlling the electricity, so he didn't understand how he couldn't get a grasp on it. Electricity and he got along well, usually. He'd begun to tame it.

Fontana craned his head and looked up at the nurse, but the woman had pitch-black hair and Army green eyes. It was Madeira, and as soon as old Dr. Shu reached for him, she slammed a punch into his head. Then she released the cold iron shackles from around his wrists. He sat up on the edge of the table and felt such a wave of gratitude that she'd come for him. He drew her into his arms, settling his lips on hers.

Fontana was aware that something wasn't quite right. When he blinked his eyes open, there should have been a little light from the windows. After his cold shower, he'd come into the bedroom and crashed onto the bed, pulling light covers over himself. But it had been early afternoon when he'd gone to bed. He'd planned to get up after four or five hours and go check on the survivors.

He felt... unsettled and aroused. Hungry, but not for food. Yes, the dream had been aggravating, but this had been the first time Jordyn had taken a role in it. He'd reached up to her at the end of the dream expecting her to be there, and she had been.

Was that what was bothering him? He'd woken up without her in his arms, aching for her.

Snorting, he flung back the covers.

Then he realized she stood in his bedroom doorway, arms crossed beneath her breasts as she watched him. Fontana pulled the covers back over himself, but he'd surely given her a show. He looked up at her face and there was a slight smile on her full lips.

"I hope I'm not interrupting," she whispered, her voice raspy. "I heard you cry out something in your sleep and just wanted to check on you."

"I'm okay," he lied.

She tilted her head to the side, trying to decide if he was telling her the truth or not. "Were you dreaming?"

"Yes," he said softly, staring at her.

There was just enough light coming in from the moon to see her silhouette in the doorway. "I had a dream as well, but it wasn't a good dream."

Fontana knew what he wanted to do, but would she actually go along with it? It seemed like they'd been together a long time, out in the jungle rescuing men, but it had only been a few days that he'd actually known her. Everything he learned about her he loved, though. The woman gave new meaning to the word strong.

"I was going to get up and go scout around, but if you need me to stay here I will."

She took a step forward, slowly, cautiously. "We could guard each other's backs?"

"Yeah," he agreed.

Taking his courage in his hands, he scooted to the far side of the bed and opened the sheet for her.

A shudder rippled through Jordyn's body hard enough that he could see her struggle.

"We're both aching," he told her, voice rasping. "If I can offer you comfort please take it. If you'd like I can roll over and face the wall. Then you can cuddle up behind me. No other stuff."

"Yes. Can we do that?"

Fontana had every intention of following through when he made the offer, but as soon as he felt her heat behind him he worried that he wouldn't be able to hold still. He trusted Jordyn, of course, but there was a part of his brain telling him that having someone behind him like that was dangerous. He couldn't relax in spite of the 'she won't hurt you' running repeatedly through his mind.

After several long minutes, she pulled away and sat up, swinging her legs to the side of the bed. Fontana sat up as well, feeling like he'd failed her. "I'm sorry."

Jordyn glanced at him in surprise. "Why are you apologizing? It's nothing you did wrong. I think we both have ghosts haunting us tonight. Rescuing that woman from the guard..."

She didn't move to leave, and he took that as a good sign, though he didn't want to talk about the guard. From the light of the moon he could see her profile, and she seemed pensive.

"When I got out of the Army, I was in a relationship," she said softly. "We'd been together for several years, married, but when I was burned, things changed. As we went to all of the doctor appointments and surgeries, he began to," she moved a hand in the air, "lose interest, I guess. I doted on that man for five years, and I guess I started to notice when I got pregnant that he didn't appreciate not having all my attention all the time."

She glanced at him and he could see in the disbelief in her expression. "Can you imagine being jealous of a child?"

Fontana shook his head, a little stunned. He'd had no clue that she had a baby. Then he grinned, because he could totally see her as a mom. A kick-ass boy's mom.

"Jason began to get more and more bitter and I knew it was only a matter of time before things imploded. But I fought to keep our marriage going... and I put up with a lot of abuse. First, he started just yelling at me, here and there. Telling me to do things, then bitching at me when I did it incorrectly. It took a while for my hands to be usable and he had to do a lot for me. Then he shoved me. I think I'd taken too long to get out of his way or something, and he just reached out and pushed. I should have put my foot down then, but I couldn't even imagine going through the pregnancy without him. I understood that his life had changed, drastically, when I was hurt. Money was tight and we were having to move out of our apartment."

Jordyn shook her head, glancing at him. There was just enough light from the hallway that he could see her profile. "I'm making excuses for him again. It used to be such a habit.

Then one day he came home and I could tell something was really wrong. He'd lost his job, and his frustration was at peak level. I don't even remember how the fight started, only how it ended ...with him raping me on the living room floor. I lost the baby a few hours after that."

Fontana just sat there, stunned at what she was telling him. Then he felt ashamed, because he hadn't taken the time to talk to her and get to know her. He'd been so focused on just getting here, getting the men out, that he'd had tunnel vision. "None of that was your fault."

"I know," she said, turning to him with a smile. "It's taken me a lot of therapy to understand that now. But I want you to understand that what happened to the woman survivor in the camp, and what happened to you in the camp, is not your fault either."

Icy fingers of fear trickled down his spine, and he was glad there wasn't a lot of light. If he could have sunk through the mattress and the floor he would have, because he didn't want anyone to know about his shame. Obviously, though, she'd seen his reaction to the guard and she'd understood.

"I'm not going to insist that you talk about it, but I just want to tell you that if you ever do want to, I'm here for you. Or if you ever want to talk about any of your other dreams, you have a safe place to do it. But I'm not demanding it."

She reached back and took his hand. He wasn't sure how she even found it in the dark, but he was glad that she did. He curled his fingers around hers and held them together on the blanket.

"I thought about the kiss in the bathroom last night, and I have to admit that you took me by surprise. I haven't been drawn to anyone for a long time. So, I just wanted to be clear on where we stood."

Her honesty deserved a response. "Thank you. I appreciate everything you've said. You've given me a lot to think about."

Jordyn gave his fingers another squeeze before she stood from the bed and moved to the doorway. "We have a few more hours before dawn. Try to get some sleep. We have a big day tomorrow."

Yes, they did.

———

Fontana tried to sleep after Jordyn left, but it just wasn't happening. There were too many thoughts running around inside his head.

At first, he'd been embarrassed when she'd said that she understood what had happened to him in the camp. It was his most guarded secret, and even Wulfe and Aiden had no idea, although he thought they might have their suspicions. It had been hard as hell not letting them into his mind to see what he'd experienced.

When Duncan had interviewed them, though, something had hit him. He wasn't sure if it was the way Duncan had phrased the question, or some burning need to make sure as many people were held accountable for what they'd done as possible, but he'd admitted on camera that he'd been sexually assaulted. It was the first time he'd admitted it out loud, and he was sure the anxiety associated with that revelation had contributed to the way he'd reacted to Madeira that first morning.

Having to look hard at your life like that really sucked.

As he began to dress for the day, he still felt a little embarrassed, but overall his feelings, his view of what had happened to him, had changed. The woman that had been raped had had no choice in the matter, obviously. She'd been unconscious at the time. *He'd* had no choice in what had happened to him. He'd been shackled down and overcome by force.

If he could overcome his embarrassment to guarantee that it didn't happen again, to *anyone*, he would do it. He could do it because he still had a voice and he wouldn't let anyone silence him ever again.

Officer Rose would be heading into the Brazilian camp later on today while Team Alpha headed to the camp in Guyana. Surely Rose would find the slaughtered guard. There was a very real possibility that Fontana would have to account for his actions.

Whatever. He would deal with it when and if it came to pass.

They were getting men out of the Silverstone Collaborative's hold. That was all that mattered.

And he realized in the wee hours of the morning that if he had people like Jordyn supporting him, he could work his way through anything.

It had been a very *enlightening* morning, kind of zen, in a way. He felt as if a tremendous weight had been taken from him. Now they had to go shoot bad guys.

As soon as he walked out of the bedroom, he spotted Jordyn in the kitchen, eating with the rest of the guys. Her short dark hair was damp in the back, like she'd wet down bedhead. The thought made him smile.

As she looked up and caught his gaze, he was still smiling. Something shifted in her eyes, and she gave him a considering look, then a responding slow grin. For a long minute she just stared at him, then she motioned toward the stove. "There's eggs and sausages. We'll be ready to go when you are."

"Is Officer Rose still in the hangar?"

Kenny shook his head. "They left late last night. Took all of the survivors with them. He said a team will be dispatched to the Taraza camp and another will be on standby for us when we need it."

Officer Rose was a determined SOB. "Okay. That's good to know. I have no idea what we're looking at with this last one. After talking to the survivors, it was apparent that several prisoners that had been at Taraza had been moved out recently, presumably to the Guyana camp. We're going to go check that out today."

The men nodded and started gathering up their plates and mess. Shane swigged down the last of a bottle of Coke, and Fontana winced. Coke at five a.m.?

Moving to the stove he threw some eggs and a link of sausage on a tortilla, rolled it up and started eating. Before she left the kitchen, Jordyn stuck a bottle of water in his hand, grinning. "We'll be in the chopper."

"I'm right behind you," he tried to say around a mouthful of tortilla.

Pablo waved at them as they entered the hangar and Fontana wondered of the man ever slept. It seemed like he was up all the time. The bent man headed to the old, lopsided tow truck to pull Margarita out of the bay where he kept her.

The helicopter looked pristine, and Fontana knew that Jordyn and Pablo had both taken care with her last night when they'd gotten in. This trip wouldn't be as long as the one to Brazil, but it would probably be even more clandestine. If this camp still had prisoners, they would have to document as much as possible before they went in.

Fontana glanced around. Payne had the camera bag over his shoulder and was fiddling with the grip on his weapon. Shane was wiping a pair of replacement sunglasses off on his black t-shirt, his single eye scanning the area. Kenny was leaning against the hangar, just looking badass and Zero was talking quietly to Jordyn. Fear bolted through Fontana. Zero and Jordyn were good friends. Would she tell him what they'd talked about last night?

He didn't think so, but it was enough that he worried a little.

Being assaulted the way he had been affected him on several levels. As a man, a heterosexual man in particular, he couldn't imagine anything worse than being attacked the way he had been. It was an affront to everything he believed in and stood for. Also, he prided himself on being strong. There at the end, his physical strength was at a low ebb and it had been easy for the guards to overwhelm him.

When the Dogs of War had broken out of the camp, the four of them had barely been able to walk.

An assault like that wouldn't happen now, or ever again. He was stronger than he'd ever been, both mentally and physically, and his attacker was dead. Fontana had killed him with his own hands. That fact wasn't as comforting as he'd expect it to be, though.

Fontana felt bad for the female survivor. When she eventually woke up— if she woke up— she would have a lot of recovery to do. What had she been doing there in the first place?

As they loaded onto the helicopter, Fontana looked the men over. Today they were wearing all the gear they'd need, and their packs and weapons were at their feet, helmets waiting on top. They needed to be ready for anything when they landed.

Jordyn climbed into the cockpit and began the start-up procedure. She blew her uncle a kiss, then slipped her sunglasses and helmet on. Suddenly, she was all business. "Let's get this show on the road, people."

There was a chorus of agreement from the back. With a final surveying glance, Fontana climbed into the cockpit beside Jordyn. She glanced over with a grin, and in spite of the gravity of the situation, there was joy in her face because she about to fly. He returned her grin as he strapped in, then gripped the handles and she lifted off from the trailer.

The morning fog burned away the higher they got into the air. It was another pristine day. He hoped it stayed that way.

CHAPTER NINETEEN

Guyana was very similar to Brazil and Venezuela in that the weather could turn on a dime. Guyana, and the area where they were heading, was close enough to the ocean that she had to deal with tropical air currents as well now, and Jordyn had to pay serious attention to what was going on.

They also seemed to be heading into a more populated area for this third camp. Not like city populated, but there were definitely more villages in the area and roads and canals stretched below them. The intel that they'd been given said that the Collaborative had a small airport at their disposal for this camp, so it could definitely be more populated that the last two.

Jungle trees obscured almost everything below, and there was a mountain to the north. The Essequibo River ran north to south and she could see boats dotted along its surface. Smoke curled up through the trees in a few areas, and Jordyn knew it was probably one of the many indigenous tribes of the country. Guyana was a bit different in that it considered itself part of the Caribbean. The official language was English, but most people of the country didn't speak it. They spoke Guyanese, an English-Caribbean cross, with words borrowed from other countries. Jordyn had been here before and found the people very down to earth and sweet; hardworkers, most of them.

Several miles away from the GPS location they'd been given, she angled the chopper high. They spotted a small plane going in for a landing, but she was far enough away that they didn't even notice her. Fontana retrieved the binoculars and surveyed the area.

"Multiple contacts," he murmured. "This is a much busier location. That plane is important, because several people are running toward it."

Jordyn peeled away from the site and angled to the north, toward the mountain. "There's a small airstrip over here my uncle has used before. He said it's very rarely used for planes anymore, but there should be enough space for me to land."

"Did your uncle know this location?" Fontana asked her sharply.

She nodded. "He said he flew a man out here years ago to speak to one of the local tribes, then flew him back out a week later. He was paid very well, and they never used him again."

She could see the frown on his face but didn't know what to tell him.

They found the old airstrip, and it was indeed at the base of the mountain to the north. The mountain would give them a great landmark. But as she'd flown she'd noticed the river and canyon that they'd eventually have to cross. There had been a bridge to the north, but it would be a hike to get there.

They landed in a swirl of red dirt and waited until the dust had settled before they climbed out of the cockpit. Once they climbed down from the chopper, Fontana rallied them quickly. If they double-timed it they could at least make it halfway back to the camp. This one was called Mourinda. He had no idea what the word meant and wasn't interested enough to figure it out. If he had his way the camp would be closed by the time they were finished with it. He wondered if the CIA would let him blow it off the face of the Earth.

This jungle was much the same as the other ones they'd been to in the past few days. Dangerous things were trying to kill them everywhere. When he heard a shout, he turned to find Payne dancing away from a tree. What Fontana had thought was a vine and shoved out of the way turned out to be a green pit viper, highly venomous. He and Payne looked at each other and laughed, but they were both shook. That would have really fucked up a day.

Once again Madeira offered to take the lead. So far, they hadn't had to get the machetes out, and until they did, he would have her take the lead through the dangers he didn't always recognize. And she set a good pace; by the time the foliage thickened enough that they needed to cut through, they were all puffing and sweating.

Madeira checked the GPS and showed Fontana the screen. At least three more miles.

Big Kenny took the lead, muscled arm swinging the machete as he plowed through literally everything. Fontana lost track of how many small trees he chopped down. If they could get within a mile of the activity they would hunker down and go into surveillance mode. If this camp was busier than the others they needed to take their time. It wouldn't do any good to get caught so close to their target.

Madeira drew them up. "There's a fairly deep ravine not too far ahead. We need to veer to the east for a while."

Zero took over the trailblazing and they started climbing a slope. Fontana could feel the pull on his glutes. Everyone went still as they heard the chug of an engine. Without saying a word Madeira pointed at the ravine and mouthed 'boat'.

Weaving through the foliage she made her way to the edge of the rock precipice. Fontana was right behind her, but he couldn't deny that he took more careful steps. He'd taken a tumble down a terrain like this before and he would not do it again.

Madeira went down on her belly and shimmied forward. She waved a hand at Fontana and he went down behind her, then crawled forward. Then he looked over the edge.

The team had been climbing for a while, but he hadn't realized how deep the ravine was. Madeira must have noticed it from the air. He certainly hadn't, even with the binoculars. As he looked down to the river he calculated they must be at least sixty feet above the murky, muddy water. There was a longboat chugging upriver. One dark-skinned man steered the boat, and there were three soldiers in the front, rifles held across their laps and ready.

"We'll have to cross that river eventually. Now we know they're patrolling it."

They backed away from the cliff and returned to the team. Fontana reported what they'd seen.

"Sounds like it's definitely an active target," Shane murmured. "Should we go ahead and call in the spooks?"

Fontana debated. They were probably going to have to call them in eventually. "Let's see what we can see first. Then we'll think about calling in Rose."

There was a round of thumbs-up and they took off again, weaving through the foliage now rather than chopping through it. Madeira had her handheld GPS out, and she checked their position almost constantly. They were a bit more than a mile away when they pulled up at the peak of the ravine. Even through the thickness of the foliage they could hear the waterfall.

"Zero and DeRossett, why don't you scope out that fall?

See if there's a way we can get across the river. There should be a bridge not too far away."

They nodded and took off into the jungle.

The rest of them settled in to catch their breath. They'd been going hard for a couple of hours now, and it wouldn't do to get too tired. Payne drew on the straw of his Camelback, a water storage system. Fontana drew on his as well. They needed to stay hydrated. Yes, there was more of a breeze here, but the heat was also more of a factor.

Madeira planted her butt on the ground and looked around. "It's going to be harder to get them out of here. If they're anything like the last group they're not going to have the stamina to do this trek."

Fontana hated to admit it, but she was right. They had been whipped when they'd gotten out of the Brazilian camp themselves and had to carry three of the survivors. If there were more survivors here, it would be that much harder.

As much as he wanted to do this himself, he was going to have to have support.

"I want to get eyeballs on it myself."

It was interminable waiting for Shane and Zero to return. The four of them scoped out the area and settled in to wait, snacking on protein bars and resting. When the two men did come back, they did so quietly, emerging from the darkness like wraiths.

Fontana spotted them first. "What did you find?"

"There is a bridge about a mile up river, but it's watched," Zero told them, taking a knee in the dirt. "There's a guard outpost on the other side. The road seems to be used by people other than just the camp, though. There's a village almost connected to the camp, so I can't tell what the guards' parameters are. Apparently, they're just watching for anything out of the normal."

"We did see troops heading into the camp, like they'd all

been called back for something," Shane said.

"If that plane brought in one of the big bosses or something, maybe it's something to kiss his ass. A show of force."

Zero shrugged. "Not sure. We couldn't see much more than that. We'll have to cross the river to get a better view."

"Roger. Zero, DeRossett, take a load off. Rest up. Tonight you're leading us across the river."

This op felt different, but Jordyn couldn't explain why. Yes, there was more danger, obviously. It was a more active camp and she had a feeling there would be more prisoners as well.

Probably more than they could handle.

Shane took point as he led them through the jungle and to the bridge that crossed the river. They all wore their night vision goggles, and the glow from the camp was enough to blind them. It was like a beacon in the black jungle that surrounded them. Even from so far away they could tell that this camp was much larger than either of the other two.

They surveyed the bridge for half an hour, watching for any kind of movement, but it was quiet. There was a village on the other side, but it didn't seem heavily populated.

Fontana keyed his mic. "I'm going to knock out that bulb in the guard shack, then we'll cross. If we can get past them we should be able to get to the jungle beyond."

Jordyn keyed her mic in an agreeing click along with the others, but she was worried. If by chance the guards had NVGs, Team Alpha would be in serious trouble.

Everything went as expected though. They crossed the fifty-foot wooden bridge to the other side and weren't spotted. There were no overhead lights and they hadn't seen a vehicle pass for as long as they'd been watching it. A dog barked in the village, but it eventually quieted.

This was going too easily. Or was she just borrowing trouble?

Insects swarmed around them as they broke into the dark jungle, headed toward the glow in the distance. It reminded her of driving across the desert toward a city, and the amber yellow glow from all the streetlights that could be seen from miles away. This camp seemed to have a steady power system. It was more than two hundred miles from the coast and fifty miles from the closest decent sized city. They were actually closer to the Suriname border to the east right now than any decent sized Guyana city. There were a few ports along the Essequibo River, which they were now paralleling, but nothing huge.

Shane lifted a fist and they crouched down. Then she heard it. There was a vehicle clattering over the bridge behind them. They waited as the rumbling engine traveled along the road and curved around to their right side. Jordyn didn't realize they were traveling so close to the road until she saw the flash of lights through the canopy before the truck passed them by.

Jordyn released a relieved breath. That had been incredibly close. She glanced up and saw Fontana looking at her. She widened her eyes at him and gave him a grin he might or might not see. Zero took point, then, and they followed along at a crouch. They were moving much more slowly now, and she was glad of that. No sense in blundering into a situation they weren't prepared for.

Zero led them north, along the Essequibo. Again, they were traveling up a slight slope, barely enough to notice, but her glutes noticed. After a while fatigue began to set in, and she noticed that Fontana's limp was a bit more pronounced. They were traveling more upright now, but it was still a trek.

Then Zero went almost completely still. Holding up a fist for the rest to see, he went down onto his belly, creeping forward through a line of thicker brush to the right. Big Kenny followed him, then Shane, then Fontana. Jordyn followed him, with Payne bringing up the rear.

As soon as they crested she had to shift her goggles up onto her helmet. They were on an elevated steppe. Similar to the cliff overlooking the ravine earlier, they were now looking down onto the well-lit Mourinda camp. The last two camps had been a fraction of the size of this one, and for the first time Jordyn felt real trepidation.

This was a legitimate compound, entirely fenced with eight foot chain-link and topped with razor wire. To the left, just outside the fence, was the airstrip they'd seen the jet come in on. It was a gleaming white jet, and it screamed corporate money. Silverstone Collaborative corporate money? There was no name on the plane, but it was probably a good bet.

She scanned the area, taking in the maintenance building, the troop barracks along with the vehicles parked in front of it. There were several different vehicles, mostly trucks with canvas tops, parked in the dirt. Then, on the right-hand side of that building, there was an added-on, low white building. She would have thought it was the med center if not for the movement in and out of the building. Uniformed men were going in and out, laughing and joking with each other. This appeared to be some kind of cafeteria.

She panned her gaze to the right. There was the med center. She'd recognize the shape of the sterile white building anywhere. This was probably what the other two camp med centers had started out looking like, but with time and disuse they'd fallen to the jungle. There were two men at the security door and two men walking around the building. It was obvious this wasn't going to be just a walk in the park.

Fontana seemed to sense it as well. "Where are the cages?" he hissed.

Zero pointed to the left and into the jungle on the other side of the troop housing.

On the one hand, it was good that the prisoners were away from the main bustle of the compound. On the other hand, it was bad because there was a decent-sized squad of military moving through the cages. At least five or six. All of the cages seemed to be closer together. And even from here she could see bodies inside. In one cage there was even a man standing, gripping the bars like he was yelling something.

More worrisome, though, were the mercenaries dressed in black that were wandering the perimeter fence. These were in addition to the ragtag military. She hadn't seen any at the last camp, so she didn't understand the significance until Fontana whispered, "Collaborative Operatives. Mercenaries. They're damn good, and the last group we ran into were enhanced, so they might have been prisoners at one time."

A chill went through her. She had seen Fontana move faster than he ever should have been able to when he'd been fighting the guard. Is that what he meant? And the shaking. She hadn't had a chance to ask him about it, but she assumed it was something related to his enhancements.

Payne drew the camera around, shielded the lens and began taking pictures. Jordyn worried that one of the men in black would hear the click of the shutter, but they were several hundred yards away. She knew for a fact they couldn't hear that far away. It was just so loud right next to her ear.

Team Alpha watched the movements of the compound for hours, logging shift changes and command structures. The guards hadn't moved any of the prisoners yet, but it was night time. Whatever medical personnel lived in the camp were probably off-shift right now. In the morning things would get busy.

There were cameras on this compound as well, mounted predominantly on the light poles that had been positioned around the area. That would be an issue unless Fontana planned on doing his *woo woo* stuff. She had no idea how strong he was in that area. Or what kind of range he had.

It was creeping toward dawn when he keyed the mic. "Let's pull back and try to reorient ourselves before the sun comes up."

Jordyn shimmied backwards through the brush, which was harder to do than expected. After hours of laying in the same position, they needed to move around and get their blood flowing. She also needed to find a bush to pee behind.

Once they were out of the surveillance area, she paused to do her business, then fell back to the group.

"I want eyes on all sides. They're probably going to start moving prisoners soon and I want it documented. Madeira and DeRossett, I want you guys to stay on this side. Payne and Zero, I want you on the north side documenting the prisoners and any movements. Kenny and I are going all the way around behind the troop barracks. Go through the fence only if you're confident that you won't be noticed. Someone came in on that plane last night and I have a feeling they'll be looking around today. I want pictures."

He looked at Payne with a raised brow, and the smaller man nodded. "Yes, sir."

"I'm going to call the spooks and see what Rose thinks," Fontana continued. "I'm sure they'll want to strike with us, but I don't know if we're going to be able to wait for them. I'll see what their ETA will be. Orders clear?"

They all gave thumbs up, then crouched down to wait for the orders to go.

Fontana moved away to make his calls, and Jordyn hoped that they could get backup sooner rather than later. They'd landed in a situation with a very high pucker factor and the more help they had the better.

CHAPTER TWENTY

Aiden fumbled the phone from the bedside stand. "Willingham."

"Hey, Will," Fontana whispered.

Aiden sat up in the bed, motioning to Angela to lay back down. "What's going on?"

Fontana relayed everything they'd done and what they were about to do, as well as their location now. Aiden took notes on the pad Angela handed him and nodded, even though he knew Fontana couldn't see him.

"How many more prisoners are there?"

"At least twenty that I can see. I'm hoping there are more in the med center itself or in cages we can't see, but twenty are definite."

He breathed out a breath, fighting the memories of the camp. They wouldn't do anyone any good right now.

Then Fontana told him about the plane. "Sounds like a Collaborative plane. Maybe they're finally trying to figure out what to do with the men."

"One of the prisoners from the last camp said that men

had been moved here, he thought, just within the past few days."

"I'm wondering if there are *only* three camps."

"Not sure," Fontana whispered. "We might find out more when we go in. One of the men we rescued in the last camp said he thought that this camp was just a stopover, and that they would be moving on."

Aiden's heart thumped in his chest and he wished he could be there with his friend. "You need to be damn careful, Fontana. I shouldn't have to tell you that, but I also know how you are. Don't go in guns blazing unless you have backup."

"Roger that," he whispered. "I'm going to call the spooks and invite them to the party. Can you see if your brother can trace a plane registration for me?"

"I can try."

Aiden copied down the registration number. "I'll text you to let you know as soon as it hits."

"Okay. I have to move."

"Okay. Keep me posted, damn it."

"Will do."

And he hung up.

A hand stroked across his back and he looked over at Angela. She was just as awake as he was, waiting to hear word on Fontana. "He's fine but they're going to be in a shit storm in a while, and I'm worried about him."

"Well, of course you are," she breathed. "It wasn't that long ago that you lost TJ. I can't imagine what you'd do if you lost Fontana as well."

The mere thought made his throat tighten. The three of them, the Dogs of War, were connected more than any other team he'd ever been a part of. Even though he was halfway around the world, if something happened to Fontana, Aiden and Wulfe would still feel it. If one died, there was a very real chance they all could.

"I'd better make some calls. And I'd better call Wulfe to tell him what's going on."

"Okay," she said softly, laying back in the bed. "When you're done come back to bed and let me hold you."

He nodded and left the room, afraid to say anything out loud.

Kevin Rose looked at the number on his satellite phone and hoped it was who he thought it was.

"This is Rose."

"Officer. This is Fontana. I'm going to send you our coordinates in a minute. We have at least twenty prisoners, possibly a high-value asset, and guards that could be enhanced. Are you in the neighborhood?"

He grinned but made sure to keep the emotion out of his voice. "Just down the block, actually."

"Team Alpha is surveilling the camp today, but I suggest you be ready to insert tonight."

"Roger. What high-value asset are we talking about?"

"Not sure. We're running the plane registration now." He gave Rose the digits. "I have a feeling it's a Silverstone Collaborative jet. Similar paint scheme."

Rose's heart raced at the thought of the evidence that could mean. So far, they hadn't gained any true proof that the Silverstone Collaborative was running these locations, only conjecture and second-hand knowledge. But if they could place a Silverstone jet on the camp itself where they were conducting illegal research on prisoners, there would be no wriggling out of the noose.

Now to keep the hothead under control.

"Your team needs to wait for us before insertion."

"We're going to try. My people are good but the odds are stacked against us here. We're going to surveil today and log movements, but if something big happens I may have to step in."

"How many troops have you seen?"

"Only about fourteen Army uniformed overnight, but ten to twelve black outfitted Collaborative operatives. Mercenaries."

Rose frowned, glancing out the cockpit window. "How do you know they belong to the Collaborative?"

"Because we've run into them before. And they were extremely hard targets. Warn your team to shoot first and ask questions later, because there's a very good chance they'll heal faster than you can get cuffs on them."

"Where did you run into them before?" Rose asked, praying that he would answer.

Fontana chuckled. "You're cutting out, Officer Rose. I'll see you tonight."

Rose cursed as Fontana hung up. God *damn*, but the man was frustrating. Rose felt like he was missing gobs of information and it was pissing him off having to go into a situation blind. *They* were usually the ones with the up-to-the-minute details. *They* were usually the ones moving on the high-value assets.

Somehow this little group of nobodies was leading him around by the nose.

But... if they did have information about the Silverstone Collaborative being dirty, he would practically arrest his own mother to be in on the takedown. Rose already had his own suspicions and had been building a file on them over the years, but if the chips fell just right, this could be the biggest takedown of his career.

Leaning forward in his seat, he gave his assistant the coordinates to take up to the pilot, then he relayed the information to Maxwell, his second. The survivors from the last camp were on a naval vessel off the coast of Venezuela, and he'd 'borrowed' this Chinook for his assault team. They were ready for insertion now, but it would take them a few hours to get within range. They would need to hike in just as Team Alpha had. If they tried to land on the airstrip, the mice would scatter and they would lose all chance of grabbing them.

Rose looked out the window at the scenery below and tried to control his excitement.

Fontana returned to the group, his gaze going automatically to Madeira in her assault gear. Tiny as hell but damn, she was such a beautiful little badass. When they got out of this mess maybe he could take her on a date or something. She drew him, and his gaze, every time she was near, and he had an overwhelming need to touch her. Even when the timing was wrong, or inappropriate. It would probably piss her off if she knew how cute he thought she was right this second.

Focus on the business at hand, he told himself.

"Rose is on his way," he whispered into the mic. "I don't think he went far. We're going to stake out our locations and monitor all camp activity. Troop numbers, prisoner numbers, medical personnel numbers. I don't want anything to slip through the cracks, especially who came in on that plane. Or who's leaving. We need to know that."

He made eye contact with each of them and nodded. They each radiated strength and determination, so he felt confident splitting up and going in. "Let's move out before it gets too light and they spot us."

With a final, lingering glance at Madeira, he turned and walked away.

Kenny moved with the grace of a much smaller man. Fontana allowed him to take point as they began working their way around the camp. They would have to swing wide to avoid detection, and the big man seemed to understand that. They hiked northeast first, then up through a rocky area that threatened to expose them as the sun began to lighten the sky. Fontana could tell that Kenny was moving as fast as he possibly could over the terrain, but it didn't surprise him when Kenny slipped at one point, one leg going down into a crevasse between two rocks. Fontana moved in to help him out but Kenny waved him away with a grin.

"If it had been my good leg we'd have been in trouble."

Fontana watched as Kenny drew his prosthetic leg up out of the hole. It was intact and didn't even look scratched, but he waited while Kenny flexed and tried it out.

The big man gave him a thumbs-up, and Fontana took the lead for a while. The morning was growing light quickly and they were going to have to find a place to hunker down, but right now he couldn't see anything suitable. They were too far away from the camp. He'd known when they started out that it was going to be a real task to make it over behind the troop barracks in time. He wondered if he shouldn't break off with Kenny and have him move in here.

The fates seemed to agree with him, because Kenny began to have a hitch in his stride. Yes, they were going through the jungle, but even accounting for the terrain there seemed to be something wrong.

"I think I may have damaged something on that rock, boss."

Fontana paused, looking back at the big man. Eventually, he nodded. "Why don't you insert here," he whispered. "Monitor what you can and try to figure out what's going on with your leg."

Kenny snapped him a salute and turned to the right, toward the camp. Fontana caught his arm. "I don't think I have to tell you how bad it would be if they caught you with your leg off."

A broad smile split Kenny's mouth. "Oh, I know. I'll be careful."

Fontana watched him go and suddenly felt very alone. And very determined. Now that he didn't have to slow for Kenny, he took off in a crouching almost-jog, circling the camp. He began to angle in toward the camp and within a few hundred yards he caught a flash of the white barracks through a break in the canopy. Slowing to a crawl, he crouched down deeper, aware that he was close enough that his movement could attract the attention of the guards he assumed were enhanced.

There was no one around and none of the cameras were pointed in his direction, so he drew out the wire snips. Before he cut anything, though, he reached out to hover over the fence with his bare hand, trying to sense electricity. Nothing. He wrapped his glove around the fence piece as he cut it, and it barely made a noise. Within just a few minutes he had a space big enough he could crawl through, even with his gear.

The guards appeared to be changing shift, which worked in his favor. He crawled in through thick foliage, angling his weapon in front of him. He found a natural depression where it seemed like the root ball of a tree had been at one time. Now it was covered over by thick, thorny vegetation. It brushed the exposed skin of his neck and fire bloomed, but he didn't dare move away from it. He was planted for the day.

Half a dozen mercenaries in black body armor and black helmets moved out between the cages, relieving the men that were already there. They didn't wear face masks, but it looked like they had mics on their helmets. It was a very similar setup to what his team had and wore.

One team was close enough that he could hear a few words of their conversation. The man going off-duty seemed aggravated, waving a hand and calling someone a 'prick'. The second guard laughed and shook his head, but the night guard persisted, motioning to the plane. He heard 'ungodly prick' as well as fucker. Apparently, whoever it was that came in had pissed everyone off.

Was this a new routine? Something implemented when the high-profile asset arrived? If it was, that would make his team's chances of success much higher. If this security team wasn't used to the new routine, it would make them easier to take over.

And less likely to notice what was going on around them, paradoxically. If they felt like they were just putting on a show for the big wig, they would be less likely to notice anything. That's what he hoped, anyway.

The prisoners seemed to be waking. He looked at the men in the cages and was surprised to realize that most of them looked okay. Not great, but definitely in better condition than the ones from his own camp. As he scanned the area, his eyes fell to one cage and the brown-haired occupant. The man was laying on his side, gaze uncomfortably close to where Fontana lay hidden. If he moved at all, the man would spot him.

Fontana held his breath as the man's eyes drifted shut, and he prayed they would stay shut for a while. At least long enough for him to shift away from the man's line of sight. There was no sense in risking anyone seeing him, at least not before he wanted them to.

Ignoring the plant sending fire down his exposed skin on the side of his face, Fontana moved out of the depression and crawled a few yards to the south, closer to the troop building.

Here he was behind a broad-leafed palmetto-type tree. It wasn't very tall, but the leaves would provide him excellent cover. He glanced back at the cage housing the prisoner that had almost seen him. The man's blue eyes were staring straight at the tree.

Fuck.

Taking a massive risk, he moved slightly so that the man's gaze could latch onto him. *If you can hear me, this is a rescue. Do not acknowledge me. This is a rescue.*

The man closed his eyes and seemed to go back to sleep, but Fontana felt like it was an act. His heart thudded in fear for a long time, but the man didn't wake again.

The sun crested over the jungle canopy and the temperature began to warm. Bugs crawled over him and he prayed none of them were venomous. With any luck, the incident last night with the snake would be his only venomous near miss.

The dayshift guards took over from the nightshift and he watched every single one of them. The way they moved, the way they looked at the prisoners, and most importantly, how aware of their surroundings they were. Most of them had been at this job for a while, he could tell, and they'd settled into a laid-back awareness that he'd seen in many former military. At a second's notice they could be on alert and ready to kill. They all carried sidearms, as well as longer assault weapons. The weapons looked very similar to the weapons his team carried.

One black-clad mercenary seemed to be in charge, standing off to the edge of the cage area. His head was on a swivel, and Fontana could tell that he was watching his own men as well as the 'military' men wandering around. The brown and black-skinned Guyanan men wore olive drab but didn't seem especially militaristic. Fontana wondered if the uniforms had been at a yard sale or something because they didn't seem like a regimented team of anything. They laughed and joked and treated their weapons, second-hand AK47s, like they were anything but something they needed to depend upon to save their lives. It was almost comical how diverse the two groups were.

The Collaborative mercenary team leader must have felt the same way. Fontana could almost see the disgust on his face. Good. If there was disorder in the ranks it could make their job easier.

It was obvious that the mercenaries in black were security, and the military in green were everything but.

Fontana used a small notepad to make a few notations. It was creeping on toward eleven a.m. when there was movement from the direction of the med center. There was a group of people there, some in medical coats and others in button-up shirts. They all seemed to be talking at a man in dress shirt and khakis. The man's arms were crossed over his chest and his thin brown hair was fluttering in the breeze, but Fontana recognized him immediately. They were talking to Anton Scofield, the public face of the Silverstone Collaborative.

Bingo, the high-profile asset.

Withdrawing his satellite phone, Fontana typed out a text and sent it to Officer Rose, Will, Wulfe, Madeira and Duncan. He was too far away from the ruckus for a phone picture, but he hoped Payne's camera was snapping away.

The look on Scofield's face was priceless. The man was used to being catered to, and high-end everything, but right this second he looked like he'd just stepped into a pile of shit with his expensive leather shoes. His lip actually curled as he looked at the barracks and cafeteria. Then he motioned to the med center. A woman in a white lab coat led him inside, out of Fontana's view.

He realized that his heart was thudding with excitement.

Apparently, Scofield had taken over after Mattingly was killed. Fontana thought the job was well beyond Scofield's abilities. The man was an ass kisser, moving from high profile government party to high profile party. If there was ever a political mover and shaker at the Collaborative, he was it. Fontana had no doubt in his mind that this was the man that had negotiated the deal between his own government and every other country involved in the Spartan program, or whatever they were calling it now.

Scofield may have had distance from the actual torture the men went through, but Fontana considered him just as guilty as Priscilla Mattingly and Damon Wilkes.

If they could secure Anton's capture, Fontana had no doubt that he would flip on Wilkes quicker than shit. The man had no morals, and he'd heard more than one story of some incident being swept under the rug for him. Before TJ had been killed, he'd created a file on the man that would make most people cringe. Stories of prostitutes being assaulted and cocaine driven parties where that and more went on. As strict and regulated as Mattingly had been, Scofield walked the edge of legal and appropriate every day.

It would be a real pleasure for Fontana to take him out, any way he could.

Scofield stayed in the med center for the better part of an hour, and Fontana wasn't surprised when one of the military guards came to retrieve one of the prisoners. They took a man out of one of the southernmost cages. The man was tall, over six feet, and towered over the shorter guards, but he didn't even try to put up a fight. There was something about the way the man carried himself that said he was broken.

His footsteps began to drag as they drew closer to the med center, but the guards prodded him on. They disappeared inside.

Time dragged then, because Fontana knew the other man

was being tortured in some way and there was nothing he could do about it. There was nothing any of them could do until Rose and his team got there. Just monitor what was going on and who the friendlies were.

So far, he hadn't seen any civilians other than the med team and Scofield's group. He couldn't assume that the food workers were civilian. One rusty truck, filled with boxes, had pulled in earlier but it was unloaded and departed within about thirty minutes.

Fontana glanced at the cages. Several of the men were looking at the front of the med center, like they knew it could be their turn at any time. He remembered that feeling, but more sharply the feeling of being vulnerable afterwards. And the fury and the shame. They'd been warriors when they'd come to the program, and left diminished.

He hadn't seen abuse like he'd been subjected to, but probably because there were so many guards.

The pervasive atmosphere of depression and fear over the camp was really bothering him. He'd reinforced his mental shields, but it was still looming, like a thunderstorm rolling overhead, heavy with rain.

Fontana waited for hours, but nothing happened. The Collaborative mercenaries rotated, taking breaks for chow and what not. The military brought food and water for the prisoners, but it didn't look like it was enough. The men ate voraciously, like they'd been starved. Maybe because the big boss was here they were settling back into what they were supposed to do. Fontana remembered perfectly how Smoke and the other guards would skim the food servings, keeping part for themselves.

Fontana drew in a swallow of water from his Camelback, as if the remembered thirst was real.

Then something interesting happened. A small engine plane circled the camp, then landed on the dirt airstrip beyond the line of trees. Six well-built men in black tactical gear climbed out of the plane and began walking toward the fence. Military stopped them at the main gate and Fontana wondered who the hell they were.

The camp was in chaos. The leader of the black-clad Collaborative mercenaries started walking toward the new group and even from a distance Fontana could see the relief in the man's expression. He stopped in front of a tall, spare man wearing a red ball cap and the two of them began to talk. The mercenary in armor seemed to be explaining himself, and the new man nodded several times before finally slapping the supervisor on the shoulder in a good ole boy way.

As the men began to walk back toward the camp. Fontana used his small binoculars to watch them, and they seemed to be having an intense, in-depth conversation, but they were trying to keep their expressions pleasant. Fontana could see anger in the new man's face, though, and he wondered what the hell was going on.

The new man walked through the cages, looking at the prisoners. It looked like he asked questions and expected answers of all the guards. Fontana couldn't figure out what was going on because he'd thought that Scofield had come to the camp because he was running it. Now this guy was doing the same thing, putting on a show like he was the cock of the walk.

As they neared the west side cages, Fontana tried to take in as much information as he could about the man. He was about fifty feet from the last cage. He used the satellite phone to capture an image of the two men together, then went still. He tried to absorb what the men were feeling. The original mercenary was feeling anxious and worried, relieved, but the new guy was calm and cool. Not much ruffled him.

"I never expected the worm to come out here, honestly,"

the new man said, a Southern drawl evident in his slow words. "Too much dirt."

The mercenary snorted. "I don't think he realized what he'd gotten into. As soon as he landed he had people hopping to do what he wanted. He went into Mattingly's bungalow and started changing things. This morning he didn't make it out until after eleven, and he's been in the med center ever since then."

"I'm sure it's the cleanest place he can be," the boss murmured.

"Yes, Mr. Truckle." The man shifted. "I tried to explain to him that you had already begun implementing new procedures, but he reversed everything, threatening to clean us out."

Truckle laughed. "He can't get rid of the mercs. We're the only thing keeping this company together. I'd like to see him try."

The men moved away, leaving Fontana with a little more information than he'd had before. He had no idea who Truckle was, but he appeared to be a former Collaborative mercenary. Or a guard supervisor? He couldn't tell exactly.

Fontana watched them walk back through the cages and he exhaled. The two of them had been a little close for comfort.

Unfortunately, if he wanted to learn anything he was going to have to get closer, because Truckle was heading to the med center. How the hell did he get in there?

The thought that flitted through his mind chilled him. No, he couldn't do it. They had enough information on the Collaborative that they would be able to put them all away. What they were collecting now was just icing on the cake. Rose would be here in a few hours and they would annihilate this entire place. There was no need to endanger himself.

"Fontana! Where are you? The guards are onto something." Madeira hissed through the radio.

As if the world were laughing at him, he realized that he hadn't been paying attention to his senses like he should have been. Three black-armored mercenaries had closed in around him, searching. He wasn't sure why they were looking here, but he had to decide if it was going to be fight or flight. Flight, definitely. There was no way they were going to put him back into a cage. He tried to project malevolence to make them turn away.

Shifting, he prepared to lunge out from beneath the tree. He'd put his hand on his weapon and was backing away from the men in front of him, who hadn't seen him yet, when lightning struck his body. Agony tore through him and he screamed out, back arching. The lightning stopped for a moment, then struck again, and he couldn't catch his breath or even see where it was coming from. Somewhere on his back. A fucking fourth guard.

Suddenly he was buried beneath men and fists were flying. Flinging up a hand to protect his head, he tried to focus on one of the guards, but the pummeling wouldn't stop. His eyes connected with one guard and he opened his mind, just before a rifle butt came down on his face. The world went dark.

CHAPTER TWENTY-ONE

Jordyn wanted to scream out against what she could see happening almost directly across the camp from her. Men had piled onto Fontana and were trying to beat the shit out of him. One man stood over him, yellow-handled Taser gun in his hand. Wires ran to Fontana's back and in the midst of the pummeling, his entire body would arch when the Taser fired. She wasn't sure why they hadn't just shot him, but she was thankful. Yes, fists and Tasers hurt, but this wasn't a lethal beat down.

They fought for several minutes before one of the guards brought his rifle butt down onto Fontana's face, knocking him out cold. Jordyn watched him for a moment, praying she would see him breathing, but she was too far away to see even with the binoculars.

Payne prodded her. "You need to message Rose, then have him dismantle that damn satellite phone. If they find that, they'll know exactly where his team is, *and us*."

Jordyn snatched the phone from her pocket and pulled up the text function.

Fontana captured. Insertion at 0038. Sat phones compromised. Dismantle Immediately.

She sent the message to Rose, Willingham and Duncan, then powered down her phone and ripped the battery from the back. Tears pushed at her eyes and she breathed through the emotion. Their operation had just gotten ten times harder, and there was nothing they could do about it until the other team got here.

Her gaze drifted across the camp. They had cuffed Fontana's hands and were dragging him across the clearing toward the med building. Oh, God. This was going to ruin him.

Payne snapped several pictures, then grabbed her arm. "We need to draw back. They're going to send out teams looking for the rest of his team. We need to get out of here."

"Team Alpha," she breathed into the mic. "Draw back. I repeat, draw back."

She received clicks for confirmation, then she allowed Payne to pull her away from their vantage point. Very carefully.

It took everything in her to not panic. Fontana was a badass former SEAL, one of the quiet professionals —trained for *anything*, but waking up in the Collaborative's custody would terrify him because he knew exactly what they could do. He knew how evil they could be. The only hope she had was the knowledge that the evil woman that used to be in charge was dead. Maybe the guy they'd seen walking into the medical building would treat him better.

She prayed it was so, because his mind was still traumatized from before. He couldn't take any more.

Anton looked up from the paperwork in front of him. The

doctors were trying to explain what they were doing to the man behind the glass but it was boring the hell out of him.

William, his personal guard, cracked open the door, furious frown marring his semi-attractive face. "Truckle is here, and they just captured someone watching the camp."

Fury ignited in his blood and he couldn't decide what he was angrier about, the fact that Truckle was here or that they'd been being spied upon. "*What?*"

William started to answer when there was a commotion at the door. Truckle shoved William aside and marched in with a phalanx of mercenaries behind him. Three of them were carrying a large, unconscious blond man wearing military fatigues. He appeared to be American.

Fear ran through Anton. "Who the hell is this? And what the hell are you doing here?"

Truckle grinned and tipped his hat back on his head, his brown beard looking wild. "Well, now, I should be asking you the same question," the man drawled, moving toward the conference table. "Because last I heard Mr. Wilkes put me in charge of this part of the operation."

Anton drew straight in the chair, refusing to react too defensively. He had every right to be here to fight for his job. "Well, Mr. Wilkes is dealing with a devastating loss right now and he doesn't know exactly what he wants. Or what's best for the company."

Truckle's dark brows raised at that. "I believe he is completely in his head, right now, and I don't think he would appreciate your assessment. Or the fact that you've gone against his explicit orders."

No, he probably wouldn't. But if Anton could prove that he was a better option than Truckle he would do it.

One of the doctors stood up from the table and walked to the unconscious man. He didn't move as the doctor rolled him over and checked for a pulse.

"So, assuming you're in charge," Truckle drawled, "what would you do about this threat to your security? I suggest you shoot the fucker."

Anton drew himself up, fighting the curl of repugnance. "Guards should be checking the area. I doubt he's alone."

The woman in charge of the medical team was leaning over the man. Leaning down, she opened one of his eyes and hissed in a breath. "This is one of the subjects that broke out of the Teraza camp."

Anton and Truckle both looked at the woman, then each other. "You're joking," Truckle said, voice incredulous.

She shook her head, face earnest. "No, sir. He was part of my test group."

Anton laughed and pushed up from the table. "Well, isn't this fun? We find ourselves with a gift in our laps, ladies and gentlemen."

"What are you talking about," Truckle demanded.

Anton gave him a condescending look. "Haven't you realized yet Mr. Truckle? This is the answer to all of the company's woes. The four that escaped, stole the formula for Dr. Shu's serum. I'm sure *he*," Anton pointed a little dramatically, "knows where the formula is, or how to get it."

Anton found himself disappointed at the dawning look of understanding on Truckle's face. The man wasn't as intelligent as he'd originally thought.

Anton waved at the guards that had come in with Truckle. "Get that guy back to his cage," he said, waving a hand into the testing room. "We need to make room for this gentleman."

CHAPTER TWENTY-TWO

They ran for a solid hour, ducking through brush and thorn trees until they got closer to the bridge they'd come over on the night before. Shane and Zero caught up with them, but they never spotted Big Kenny.

There were tears filling her eyes as she braced herself on her knees and panted. They had left him behind.

A hard hand gripped her shoulder, and she looked at Zero as he knelt beside her. "We'll get him out. Don't worry. The spooks will be here any time and we'll go get him."

"What if they hurt him? Or kill him? What if they move him out?"

"I don't think they'll kill him. They'll want to know what he's doing there."

She waved a hand in exasperation. "So, they'll hurt him, then. Torture him."

Zero's eyes were cool, but his face calm. "They may. But you have to consider what he's already lived through. A few hours of beating will not break that man. I promise you. He's a Navy SEAL. We're harder to break than that."

She breathed through her nose, praying Zero was right. No, she knew he was right, but it hurt her heart to think about the fear Fontana must be feeling.

"We need to rethink this plan, okay?"

"Okay," she nodded.

"When Officer Rose gets here we'll put our heads together and decide the best plan of action. He has to cross this bridge to get to the camp, correct?"

She thought for a moment. "Yes. Unless he plans on letting them rappel from his helicopter, assuming that's how he's coming in."

Zero shook his head. "It would make too much noise. He and his team will be coming in covert on foot, which means we'll meet them right here. Okay?"

She nodded, looking toward the bridge. It was less than a half mile away from their location.

"Now," Zero said in his best Big Brother imitation, guiding her toward the base of a tree. "Sit down, drink water and eat something. If you can, rest. We're going to need energy tonight."

Jordyn took his advice, but it was hard. The protein bar tasted like cardboard in her mouth and the water from her Camelback was swampy. She watched and listened for any kind of movement or sound from the guard shack at the bridge crossing.

At one point they all heard a mic click. They looked at each other to confirm that none of them had done it, then they listened even harder. But it didn't come again.

It wasn't until almost twenty-one hundred that the nocturnal creature sounds quieted.

A form they assumed was Officer Rose walked out of the brush, arms up. Jordyn had her NVGs on, and he looked equipped the same way they were, but he held a badge out before him to be seen. That was smart, and probably the only way they could have met up considering their communications were compromised.

"Who's in charge?" the man asked.

Madeira stepped forward, into the small clearing. Officer Rose nodded to her.

"I'm sorry about Mr. Fontana."

"Don't worry about it. Let's just go get him. Our team is at four. Big Kenny went out with Fontana and hasn't found us yet."

"I have twelve, not including myself, and I have a Chinook helicopter on standby. It can be here in five minutes."

Madeira nodded. "We have a good ways to go." She described the camp to him, and where everything was located. "We'll lead you there, then follow your lead in the assault. Then I'm on the medical center and Fontana, no matter what."

Officer Rose seemed satisfied with that. After they worked out a few details, they moved out together. Madeira wanted to run full-tilt into the camp, but she knew she needed help. There were just too many bad guys. So, she kept her pace at a jog, weaving in and out of trees. Once they got within a half-mile of the camp, they spotted a two-man military patrol. She'd barely had a chance to point before two of Rose's men had taken them out, swift and silent.

Rose broke up his team into two-man teams, and by the time they crested the rise to look down onto the camp, they were already moving into position all the way around. Jordyn was amazed at the efficiency of his crew. It was obvious they'd worked together a long time.

She hoped that smoothness worked for them tonight, because their lives were on the line.

DESTRUCTION

Fontana woke to the most terrifying thing he'd ever felt—the cold metal of the medical table he lay upon. He tried to lift his arms, but they were cuffed to the table with iron shackles. Horror tightened his gut and he thought for a moment he was going to throw up on himself. His breaths began to chase each other, faster and faster, but he couldn't get any oxygen into his lungs.

"You need to relax. You're hyperventilating."

If anything, that voice made him breathe even faster. He remembered that voice. It had usually preceded pain. Panic chewed at his mental shields, and he wanted to run. Jangling the cuffs, he knew that he couldn't. Lifting his head, he looked around the room. People surrounded him, mostly mercenaries in black body armor, and the doctor that had spoken to him initially. She'd been one of Dr. Shu's assistants from the old camp, eager, and her personality had an edge that allowed her to distance herself from her patient's pain. It was what had made her such an effective assistant in the program.

Fontana realized he had a needle in his arm, and blood was draining down into a collection bag. Obviously, they were getting samples while they could.

Drawing in a deep breath, he forced the panic away, and looked for a way out of the situation. There were six people in the room, a lot to try to control mentally. One or two at a time was easier. His influence lost its power when spread over more people. The shackles shouldn't be a problem. He could either manipulate the locks on them or get one of the guards to free him.

Timing, that was the thing.

Then the bearded man stepped forward in the red 'Roll Tide' ball cap, the same guy that had come in on the plane.

Tall and strong, he stood hip-shot. His right hand rested casually on his sidearm, and his dark eyes were direct. "It's a pleasure to meet you, Mr. Fontana. I don't think we've officially met before."

Panic surged again. How the fuck did they know his name?

The man must have understood his confusion because he nodded at the female doctor. "Dr. Levalee here remembered you from the Brazilian camp. It's like old home week. It took a bit of digging to figure out which one you were, but we did it. It's a pleasure to have you back, Mr. Fontana."

"Fuck you," he growled.

The easy going light left the man's eyes. "Now, I did not offer you that kind of disrespect. Why not behave like a grown man?"

Fontana narrowed his eyes on the man and knew that this was the one he wanted to ruin. It was too soon, though. He wouldn't use his ability until he absolutely had to. "Behave like a man that tortures military personnel for profit? His own countrymen?"

The man grimaced. "I'll admit, that little part of the job has been ... challenging. I'm a former Army man, myself."

Fontana snorted. "Way to represent your country, big man."

Anger glistened in the man's dark eyes, but he held his easy going pose. "You know, I was going to be all nice about asking you where the rest of your team was. Now I think I'm going to enjoy finding out the other way."

Fontana wasn't especially worried. He'd been beaten by some of the best. Glancing around the room he looked for any indication of the time of day, but he seemed to be completely secluded. There were no windows here, only a one-way mirror along one wall, and he felt a little blinded.

Closing his eyes against the light he tried to take inventory of himself. His back muscles were sore, even laying here on the table, but he didn't think he had any other injuries. He still had his t-shirt and BDUs on, which surprised him. They must have been worried about him waking up before they were ready for him. His body armor and weapons were gone of course, as well as his helmet with the mic. The satellite phone had been in the breast pocket of his vest, surely, they'd found that as well.

So, what was he left with? His mental abilities. And a team on the outside that he knew would make some kind of move tonight. Jordyn had probably seen what had happened to him when he was taken but she would have had to draw back as well. Once he was captured, the Collaborative mercenaries had probably known that he was part of a team. If Fontana were in charge, he would have sent out every man he could spare to look for the surveillance team. Then he would have brought them back here or put them into the spare cages, if not killed them outright.

What if they had already been captured?

This man above him had the answers. He just had to tease them out.

"Maybe we did get off on the wrong foot," Fontana said. "Did you take over from the Bitch in Blue?"

The man tipped his head back and laughed. "You know, I used to call her that in my mind, but I didn't dare ever say it aloud. I would worry about her hearing it on the air, or something, and haunting me for the rest of my days." He shook his head. "As for the command structure, that's a bit contested at the moment."

"This isn't the job for Anton. He doesn't like to get his hands dirty."

The man in the ball-cap snorted. "You are right about that. My name is Dustin Truckle. Wilkes named me Priscilla's replacement when Anton couldn't do the job."

Fontana forced a slight smile. "Yeah, thought so. I would say it's nice to meet you, Mr. Truckle, but I wouldn't mean it. And I'll probably have to kill you soon, so I'm not going to get attached."

Truckle's gaze narrowed dangerously, and he nodded once to whoever Fontana suspected was behind the one-way glass. "Dr. Levalee has created a cocktail that you might be interested in, Mr. Fontana. Rather than go weeks between testing every disease, she found a few combinations that work very well together, and really knocks the patient down. She's curious to see if the serum Dr. Shu created is still working in your body." He turned to glance at the woman. "Remind me, Robyn, what's in this?"

"It's a mix of Tetanus, Shingles and Malaria. Should cause plenty of external manifestations we can monitor. Muscle spasms, persistent itching rash, possible convulsions. The pain, unfortunately, will be debilitating." There was a glimmer of humor in her dark eyes. "We'll make sure you don't choke on your own vomit."

Yeah, right. She didn't think it was unfortunate at all. Fontana could hear the subtle excitement in her voice. Rocking his head on the hard metal table he looked at her. The woman had pulled her dark blond hair into a business-like bun, and a pair of wire-framed glasses sat on the bridge of her nose. Her mind was excited, and more than a little sociopathic. He could feel that just from looking at her. He glanced at Truckle. The man was reluctant but determined. He would do what needed to be done for the company.

"You're not going to inject me with that," he told the woman.

She lifted both her brows in disbelief at his words. "Really?"

She made a motion with her chin and four guards moved in to hold him down against the table. Without consciously thinking about it, Fontana braced, preparing. There were too many emotions fighting in his gut to be still.

Each man took an extremity, latching on hard. Fontana fought the shackles that were around his wrists and ankles, as well as the men that had piled on. He arched on the table, trying to get away from the doctor as she moved in, needle exposed.

"Hold him!" she snapped.

Truckle moved in to put pressure on his chest and keep him from arching again, and as soon as the slow-speaking guard touched him, Fontana knew Mr. Truckle had a very dangerous secret. He'd been tested on as well. Fontana lost his breath as Truckle, unnaturally strong, forced him down. Truckle used his hands to grip each side of the table, pushing his own weight down onto Fontana. It was exactly what Fontana had been waiting for.

He looked at the female doctor and projected into her mind, *Mr. Truckle wants to try the shot first.*

The woman blinked and hesitated, her mind struggling against his hold.

Inject Truckle! Fontana screamed at her, using every bit of mental push he had.

Veering her trajectory slightly, she sank the needle into Dustin Truckle's neck and pushed the plunger.

Truckle looked up at her in shock, then down at Fontana. He slapped a hand over his neck, like he could grab back the fluid. He glared at the doctor, who backed away from the table.

"What the fuck did you do, woman?"

The doctor appeared dazed as she glanced from Truckle to the syringe in her hand. Confusion crossed her features, just before Truckle's fist slammed into her face. The woman sprawled inelegantly across the floor.

Fontana barely saw the same fist coming at him, Truckle

moved so fast, but he certainly felt it. His head rocked on the table and blood sprayed across the wall from his mouth. Then the rest of the mercenaries began whaling on him. This was really going to hurt.

Fontana drew into himself and just let them do what they were going to do. The guards rained blows to every part of his body. Fontana pulled at the shackles out of instinct, but Truckle landed several good solid hits to his ribs, and he felt them crack. With another punch they broke. Truckle seemed to know that he'd found a weak spot, because he struck him in the same spot one more time. Suddenly, Fontana felt his breathing become compromised. Fuck, he'd punctured a lung.

Luckily for him, Mr. Truckle suddenly began feeling the effects of the shot. Drawing back, he had a dazed look on his face, and he looked like he was going to vomit.

For the tiniest split second, Fontana felt bad for him, until Truckle's gaze swung back to him. There was fury in his eyes. "You did this," he hissed, before he went down to his knees. He reached for his sidearm, then detoured the motion to clutch at his throat.

Two of the mercenaries moved to help him and Fontana lost sight of him behind their bodies. Taking a second to center himself, he closed his eyes and focused. No one heard the locks release on the shackles over the sound of Truckle vomiting. One of the men were calling for nurses for the downed people, and maintenance to clean up the mess. In the midst of the chaos, Fontana looked at the mercenary to his right and mentally suggested that he close his eyes so that he didn't have to see the carnage. The guard closed his eyes. Very calmly Fontana released his wrists from the shackles, reached out and lifted the gun from the holster on the mercenary to his left, who had turned to watch Truckle puke. His ribs screamed from being curled up, but he blocked off the pain as he put the muzzle of the weapon to the man's spine and pulled the trigger. He dropped like a sack of potatoes.

Fontana shot the mercenary to his right, who still had his eyes shut, sat up, and shot the two mercenaries who were trying to help their boss. He underestimated Truckle though. The man had managed to grab his sidearm in spite of the pain and before Fontana could slide off the table, Truckle shot him. One shot skimmed across the back of his head, through his scalp. The second skimmed across his ribs as he turned, almost exactly where Truckle had already punctured his lung, and the third took him in the meat of the left thigh. Then Truckle went down, his body arched into a rictus of pain.

Fontana was struggling with his own searing pain. It hurt so bad, it stole his breath. He clenched his teeth and tried to block it off, but it was more than he'd been trained for. Knowing he had to move, he tried to psych himself up, and Jordyn's face popped into his mind. He wanted to see her again; the way she smiled at him, and fuck, that rockin' body. If he got out of here alive, he *would* be taking her out.

Rolling off the far side of the table, Fontana tried to brace for the fall, but it was too late. He clattered to the ground in a heap. He'd been hit good, and nothing wanted to work correctly right now. In spite of himself, he had to respect Truckle's grit. He tightened his grip on the gun in his right hand, afraid to lose it. He knew that within seconds, more mercenaries would be pouring into the room.

Shoving his pain to the side, he looked at the mercenary he'd landed on. Fumbling at the man's utility belt, he found the mag pouch and pulled the extra mags out, trying to get them into his own pocket.

Everything seemed to be moving super slow, including him. There was a scalding sheet of heat running down his back which he assumed was blood from his scalp wound. He was gasping in little puffs of air because his lungs wouldn't draw any more than that. His entire left side was a blaze of pain, and he prayed that his engineered healing ability would kick in.

Peering through the legs of the medical table he looked for danger. Truckle was still arched in pain, his muscles straining all across his body. He'd long ago lost his hat. His dark, bulging eyes were latched onto Fontana though, and the gun was still clutched in his right hand, his knuckles white with tension where he gripped the weapon. Fontana wondered if his fingers would snap.

As if in response to his thought, another shudder rippled through the man, and his muscles contracted even tighter. It must be the tetanus hitting him so hard. Something gave a meaty, viscous pop and the man grunted with pain, his teeth clenched and bared, jaw locked. Then something else snapped, and the man's eyes widened. His mouth opened in a silent scream.

Fontana had no idea what had broken, but the look in Truckle's eyes had changed. They weren't angry any more, they were pleading.

Fighting the pain from his gunshot wounds, Fontana forced himself to his feet, using the metal table as leverage. The thigh wound was still bleeding, but the leg was usable. Sometime during the fight, the needle had come out of his arm. The heavy bag of his blood was on the floor, completely intact. He almost passed out leaning over to pick it up, but he managed. Using one of the clamps on a nearby table, he crimped the hose, then stuffed the thing into the thigh pocket of his BDUs. He might need that blood if he kept leaking the way he was. There was a roll of adhesive sports tape on the table. Using a fingernail to find the end, he stretched it out and wrapped it several times around the gunshot wound in his thigh. Not perfect, but maybe it would slow the bleeding.

Stepping over arms and legs and puddles of blood, Fontana made his way to the door. He looked at Truckle. The man's eyes were desperate now, begging for death. Fontana could remember feeling that way many times.

Turning, he limped out the door, leaving Truckle to his agony.

CHAPTER TWENTY-THREE

Anton didn't hear anything his guard William was saying. His feet moved automatically as the big man dragged him out of the room with the one-way mirror and through the hallways, toward the front entrance of the medical center and presumably safety.

The man on the medical table had been phenomenal, exactly the kind of super soldier they'd been trying to create. Even shackled to the table the way he'd been, and with the guards beating him, he'd still managed to prevail. Truckle had done his best to put him down, but Truckle was now writhing on the floor as his own muscles were dislocating his joints. Anton had gagged when he'd seen that, right after Truckle had shot Fontana three times while he was still on the medical table.

Anton had seen more violence in the past five minutes than he had in the past five years. It was terrifying and arousing at the same time. His blood was pumping with excitement, with a strong edge of fear. If Fontana spotted him, he had no doubt he would die.

Anton's shoulder slammed into a door and he realized

they were outside. William was yelling at a group of the uniformed military as well as some of the Collaborative mercenaries to pull in, they were heading to the airstrip.

"No," Anton said suddenly. "I can't leave my laptop, my things."

Williams looked at him incredulously and Anton realized what he'd said was incredibly stupid. Of course, his life was more important than the material things in his cabin.

Pulled along by William's hand clutching his arm, Anton ran faster, his blood suddenly chilling with fear as he observed Collaborative mercenaries being shot down one after another. Blood was flying everywhere and Anton screamed as one of their guards collapsed right in front of them, making them go down in a tumble. William jerked his arm to pull him back up to his feet.

"I'm trying, asshole," Anton snapped, just as a red hole appeared in William's forehead. His longtime bodyguard crumpled to the ground, lifeless.

Anton stared in horror, the very real danger he was in suddenly slamming home. He looked around and realized that all of this guards had been taken out, and a group of men dressed a lot like his own were overwhelming them. Raising his hands into the air, Anton held his breath as they encircled him. Before he could open his mouth to say anything, something struck his head violently and his world turned dark as he went down.

The camp was lit up like the Fourth of July. Something had happened. Or was happening. Even as she watched, a group of heavily armed black-clad mercenaries began herding a man toward the airstrip. Gunfire sounded from somewhere to the right. From the medical center? And even more people started running, muddying the field of battle.

Jordyn pointed at the group of mercenaries huddling around the man in civilian clothes. "That must be Anton under there," she cried.

Officer Rose nodded and made a series of hand motions to his people. "Mics on people!"

Yeah, he was right. She seriously doubted anyone would be listening to their transmissions now. They were all too busy running for cover.

"Team Alpha, let's find Fontana."

Crouching low, weapon high, Madeira led her team into the chaos.

Fontana lost track of how many men he killed. If they were in his way, he took them out, no hesitation. He'd seen Anton's head moving through the crowds a minute ago, but he'd lost him. It seemed like they were heading toward the airstrip. If his world started falling down around his head that's where Fontana would go too, in the hopes that he could escape.

His vision was tunneling. Fontana knew he'd lost a lot of blood. Using his mental ability as sharply as he had didn't help with his energy either. Mental exercises drained them, bad. And he couldn't seem to get enough oxygen. As much as his body worked, it didn't seem like he could breathe.

Pausing at the back bumper of a truck, he realized there were men being shot down and he wasn't doing it. Looking around he saw covert figures moving into the camp, weapons blazing. The cavalry had arrived, finally.

If he could have cheered he would have, but he could barely stand on his own. Three men ran around the truck, weapons raised. They were in the olive green military uniforms and seemed to be fumbling with their guns, trying to pull back the slides. Fontana realized they couldn't be very old and had obviously not been trained at all. They looked up and saw him staring and went still. Then, one by one, they dropped their weapons and backed away.

Fontana let them go, because he knew they hadn't been complicit in what was going on here. Scanning the field of fire, he looked for targets. He thought he'd seen Scofield running in this direction.

Just as the thought materialized, he spotted them. The guard that normally protected him was shot down, and Anton held his hands in the air like the coward that he was. Officer Rose's CIA insertion team, he assumed, encircled the man, and one of them knocked him out with the butt of his rifle.

Fuck, yeah.

Pushing away from the truck, he started toward them, but his vision swam. His stomach lurched with nausea and he stopped, waiting for his body to rebound. The blood loss was getting to him. Gasping air, he tried to blink the world into focus. Even that hurt because of the beating he'd taken. Oh, and he thought that was the same side the rifle butt had hit him on.

Something slammed into him from behind, sending him sprawling across the ground. He turned to fight instinctively but the Collaborative mercenary got in the first punch, dead center of the gunshot across his ribs. Fontana swung wildly, managing to connect to a piece of body armor. Well, fuck. That wouldn't work. Blinking, he tried to focus on his assailant, but he couldn't breathe. The Collaborative mercenary drew back and reached for his sidearm.

A massive form took the man down to the ground and they rolled away. Fontana dropped to a knee as Big Kenny plowed a fist into the guard's face, beneath the helmet. Two more strikes and the man was unconscious.

Fontana lost time then, because he blinked and realized he was lying on the ground now, and Big Kenny was leaning over him. His mouth was moving but Fontana couldn't understand what he was saying. Then Jordyn was there, her beautiful face scowling as she looked down at him. He couldn't understand what she said either, but he felt her hands as she cupped his cheeks. Staring into her beautiful eyes, he tried to gulp in air, but his chest was so constricted. Well, if he had to go, at least he would be looking at beauty.

―――――

Jordyn screamed for a medic as Fontana's eyes closed and he fell unconscious. He was doing this weird gasping thing, like he couldn't get breath into his lungs. Blood coated him from head to toe, and she couldn't tell where it was all coming from. There seemed to be a wound in his ribs, and she wondered if that wasn't why he was gasping. There was also some kind of bandage around his upper left thigh, which looked deep.

Keying her mic she demanded medical help, then gave her location. Within seconds a man ran out of the fire and smoke toward them. Kenny waved an arm to bring him in, and the man, dressed in a hodgepodge of camo and black, went to his knees on the other side of Fontana. There was a large red cross on his right arm, denoting medical. Immediately, he started assessing Fontana's vitals; blood pressure seemed low and his pulse was sluggish as well. Jordyn had had basic medical training and she knew that much, but the medic was frowning hard. He didn't like what he found.

"I'm Dr. Giraldi," the man said, glancing up at her. "I'll be taking care of Mr. Fontana. What can you tell me about his condition?"

"I just got here, too. Looks like two bullet wounds, chest and leg, but I haven't gone any further than that."

Giraldi nodded, and she stared at the man as he did his evaluation. Commonly on high-risk ops like these there were medics, or corpsmen, but very rarely actual doctors.

"My assistant is triaging other wounded. Would you mind helping me roll him over, very carefully? I'll stabilize his head."

As Big Kenny stood over them in guard position, she and Giraldi rolled Fontana up onto his side. Jordyn realized a lot of the blood was coming from a cut on the back of his head. Dr. Giraldi spotted it at the same time and quickly applied a bandage that looped all the way around. Then he began cutting the clothes from his body. They found the gash in his ribs, and the weird bubbling in the blood there. "He's punctured a lung."

Giraldi dug in his kit for a minute and withdrew a round piece of bandage. He removed the sterile packaging, wiped the area around Fontana's injury clean, then applied the bandage. It may have been her imagination, but she thought he took a more sure breath that time.

"Hopefully that will keep the air out of his chest and keep the lung from collapsing." He gave her a bright smile. "That won't kill him."

Giraldi continued down, cutting Fontana's pants from his legs. They peeled away wetly, almost completely saturated with blood. It was as he was cutting them away that he pulled something heavy from one of the cargo pockets.

"Is this a bag of his own blood?"

Jordyn looked at it in confusion. "I have no idea."

"We'll set that aside for now. If he comes to and confirms it's his, we may just roll it right back into him. It would help with his blood pressure."

She nodded, wondering where the hell it had come from. Had they been drawing his blood for experimentation?

Giraldi cut off the makeshift bandage on Fontana's thigh and it started bleeding again, more than just wound bleeding. "Okay, this is enough to kill him. He's nicked an artery. Can you assist?"

Jordyn nodded, knowing that she would do anything she needed to do to keep Fontana alive. Packing the wound with dressings, he told her to hold pressure on it, then he started an IV. Big Kenny moved close enough to hook the bag onto one of his pockets as he continued to cover them.

Jordyn did as she was told as Giraldi prepared to try to stitch the wound closed. She glanced around the area. It seemed like most of the shooting was done and now the CIA team was rounding everyone up. They were also going cage to cage and checking on the survivors.

There were a lot of dead here, but it looked like the good guys had prevailed. She spotted Zero and Shane moving through the captured prisoners, and Payne had the camera to his eye, documenting the rescue of the caged survivors. Officer Rose stood over an unconscious a man in civilian clothes, scanning the scene around him and talking into his satellite phone.

She glanced down at Fontana. It wasn't her imagination. He was definitely breathing better, but still not normal, full breaths.

Jordyn held a focused flashlight beam and several tools she had no name for as the doctor dug into Fontana's leg and stitched the bleeder closed. It had to be damn near the *least* sterile environment ever, but she had no doubt that Fontana would be able to walk afterward. And if his healing abilities were as good as he said they were, he would be up and around in no time.

Giraldi bandaged the leg and pronounced him ready to

transport. Stripping off his gloves the doctor keyed his radio and talked to someone. Over the din of fighting and yelling, Jordyn had heard the steady *whomp whomp whomp* of rotor blades coming close. That was definitely a Chinook.

"Are you going with him?" Giraldi asked.

"Yes," she said, no hesitation. She was not leaving Fontana now.

There was something over his face, cutting off his breathing. He lifted an arm and tried to pull it off, but the wind was blowing so hard that he couldn't.

"Leave it, Fontana," he heard Jordyn say. "We're almost loaded."

Though it made him a little panicked he left the fabric over his face. The wind eased as he felt himself being carried up onto something, and his cot being set onto a floor. Noise was all around him and he blinked into the darkness.

Then Jordyn was leaning over him and smiling down into his face. "Hey, we're loaded. How are you feeling?"

He blinked up at the line of lights above his head. "Helicopter?"

"Yeah, we're in a Chinook headed who knows where. The CIA is driving."

He nodded, then winced as fire blazed across the back of his head. He must have made some kind of sound because she squeezed his hand. "You're okay, but you have a cut on the back of your head and a punctured lung. You're not as pretty as you used to be with your face all swollen. Your left thigh took some heavy damage as well. But you're stitched up enough to get the hell out of the jungle. Okay? I'm going to stay with you until you're stabilized."

That one sentence made him feel better than anything. "You'll stay with me?"

"Yes, I will," she said firmly. "I'll watch over you until you wake up, okay? Don't worry about anything."

Yeah, he believed her. Jordyn Madeira was a beautiful woman with an amazing heart, and if she said she would watch over him, he believed her.

"Hey, Fontana. Is that your bag of blood we found in your pants pocket?"

"Yes," he said, voice drowsy. "Mine."

"Okay."

He felt her fingers in his hair and even though it hurt to move, he turned his head toward her. Then he let the world drift away.

CHAPTER TWENTY-FOUR

Jordyn wanted to throw up, but she'd have to let go of Fontana if she did. The helicopter thrummed beneath her. She sat on the floor next to Fontana's four-inch tall cot, her hand buried in his hair. If he had any idea what she'd done for him...

Glancing around the cargo hold, she looked for familiar faces, but there were only one or two who looked vaguely familiar. They'd been on Officer Rose's team treating the Brazilian survivors at her uncle's airport. The rest of the people packed into the hold were survivors from this camp, or other critically wounded CIA officers. Giraldi was at the far end of the cargo space, leaning over one of the critically starved men. He'd been moving back and forth almost constantly, putting out medical fires as he came to them. As soon as she confirmed that the bag of blood was indeed Fontana's he'd changed out the bag of IV solution for the blood. Fontana had improved to the point that once the blood was gone, Giraldi removed the needle completely.

"Just let me know if you see anything I need to worry about," he warned.

Fontana had steadily improved, though.

"Where are we?"

She looked down at him, surprised that he was able to even talk. "We're in the air, flying over the ocean. I believe we're heading to a carrier or something in the Atlantic, maybe the Caribbean. No one will say exactly."

His eyes closed for a minute, and she wished she had better light to see him by. There was minimal lighting in the hold, just enough to get around. Giraldi was working by flashlight.

Fontana suddenly sat up enough to look at her, propping himself on an elbow. It had to be painful, but he gave no indication of it. "You're on a helicopter."

Jordyn smiled grimly. "I am." Her eyes held his for a long moment. "Only for you."

Fontana blinked and some expression crossed his face. Tossing the sheet from himself, he rolled off of the cot to the floor. He gasped in pain but seemed determined. Jordyn was leaning against a heavy metal crate. Fontana maneuvered himself until he was laying over her lap on his right side, his heavy arms wrapped around her waist. His head ended up resting in her left elbow, her right arm over his back. It definitely wasn't a long-term comfortable position, but it was exactly what they each needed in that moment. Jordyn felt her anxiety ease. She reached out for the sheet he'd pushed away, and she drew it up against his back. He still wore his blood-stained underwear, but she thought that maybe being that exposed would cause him to be uncomfortable.

There was a nip against her left breast, hard enough that she felt it even through her uniform and bra. It had been just at the edge of her bulletproof vest. She looked down at him and saw a flash of a grin, and the dimple in his cheek. He tightened his arms around her, and she around him. Yes, this was exactly what they needed.

They flew for at least two hours and Jordyn had to admit it was one of the smoothest flights she'd ever been on. So smooth that she fell asleep herself... with the solid warmth of Fontana cradled in her arms.

Fontana woke when the bottom fell out of his stomach. The noise around him was almost concussive, it was so loud, but he realized they were landing. Jordyn's arms were strong around him and he wondered how long they'd been in the air.

His body felt like he'd been run over by a truck, but he was breathing normally now with no pain in his ribs. Pulling his arms away from her luscious body, he pushed himself into a sitting position, and found himself looking at her full lips. Without thought or hesitation he leaned in and captured her mouth, trying to convey how much he appreciated what she'd done for him.

Jordyn rested a hand on his cheek and smiled against his mouth. "How are you feeling?" She whisper/shouted over the sound of the engines.

He pulled back to look at her. "I'm fine."

As soon as he sat up she shifted her legs, stretching her booted toes flat, then vertical. He must have been a hell of a burden for her. "Sorry," he mouthed. He was lucky he hadn't crushed her.

She shook her head and leaned close to his ear. "I wouldn't have had it any other way. Thank you."

The fact that she'd flown with him, and hadn't been in control of the stick, was really something to him. Would anyone else in his life had done something so selfless for him? The other Dogs of War maybe, but they weren't here right now. And it wasn't on the same level as what she'd done for him. It was a true, emotional sacrifice.

Fontana looked out one of the windows but all he could see were misty clouds, lit by the green flash of the position light on the chopper itself. They were landing but he couldn't see what they were landing on.

Scooting his butt back against the floor until he leaned against the same crate as Jordyn, he pulled her in tight against his shoulder. She sagged into him, arm draped carelessly over his lap. Fontana tried not to react, but he couldn't help himself, and he knew the moment she felt him. She looked up at him incredulously. "Really?" she chuckled.

He gave her a shamefaced look and shrug. "What can I say?"

She rocked her head against him. "You have life threatening injuries. There's no messing around until you're completely healed."

Fontana took stock of how he felt. His pain level was at about a three, negligible. There was some achy pain in his thigh, but not enough to keep him from walking off the helicopter. His scalp wound itched and he was breathing like normal. More importantly his body was telling him that it needed more of her. Maybe she was the reason he'd healed so well. "I'm fine, seriously. I'll walk off this chopper."

Jordyn frowned, and he could tell she was wondering how much of what he told her was bravado.

At that moment the engines whined and a glow began to build outside the window. They were landing on something dangerous, and he could feel the anxiety she tried to fight.

You'll be all right, he told her mentally, somehow knowing that she would be able to hear him. *I'm holding you and I would never let anything hurt you.*

Her big eyes blinked at him and he knew she'd heard him, but she didn't respond. He thought he might have heard *oh, fuck*, but he wasn't entirely certain. Either way, it was enough to distract her until the Chinook was solidly on the asphalt platform of whatever ship was providing their refuge.

Once they were stable, Jordyn pushed to her feet. He accepted her help to stand because he couldn't bend his thigh the way he needed to without ripping stitches, but he was steady on his feet once there. They waited against the bulkhead of the ship for their turn to leave. He wound the sheet around his hips and tucked it in like a towel.

A man with dark hair started directing Navy medics on the unloading of patients. He stopped short in front of Fontana and stared, frowning. Flicking on a flashlight, he leaned in to look at the bandage over his ribs, then pulled the sheet out of the way of his damaged thigh. Flicking the light into Fontana's eyes he checked his reaction, then pressed a stethoscope to his chest to listen. When he pulled back he wore a puzzled expression.

"Let the more injured off first, doc. I'm fine."

Blinking, the man nodded. "Yes, I think you're right. I'll have someone park you somewhere so I can check you later."

Then he was gone, directing again. Jordyn laughed when the man kept glancing back, like he was waiting for Fontana to fall over, but he had no plans of doing that.

It was twenty minutes later before they were finally led off the Chinook. Fontana had looked out the windows and realized they were on an amphibious warfare ship. Ospreys, Harriers and AAVs— amphibious assault vehicles— lined the expanse of the ship's deck. Nostalgia surged in his gut. This had been his old stomping ground, so to speak, but he didn't recognize this one in particular. He asked the young man leading them across the landing strip the name of the vessel.

"This is the USS America, sir. She's fairly new."

"Apparently."

The sailor led them under cover and into what was obviously a temporary hospital. There were several partitioned areas, not exactly private but not out in the open either. When the curtain was pulled they would have a modicum of privacy.

"Think you can find me some clothes, sailor?"

The young man nodded. "Yes, sir. Your sizes?"

Fontana reeled them off. "Something combat-worthy if possible."

The man blinked, then nodded. "I think I can do that."

And he disappeared.

Fontana sat on one of the chairs, leaving the other for Jordyn. There was an exam table on the other side of the little area, but he definitely didn't want to sit there. His left thigh was itching like a bitch and he pulled the sheet away. The gunshot wound where Truckle had shot him had completely sealed up and the stitches that the doctor had put in were beginning to fall out.

"Jeez," Jordyn breathed. "It looks like it happened two weeks ago. How the hell is that possible?"

Even he had to admit that the speed of the healing was faster than normal. "I'm not sure exactly."

He started plucking at the black stitches, but she waved his hands away. "You're making them bleed. Quit pulling on them like that."

She leaned over his leg and began teasing out the threads with her short, pretty fingernails. He had to admit that she was much gentler than he'd been to himself. Once she had a handful of stitches, she rubbed her hand over his thigh, wiping the few bloodstains away. It didn't hurt, but it did make him shift for another reason.

Jordyn seemed to realize what she was doing and pulled away, but he caught her hand. "I wanted to thank you," he said softly, "for being there for me."

Her eyes filled with tears and he was truly shocked. Jordyn was too strong of a woman to cry. "I had to leave you first, and it was one of the hardest things I've ever had to do. When I saw them attack you... I thought I'd never see you again, and it scared me. Oh God, it scared me."

Reaching out, he wiped her cheeks with his thumbs. He couldn't remember anyone ever crying over him. "I'm sorry it scared you. They were on me before I could retreat. With Anton there, I knew they wouldn't kill me outright. He would be curious about who was watching him. Actually, though, he wasn't the dangerous one."

He told her about Dustin Truckle, and the pain he'd left him in.

"Good," she snapped. "It was no less than they did to you for eight months."

Yes, that was true, but he still felt a little guilty. "We need to bring him in for questioning if he's still alive. Have you seen Rose?"

She shook her head, her dark hair falling over her eyes. "I think he was still at the camp when we left."

Drawing her into his arms, he rested his chin on top of her head. "And I assume the rest of Alpha Team is there."

"Yes. None of our crew was hurt."

That was excellent news, and no less than he'd expected.

"Some of the mercenaries they fought were harder to take down than expected," she said softly. "I know it took Big Kenny and Zero both taking one guy down. They didn't want to shoot all of the guards because Rose wanted to take some in for questioning. I know they retrieved a few before we took off."

Fontana sighed into her hair. That was good news. Everything was happening the way he'd wanted it to. Anton was in custody as well as several of his men. Truckle, maybe. And the men that had been repeatedly tested upon were safe.

All in all, Operation Absolution had been a success, other than the dead they'd found in Venezuela. They'd confirmed a lot of things, and rescued men who'd had no say in the path their lives had taken once they'd volunteered for the project. Fontana knew that those men would have a lot of adjusting to do. But before they even returned to civilian life they would have to be tested or monitored for a certain amount of time to see what abilities they did or didn't have.

Even as his brain thought through the details, his body seemed determined to go in a different direction. It liked the closeness of Jordyn and wanted to be even closer. He tried not to be assertive, but even standing loosely in his arms she felt him respond. Looking up, she gave him a thoughtful smile. "You know nothing can happen here."

He shrugged lightly. "I know, but it doesn't mean I can't enjoy holding you."

That seemed to satisfy her just fine, because she parked her head against his chest again. They stood there, holding each other against the sway of the massive ship beneath them, until someone called from the other side of the partition.

Jordyn backed out of his arms. "Come in," she called.

The medic stepped in, looking him up and down. A nurse in uniform stepped in right behind him, smiling.

"Fontana, this is Dr. Giraldi," Jordyn said. "He operated on your leg in the field."

Fontana held a hand out to the man. "Doctor? I expected a medic. You did a fantastic job, Doc."

Giraldi waved a hand. "I'm honestly amazed to see you on your feet, Mr. Fontana. That was a pretty devastating injury. Mind if I check you over?"

Fontana moved to sit on the exam table and scooted back. "Maybe you can take the head bandage off first. It's bugging me the most."

Giraldi looked at him oddly but reached for the wrap around his head. Fontana would have blushed if the doctor had insisted he start lower. This would give his body time to chill.

Jordyn crossed her arms beneath her breasts, and he realized she was still completely dressed for combat, only her helmet was missing. Damn, he must have been truly out of it if he hadn't noticed all that. She looked glorious, petite and fierce, her mussed hair down over her eyes. More importantly, there was worry in her eyes. For him.

He forced a grin as the doctor removed the last of the bandaging. Giraldi handed the gauze away to the nurse, then wet down a wad of cotton with water and started scrubbing his head. There was no pain, just a bit of an itch.

Giraldi stopped cleaning and stepped in front of him. "I *know* you had a wound, there. Now there's barely a scar."

He tugged on Fontana's sheet and looked at his rib injury, then drew back, frowning. Removing the stethoscope from around his neck he plugged the earpieces into his ears and held the end to Fontana's chest. "Breathe for me. Deep breaths in ... and out. Again. Once more."

Fontana did as he was told, knowing that their recovery abilities would be an issue sometime, but not sure how to get out of it.

Giraldi removed the stethoscope and pulled the sheet further away to look at his legs.

"Where are the damn stitches?"

Fontana glanced guiltily at Jordyn. "We took them out. They were itching."

Giraldi touched the wound. Even the little tiny blood spots were gone now. "How in the *hell* is this possible? I put those stitches into a gunshot wound, after surgical repair, less than *five hours ago*."

Fontana winced. He hadn't realized how little time had passed. Shrugging, he looked the doctor in the eye. "I'm really not sure."

That was the truth, but Fontana was fudging it just a bit. He knew it had been the serum he'd been given two years ago, but there was no way he could tell the doctor that. Aiden still had some of the serum somewhere, but he hadn't seen it for a long time. Fontana wasn't sure where his buddy had hidden it.

"Can you stand up for me, please, Mr. Fontana?"

Standing, he went through the small exercises Giraldi asked him to do. His leg twinged a bit, but not too bad. And his lungs seemed be just fine. He ran a hand over the back of his head. There was a line of stubble where the bullet had grazed his scalp, shaving hair. It would grow in eventually.

Giraldi had planted his hands on his hips. "I don't know what to say. I wish all of these men we found out here could have a tiny portion of the healing ability you've exhibited. It's going to take them months of steady care to get back to where they need to be."

"Years," Fontana corrected, and he let the doctor see the experience in his expression. "At least two."

With a single, thoughtful nod, Giraldi marked something on a tablet the nurse held. "If you don't mind I'd like to take a blood sample."

"I do. We need to get out of here. Have you seen Officer Rose?"

Giraldi frowned. "No, not yet. You won't give me a blood sample?"

Fontana shook his head. "Not right now. I need to get back with my team."

The doctor frowned and looked Fontana up and down. "I guess I have no reason to stop you. I really wish you'd reconsider, maybe take some time to sleep."

He glanced at Jordyn with a slight smile. "I slept on the ride in."

Giraldi waved his hands. "I can't really stop you then."

As if in answer the young sailor brought a pile of clothes into the space. "Here you go, sir."

"Thank you, O'Connell."

The young man left, and right after Dr. Giraldi and the nurse. Jordyn looked at him with raised brows. "I can't believe you got away with not giving him a sample."

Fontana smiled and shrugged as he dropped the sheet to the floor. Jordyn blinked, and her cheeks flushed. The scarred skin on the right side of her face mottled with color, like it wanted to blush but couldn't any longer. Grinning, he stepped toward her, till there was less than a breath between them. Reaching behind her head, he sealed the partition closed as much as it would go. Her eyes rolled slowly up to his, taking their time getting there as they scanned his body. Not for injuries, like she had before. Now she was looking at him like a woman looked at the man she desired. He would cherish that slow look in the depths of his heart. Her eyes dilated with arousal and her tongue flicked out to wet her lips. The wanting was there on her face, like she was looking at a decadent cupcake.

Not one of these things did she do deliberately, which made them all the more dear to him. This entire Collaborative situation was about to blow, and when it did the reverberations would be echoing across the country. Hell, the world. But for that second in time, he could see in her eyes that he was the most important thing to her.

Fontana reached out to cup her face in his hand, and his thumb stroked over the scars on her cheek, then they traced back through her hairline and over her damaged ear. A shudder rippled through her and her eyes fell. Cupping the back of her neck in his hands, he leaned down enough to whisper against her lips, "I love the way you respond to me."

Then he kissed her like he'd been wanting to for days, his tongue slipping into her mouth to taste. She moaned and gripped his face in her small, strong hands, tilting her head up for him so their mouths aligned better. There was a good bit of height difference, but he didn't mind bending down for her as long as she would meet him part way.

One of Jordyn's hands ran down his shoulder, then along his arm till she gripped his wrist in her hand. He thought she was going to push him away, but she didn't, just held him as if she didn't want *him* to let go. Fontana shifted, allowing his body to rest against hers. If she didn't have her combat gear on, this would be much more enjoyable.

She seemed to come to the same conclusion, because she drew back, laughing a little. "You are *bad*, that's all I can say."

She leaned into his hold on her neck, but he didn't let her go. Instead, he brought her in for another quick kiss, lingering over the taste of her bottom lip. She moaned, and her hands fell to his chest. Those short, feminine fingernails scratched through his chest hair and he gasped, loving the feel of her hands on him. Swirling her fingers, she danced them down his ribs to rest on his hips.

Fontana wished they had more than a thin partition between them and the world, because he would take her in a heartbeat. As it was, they could be giving someone an auditory thrill if they were close.

He drew back this time, his body rock hard and aching. "My name is Drake."

Jordyn tipped back her head and laughed, her eyes creased with sudden amusement. He'd remembered what she'd told him in the bathroom at Pablo's, that she wouldn't sleep with a man she didn't know. He didn't think she could know him much more than she already did, but he would give her that part of himself.

"Are you serious?"

He nodded, mouth spreading in a smile. "Why?"

"My best friend's name is Drake, and now my ... other,

sexy friend." She giggled, and it was the most lighthearted he'd ever heard her. Then her eyes flicked to the floor and he knew when she caught sight of his body. Her expression sobered and she gave him a thoughtful look.

"It is my true pleasure to meet you, Drake. I hope we're going to get much better acquainted."

Oh, fuck yes.

CHAPTER TWENTY-FIVE

"Ahem," a voice said from the other side of the partition. They jerked apart guiltily, then grinned at each other.

"Just a minute," Jordyn called.

Then she just stood there and watched Fontana, *Drake*, get dressed. Oh, he was so damn lickable her mouth actually watered. And that tight underwear did nothing to conceal him from her eyes. If anything they outlined and teased.

She huffed out a breath and turned away, not sure exactly what she was going to do now. Actually, she knew what she needed to do. She needed to go get Margarita. The poor thing was all alone out in the jungle. Her uncle would never forgive her if anything happened to her. If she were honest with herself, though, she would admit that the last thing she wanted to do was leave Fontana. There was a throbbing need in her blood that he had stoked and needed to be satisfied. It had been at least a year since she'd been with anyone, and her body craved his touch.

Tightening muscles low in her body, she stepped back from temptation.

Fontana dressed quickly, and everything seemed to fit him the way it was supposed to. His eyes met hers and he smiled, understanding the frustration of being in the wrong location at the right time. Or was it the right location but the wrong time?

Officer Rose stood waiting on the other side of the partition, and he didn't look happy when they stepped through. His arms were crossed and he looked frazzled, like the past twenty-four hours had taken a lot out of him. And they probably had. The biggest takedown of his career was within his grasp. As long as he could gather all the parts together.

"Come with me," he said shortly, and turned away.

Jordyn wasn't sure if he'd been speaking to her or just Fontana, but with a look at Fontana she decided to follow along. Rose led them to a small conference room with a long window that looked out onto the deck of the ship. It was lit as bright as day, and there were people moving around in every direction. She looked at the watch on her wrist. Just going on four am. Seriously?

"You need to tell me what happened at that camp."

Rose knew what had happened on her end, he'd been there, but Fontana shifted.

"We'd moved close and I spotted Scofield when he went into the medical center. Then the second plane came, bringing Dustin Truckle. Did you find him? He was probably curled up on the floor in pain with a bunch of dead Collaborative mercs around him."

Rose frowned and spoke into a handheld radio, then held a finger to an earpiece. It was obvious he was listening to a response, but when he was done he shook his head. "Give me a description."

Fontana did that, sinking down into one of the conference table chairs. Jordyn sat down beside him and rested a hand on his knee, beneath the table. He gave her an appreciative look, then turned back to Rose.

"No bodies with that description, are you sure he was in that room?"

Fontana sighed. "Yes. The doctor that was in there injected him with a cocktail of illnesses that caused him to be in intense pain. He was literally curled up on the floor damn near bawling like a baby when I left him."

"Why didn't you kill him?"

"Because I wanted him to suffer like I suffered two years ago."

Officer Rose shook his head and scrubbed a hand through his hair. "I'm coming into this late, but I think I've pieced a few things together. The Dogs of War — you and Wulfe, were prisoners in the Brazilian camp two years ago. And somehow you broke out, stealing information when you did?"

"Yes," Fontana confirmed.

"I don't understand the two-year gap."

Sighing, Fontana rocked back in the chair. "There were four of us that broke out. When we left we each took part of the evidence, one of the four stick drives of Dr. Shu's personal notes. We scattered, knowing that they would be trying to track us down. But those drives had to be together in order to work. TJ was killed delivering his drive to Aiden Willingham, our fourth. The Lost and Found Investigative Service has been helping us with the technical aspect, keeping the drives secure and compiling the evidence."

Though he wasn't writing anything down, Jordyn knew that Rose was committing everything to memory. She had no doubt that within minutes of this interview LNF, its partners, employees, history, financials and business dealings would be under investigation. Hopefully Rose wouldn't piss them off too much before he asked for all of the info they'd compiled...

"I'm going to need a copy of everything they have," Rose started.

"You'll get it, after we get some assurances."

Fontana folded his hands together over his stomach. Officer Rose got an odd look on his face. "What kind of assurances?"

Fontana rocked forward and looked at him for a long moment. "We need your promise of protection. We've done some things that would definitely fall into the gray area of the law in order to make sure that this company was brought to justice. Literally, we've had to fight for our lives over the past two years. It will be a blanket protection for all the members of the Dogs of War, as well as the Lost and Found Investigative Service, all of their officers and employees. We want a get out of jail card for all past, present and future indiscretions against the Silverstone Collaborative and/or her officers and employees."

Jordyn thought Rose's eyes were going to pop out of his head. "I can't promise anything like that! Are you off your fucking rocker?"

"Sure, you can. Make us covert CIA operatives if you have to," Fontana laughed, "placed in the field retroactively or some shit. Then I want your promise that our military careers will be reinstated, as well as that of every American we've rescued. We will also be given the option of retirement with full benefits or employment in another agency. The younger survivors might want to go back to their branch of service, if they want to do that, they can. Military personnel from other countries are to be offered asylum from their home country if they desire it, considering they were sold out to the company, or immediate return home. Bottom line is, these guys— American and all the other countries— were sold a bill of sale *by their governments* that they were going to be super soldiers and heroes by the time the Collaborative was done. All they did was make them, *us*, into lab rats."

Officer Rose seemed shell-shocked, and she kind of felt bad for the man. So far she hadn't heard Fontana request anything she disagreed with. Then something occurred to her and she squeezed his knee. "And for all those that have died ...they need to be honored posthumously, with full military benefits to their families. And they need to be told what actually happened, not some bullshit story."

Fontana nodded. "Agreed."

The man across from him shook his head. "There's no way I can authorize any of this."

Fontana waved a hand, a slight smile deepening the dimples in his cheeks. Jordyn wanted to kiss those dimples, but she figured Rose had been shocked enough for this meeting.

"Do you still have people at Mourinda?"

"Oh, yes. We're still documenting and collecting evidence."

"We need a ride back out there," Fontana told him, pushing up out of his chair. Jordyn followed.

Rose frowned and shook his head. "There's no reason for you to go out there, again. We have everything under control."

"I have to get Margarita," Jordyn told him. "My helicopter."

"Margarita?" Rose shook his head, waving it away. "Whatever. Fine."

"And I need to get Truckle."

Rose narrowed his gaze on Fontana. "Why is he so important?"

"Because he was appointed to take over the research program by Damon Wilkes. And right now, Wilkes has no idea what's going on. But as soon as Truckle gets his happy feet to a phone, he's going to go tattling to Wilkes and all your months of investigating Wulfe said you've done will be down the tubes."

Jordyn thought she was going to have to grab Officer Rose before he keeled over, but he caught himself.

"You'll be on the next chopper out," the officer promised.

Fontana winked at her. "Yeah, I thought so."

The Chinook was originally slated to return to Mourinda in five hours. Rose got that shortened to two hours. It would take just that long to clean, restock and refuel the one they'd been on before. Fontana hoped they found a fresh pilot as well.

Two hours wasn't enough time to really wind down, but it was enough time to get a bite to eat in the mess and for Jordyn to get cleaned up in one of the DV staterooms O'Connell led them to after the mess. Fontana laughed to himself, they were visitors, all right but he wasn't sure they were Distinguished Visitors after all that time in the jungle. She still had her pack with her, so she went in and took a shower while he waited outside, trying not to imagine her in the nude just on the other side of the door. When she returned she smelled of Irish Spring and loveliness, and he couldn't resist bending down to kiss her.

"We can't do that here," she hissed, dodging his mouth.

"Sure, we can," he argued. "Technically, we're civilians."

She allowed him to catch her for a kiss, then lifted her brows at him as pulled back. O'Connell stood down the hallway, trying not to watch. "Not if you get reinstated," she chuckled.

"I'll worry about that later," he said, pulling her hips to his with fingers in her belt loops.

He was just sinking into her mouth when their shadow cleared his throat. "Sorry, sir, ma'am. That chopper will be in the air in twenty minutes and I have to make sure you're on it."

They pulled apart reluctantly, nodding at O'Connell. "No worries, buddy. We'll be on it."

The chopper lifted off the deck of the USS America exactly twenty-two minutes later. Jordyn and Fontana were on it, as well as Dr. Giraldi and a few medics who were heading back into the jungle.

Fontana had been issued weapons and combat gear to go with his borrowed clothes, and he prayed they worked as well as the gunnery officer had promised. Right now they didn't sit on his hip as well as his regular gear but it would have to do.

Rose was staying on board the America to talk to the powers that be about Fontana's proposal. Officer Maxwell was handling the rest of the cleanup duties on the ground. As Fontana was getting on the Chinook, he'd glanced back at Officer Rose. "I haven't even told you about the senator and the congressmen involved, or the other names we've collected."

Rose's mouth had dropped open, and Fontana had a feeling that they'd have some kind of written promise in hand by the time they got back.

Before they'd lifted off he'd called Aiden to warn him about what he'd proposed to Rose, and Aiden had laughed. "I think that's perfect. Good thinking."

He also told him about the loose cannon he was going back into the jungle for.

"I don't think I even recognize Truckle's name," Aiden admitted. "I'll search the information we have to see if we have any kind of background on him. And I'll call Wulfe. Maybe his informant can give us something."

"Do you have any idea who it is?" Fontana asked.

"Nope. Not a clue. We've been apart for two years, so we don't know everything about each other's lives right now."

That was very true. "Let me know if you hear anything. And of not, I guess I'll talk at you when I can."

"Stay safe, Fontana. I can't take another death of a friend."

Yeah, neither could he. "I'll stay as safe as I possibly can, Will. I have a great team with me."

Jordyn sat strapped into one of the seats, her mouth tight with tension. She didn't balk at getting on the chopper, but she did give the pilot a good hard look. Sitting in the chair next to her, he took her hand in his.

You've got this.

She jerked her head around to look at him. "How do you even do that?" she called over the sound of the engines.

Fontana shrugged. "I can feel the weight of your worry. I don't shield against your emotions like I do most people. I'm not sure I can."

She shook her head and rested it back against the head rest, not saying anything. "Is it only one way?"

He shrugged. *Try it.*

Frowning, she stared at him for a long minute.

I want to lick straight down your abs.

The thought came through so strong his breath sped up with excitement, and his cock immediately hardened. *And where will you stop licking?*

Her mouth dropped open and she paled. "You heard me?" she mouthed.

Nodding, he reached out to brush a finger over her lips. *I would love to feel your lips on me.*

Her eyes took on a glitter of laughter. "Well, now that I know your first name..."

Grinning, he quirked a brow at her. "Let's get through this and we'll find a place where we can do anything we want." *Because I've dreamt of gripping your ass as you ride me.*

She gave a long, slow blink, and looked away, flustered, then saw the rest of the people in the hold with them. None of them were actually looking their way, but he saw her retreat just a bit.

Jordyn held his hand as they flew over the ocean and back into Guyana, to the camp. Her anxiety had eased, until they went in for the landing. Then she tightened up, her hand gripping his like he was her life preserver. "Hey," he said. "Look at me."

Her big eyes met his and he could feel the screaming anxiety in her. He could also feel how much she appreciated his hold on her. If he could take some of the fear from her, he totally would, because that was one thing he'd dealt with a lot himself. Not that he'd mastered it, but he'd definitely learned to not let it control him.

Fontana picked up her hand, with its pretty nails. "How do you do this?"

"I go to a nail salon and tell them what color I want," she laughed. "I need some outward expression of my femininity. I could lose myself if I'm not careful. But this is a special kind of varnish that's super strong."

"I like that you do it. What color is your underwear today?"

"What?" She stared at him.

"What color is your underwear?"

Frowning, she looked out the window as they hit a little turbulence, her grip tightening on his hand.

"Jordyn, what color is your underwear?"

Her attention came back to him and she shook her head in exasperation, her eyes a little dazed. "Um, flowered, I think, mostly black... with a red bow on the front."

He grinned at her lasciviously. "Maybe I'll have a chance to take those off of you later."

The look that crossed her face almost made him laugh. She thought he was crazy. Just then they thumped to the ground and she looked out the window in shock. Then she looked back at him. Her face relaxing, she leaned into him for a kiss. "Thank you, Drake. That was very sweet of you to distract me."

He made a face at her. "That wasn't a distraction. I totally want to get you out of your underwear," he laughed.

Laughing, she leaned into his shoulder for a moment. When she climbed to her feet, her eyes promised him that that time would be soon.

CHAPTER TWENTY-SIX

Zero spotted them as soon as they disembarked. He jogged up, weapon held low ready.

"Glad you came back, guys. We have an issue."

Fontana could feel the anxiety rolling off the former SEAL, which was a little shocking in itself. He was normally so self-contained. "What's wrong?"

"One of the mercs here managed to grab a weapon and take off. He was moving... well, he was a blur. I can say that much. He shot several spooks and Payne took a bullet in his good arm when we went after him. I just got him back here for medical."

"Fuck," Fontana breathed. "How long ago was this?"

"It was just after you guys took off, maybe zero five thirty? Sky was just getting light."

"Did he have a beard?"

Zero nodded. "Do you know who it was?"

"Yeah." Fontana cursed himself, because he should have dispatched Truckle when he'd had the chance.

The satellite phone rang in his pocket and he answered it.

"Yeah, Will."

Aiden sighed on the other end of the line, and his voice broke up into static. "I can't make this shit up."

"What?"

"The only Truckle we found was an Army serviceman who took part in the program three years ago." Static cut in, obscuring the rest of what he said.

Fontana cursed and looked at the phone. There were five reception bars. Their connection should be good. "Say again, Will."

"He was in our camp, Fontana."

That part came through crystal clear, and he rocked on his heels in shock. "No fucking way," he breathed.

"Did you recognize him?"

Fontana shook his head, then realized Aiden couldn't see that. "No, he has a beard. He is definitely enhanced, though."

"Did he talk to you? Does he know who you are?"

"I talked to him," he admitted, "and he did say something about old home week or something. But I didn't make the connection."

"Well, you need to be careful. If he was in our program, receiving the original serum, he won't have the drawbacks that the later subjects did."

Priscilla Mattingly had taken part in a later program, and she'd suffered adverse effects when she used her power to stop them in the train depot. "Noted. I'll call you when we get back."

Pressing the disconnect button he looked at Zero. "Where's the rest of Team Alpha?"

"Guarding mercs."

"Tell them we're moving out."

Zero took off, heavy-duty K-Bar knife flashing in its sheath at his lower back.

Dr. Giraldi was heading toward the triage tent the CIA had set up outside the med center. There they could see prisoners to document their condition before they were shipped to the USS America. They'd already gone through the group once to choose the most seriously ill. Those prisoners had flown out on the same flight with Fontana.

Now they were wading through another group. Fontana wanted to go up to one of them and demand answers, because this didn't seem to be enough men. And he didn't think they'd discovered any mass graves or anything either. Aksel had said he thought this camp was just a stopping off point.

"Do you think he recognized you from the camp? Or just knew that you were one of the ones that left?"

He looked down into Jordyn's concerned face, thoughtful. "I'm not sure. When we left there couldn't have been more than one or two guys left. And they were in really bad shape. If they couldn't talk to us mentally like the rest of the team, I think we assumed they weren't strong enough to make it out with us. And we certainly didn't have the power between us to carry anyone out."

She nodded, looking just as thoughtful. "Well, then there's the chance he did recognize you and has a hell of grudge to settle with you."

Fontana frowned. "If he did, I kind of don't blame him."

One of the men in the triage tent moved, leaning forward in his chair and drawing Fontana's eye. He thought it might be the prisoner that had spotted him before he'd gotten caught. Curiosity piqued, he walked forward.

The man was emaciated, one of the worst in the group. Sallow skinned, it looked like he'd been soaking in a pool for the past three days, his skin sloughing off in places in large sheets. Fontana had no idea what could have made it do that, because he'd certainly never heard of a disease with the same symptoms. Hair had fallen out in clumps as well, and the man's gray-blue eyes were dull.

The skin was the number one defense against diseases and

other illnesses. Even as a non-medical person he knew that. He wondered how many other issues this guy was going to have to battle before he recovered.

As soon as Fontana stopped in front of him, the man pushed to his feet, a little unsteadily. His emotions reeked of guilt and anxiety, like he'd been caught by the principal smoking in the bathroom. The spooks had given them hospital gowns to wear, and his billowed around him like it was three sizes too big. But he made direct eye contact and even held out a hand.

Fontana didn't look at what the man's palm looked like, just shook it, then planted his hands on his utility belt.

"My name is Wheeler. I have to apologize to you," the man said, speaking perfect well-enunciated British English. "By turning you in, I thought I would get some acknowledgement for a job well done. But I didn't."

Fontana shrugged. "If I were in a similar position I might have done the same thing."

Not really. There was no way he would have turned in a possible rescuer.

The man seemed defeated. Swaying on his feet, he looked Fontana in the eye, and something about the look had Fontana slamming every mental shield he'd ever created into place. The man blinked, and nodded his head, dropping to the seat of the chair. He looked even more tired and drawn, if that were possible. "The man you're looking for headed southwest," he told them, voice no more than a rasp. "He crossed beneath the bridge less than an hour ago. He's in pain but mobile, and he'll take the path of least resistance through the jungle to find escape."

Fontana looked at Jordyn. "If he made it over the bridge and finds our trail, we cut him a path right to the chopper."

Her jaw clamped with anger and her hands tightened on her MP5.

"Are you telling us the truth? Or covering your own ass again?"

Fontana cracked his shields enough to feel the man's regret at what he'd done, and the determination to make it right. He thought what he was reading was true. The man was so depleted he didn't have the same kind of shielding Fontana did. Or was that what he was projecting?

The man beside Wheeler leaned into him, holding his arm. "He's telling the truth."

Fontana looked between the two of them and decided to go with his gut, which said the man was speaking truth. Turning away, he looked at the other four members of Team Alpha, brow raised in question.

"I say we go for it," Zero said. "We've scoured the area and he's nowhere within about three square miles. But we didn't go over the bridge. Payne got shot circling the village. Maybe we were just too close."

Jordyn nodded. "Agreed."

Shane and Big Kenny tipped their chins in agreement.

"Okay, let's move out. This fucker is determined to survive, so be aware."

They took off at a slow jog, back through the holes they'd made in the fence. The team was immediately back on their own trail. It was light enough, and the trail was clear enough, that they were bound to make up time.

They reached the bridge less than thirty minutes later. The CIA had taken over this guard post and waved them through. Fontana paused at one side, though. "Did Wheeler say he went under the bridge?"

They all leaned over to look. The river was a torrent beneath them. "There's no way he crossed that," Shane breathed.

"Maybe he climbed through it," Kenny murmured, waving at the beams that stretched beneath.

"Is the man suicidal or what?"

"Determined," Fontana corrected, and took off into a lope.

They ran for a solid hour looking for some sign of Truckle. During a pause for Kenny to adjust his prosthetic, Fontana told them about his altercation with Truckle in the med center. "When I left him on the ground it sounded like bones were breaking or joints were dislocating under the strength of his own muscle contractions."

Shane cursed. "That's fucked up."

"I agree," Fontana told him. "That's what they were going to inject me with. I feel no guilt for leaving him there like that. I do, however, feel like I need my ass kicked for not suspecting that he could pull out of it enough to wreak havoc."

Jordyn reached out and punched him lightly in the arm. "I'll kick your ass later."

"Ew," Shane said. "Are you guys hooking up?"

Fontana blinked, then glanced at Jordyn, which was exactly what he shouldn't have done. Her skin had mottled with color.

"You *are*," Shane cried. "Oh, that's so wrong!"

Fontana shook his head, sighing. If they denied it the ribbing would be worse.

"Whatever," he said. "Big Kenny, you ready?"

Kenny strode forward. "Yes, sir."

"Okay, let's get this bastard. Madeira, if there's some kind of altercation I want you to move ahead and secure the machine."

"Roger!"

They took off again, this time with Zero on point. He found the path they'd hacked in on, and started following it. Every once in a while he would pause next to a depression in the earth. "It looks like he's struggling here. Like he's wallowing on the ground trying to get away from the pain or something. I may be reading too much into it, but he definitely paused and laid down. Not for very long, but maybe long enough to catch his breath."

They took off again, scanning the path from side to side. Fontana knew they were getting close to the chopper; he recognized the terrain. It was mostly downhill now.

Lifting a fist at a break in the trail, he called a halt. "Catch your breath," he said, "then we're splitting up. Shane and Zero, I want you to swing west and come in from the side of the old airport if you can. We'll give you a few minutes head start. If he makes it there before us we have to assume he'll be waiting to ambush. It's extremely unlikely he has his helicopter license. Which makes Madeira here, valuable as fuck."

Jordyn rolled her eyes. "Great..."

"I don't know what kind of weapon he has, but we're going to assume the same thing that we're carrying. Probably limited ammunition though. If you have contact, shout out, either on coms or out loud," Fontana told them firmly, meeting everyone's gaze. "Don't try to take care of this yourself."

There was a round of agreement, then Shane and Zero took off. A light rain began to fall, just enough to minimize visibility. Fontana sat where he was, very conscious of Jordyn right beside him. In a short amount of time she'd become very important to him, and he wouldn't risk her for anything.

They gave Shane and Zero a ten minute lead time, then began moving in. They followed the trail they'd cut into the bush, but Fontana opened his senses as wide as he could, searching for something. He recognized the feel of Jordyn, and even to an extent Big Kenny, moving off to the left. So when the feeling of danger began to crowd him from the right, he acknowledged it.

"Potential on the right," he whispered into the mic.

His team clicked to acknowledge, but they didn't react too strongly. Big Kenny started moving a little closer, subtly. Fontana didn't turn his head to look, even though he wanted to.

But the danger didn't move in. It followed along as they continued down the trail.

Fontana didn't relax his guard, though. He knew that as soon as he did that Truckle would move in, because if he was sensing him, there was a strong possibility that Truckle was sensing him as well. If they had been part of the same research group, there was a very strong possibility that his abilities had developed the same way.

His mind was racing as they drew closer to the old air strip. They had to be less than a mile away at this point.

They reached an open meadow where they hadn't had to chop their way through, and he felt frustration from the right. It had to be Truckle. He wasn't sure how to cross the expanse without being seen, and circling around it would take too long. Then Fontana felt pain, and the sense of the man following them fell away. Was his body still contorting as it dealt with the injection he'd been given? The man had been following them for fifteen minutes with no indication of it. Maybe the adrenaline had worn off.

He had a split second to change course and attack when he knew he had a chance of taking the mercenary down safely, without endangering the rest of his team.

"Kenny!" And he took off running toward the danger. "Madeira, get to the chopper!"

He didn't pause to look to see if she listened, he just took off running toward where he could feel the energy writhing, struggling. He hurdled trees and crashed through palmetto as he tried to pinpoint the location. *There*, to the right and back, down over that little bank.

Truckle knelt on the ground, one hand down, the other

still curled around his weapon. Lines of saliva hung from his beard where he'd just thrown up, and Fontana could see blood on the ground beneath him. He was looking directly at Fontana as he crested the rise, though, and drew his weapon up.

Fontana had a split second to decide whether or not to take the rifle fire, and he stayed his course. Big Kenny was literally right behind him, and if he did dodge, Kenny would take at least one round to the chest. Even with the vest on, he wouldn't survive it, but Fontana might.

Time began to crawl as he sped up those last few feet, in the hopes of derailing the shot.

Truckle pulled the trigger.

Fontana tensed, waiting for the shot to hit, but it never did. Zero, crashing out of the brush from the left, slammed into Truckle a split second before Fontana. Fontana was running too fast to veer off course, so he ended up crashing into Truckle and Zero both. There was a bit of a struggle as they fought with the mercenary over the weapon, but Zero managed to get it out of his hands as Fontana drove a fist into his jaw. He felt it break beneath his fingers, and he felt the mental pain from Truckle, then the release as he fell unconscious.

Fontana looked up at Zero, and held a fist out. "Where the fuck did you come from?"

Zero bumped his knuckles, grinning. "We cut behind him when we separated, and I could see his trail. I sent Shane crashing on ahead as a distraction and I took my time, watching. I think we both timed that just right."

On the ground, Truckle's body arched in pain, even unconscious. They needed to get him secured. Fontana patted his borrowed equipment. "I don't have cable ties."

Zero handed him a set, then hunkered down to put some over his ankles. "I've only got two."

Fontana secured his wrists and handed the weapon up to Kenny, who stood behind him protectively.

"What the hell do we do with him?"

Fontana sighed. "We take him back to the camp, get the docs to knock him out with drugs and hope the CIA has a way to control him when he gets back to the states."

None of them were happy about the options, but Kenny and Zero each hooked an arm under Truckle's. Fontana grabbed his feet and they headed back to the trail.

The sound of Margarita's engines whirring to life was one of the best sounds he'd ever heard, and seeing Jordyn's grin beneath her flight helmet one of the best sights. Shane stood guard outside and helped the men get Truckle into the passenger compartment. Fontana crawled in behind, because if the man roused, he wanted to be here to try to control him.

"Fly us over to Mourinda, Jordyn."

"Roger."

They were in the air within seconds. It only took a few minutes to hop a few miles over the river to the other airstrip, and Jordyn set the chopper down like a pro beside the much larger Chinook. CIA Officer Maxwell, Rose's counterpart on site, looked at them with a frown on her face as they carried Truckle back into the camp and placed him on the ground in front of her.

"Is this the one that took out two of my officers during his escape?"

"Yes," Fontana told her. "He needs to be sedated. Heavily."

Frowning like she'd rather just shoot the man and get it over with, she called for one of the nurses standing nearby. "Get me Giraldi."

Fontana felt awareness return to Truckle, but the man didn't by move or sound betray that he had woken. He continued to lay there, quiet.

"Why does he need to be sedated?"

"Because he was injected with a cocktail of diseases," Fontana told her. "Tetanus, Shingles and something else debilitating. I forget what the doctor said. His body is fighting it off but he's still dealing with a massive amount of pain."

She blinked down at the man, but her smooth face betrayed none of her emotions.

"He also needs to be sedated," Fontana continued in a warning tone, "so that he doesn't overwhelm anyone mentally."

Maxwell made a face and planted her hands on her hips. "I've been briefed a bit on this, but can you clarify?"

Truckle tensed like he was about to do something, and Fontana dropped down onto the man's back, wrenching his bound arms high to make him focus on the pain. Running his left arm inside Truckle's bound arms, Fontana rested a hand on the man's shoulder and leaned into the arm bar. Truckle cried out and struggled, but Fontana knew he had him secure. The rest of his team stood close, ready to help.

"I'm not fucking doing anything," Truckle cried, spitting dirt from his mouth. It wasn't moving exactly right, thanks to Fontana's fist from earlier.

"You were about to."

"Get the hell off me, you bastard."

"Not right this second," Fontana said calmly. "It didn't have to be this way, Truckle."

"Yeah," the man gritted out. "You would have been fine leaving me in pain just like you did the last time."

Fontana's conscience prickled, because what the man said was truth. "So you *were* at the other camp when we broke out."

"Yes," the man beneath him hissed. "You looked right at me, didn't say a word, then kept right on walking."

"I thought you were at death's door." *I tried to speak to you like this and you didn't respond*, he continued, curious to see if he would react.

Truckle went completely still beneath him. Even his breathing stopped as he twisted enough to look up at Fontana.

Did you hear me?

"Yes." *Yes.*

"You didn't respond and there was no way we could have carried you out of there. We were lucky we were on our feet at all."

Truckle put his head down into the dirt, and Fontana could feel the confusion in him. Then the building resentment.

"If you're not a dick, I'll turn you over."

Truckle nodded once, and Fontana could feel the agreement. He released the arm bar and turned Truckle over so that he could sit on his ass. The mercenary glanced at the faces around him, as well as all the guns.

"You all act like I'm the Bogey Man or something." He grinned at them, then a spasm of pain rippled through him and he had to gasp for breath. When he could finally control himself, he glared at Fontana.

"We suffered there for months after you left," he said eventually. "They brought in other test subjects, but my buddy Rafferty and I were the only ones showing progress. We were the only ones recovering. We eventually got strong enough that she offered us an opportunity to get out of the cage."

The mercenary looked away and wiped his mouth on his shoulder. Fontana crossed his arms, waiting for him to continue.

"If we helped the doctors reverse engineer the serum, which you guys stole when you escaped, and be their willing volunteers, they would give us a job and our lives back. We had to work for the Collaborative, of course, but it wasn't so bad after a while. We had all the food we wanted and a decent place to live. We were fine for a couple years. Then Rafferty went loco and I had to blow his brains out across the lab."

"Why did he go loco?" Fontana asked.

Truckle shrugged and a hard, uncompromising look came into his eyes. "I think he was having a flashback or something. They'd strapped him down for a test. Anyway, they kind of frown on killing doctors in a research facility. Mattingly appreciated that I stopped it, though. So much so that she brought me into her inner circle of guards, promising that if I ever wanted a chance at the four escapees, and you in particular, I could have it. Made it easy too, keeping track of the trail of havoc you left behind you. I've waited years for a chance at you."

Fontana shook his head, amazed, and still feeling guilty. "I had no idea, dude. If I'd known you could have survived the trek out of the jungle, I would have thought about breaking you out. But it took us weeks to get out of that jungle. Weeks, on foot. And it wasn't like we had it made when we got home. We didn't."

Truckle stared at him for a long time, before looking out over the camp. His emotions were in a huge tangle, and Fontana's weren't much better at that moment. Needing something, he looked around the faces. Jordyn stood just in front of Big Kenny, and was looking right at him, a sympathetic look on her face. If he could have gone to her then and wrapped his arms around her for comfort he would have. In a heartbeat.

Truckle was a dangerous individual, though, and he was willing to talk, so they would let him. Giraldi joined the group, a medical kit in his hand.

Truckle's face tightened, and fury curled his lips beneath his beard. "So, you're going to sedate me and do what? Put me in one of those cages so that you can study what the company did to me? Isn't that ironic? You motherfuckers. Just kill me and get it over with," he growled. "I'm done being everyone's bitch."

For the slightest second empathy filled Fontana's heart, and it was exactly the opening Truckle had been waiting for. With a mighty heave he strained every muscle in his body, snapped the cable-tie restraints and lunged to his feet. Straight at Jordyn.

Fontana had his weapon up faster than he'd ever drawn it before, and he fired without conscious thought. Truckle went down in a heap at Jordyn's feet, Fontana honoring his last request.

CHAPTER TWENTY-SEVEN

Jordyn could tell that Fontana was glad that he'd killed Dustin Truckle. She wasn't as sensitive to others' emotions the way he was, but he had to be dealing with a massive amount of guilt at the same time. And relief. She knew she was relieved that Truckle hadn't reached her.

There had been something she'd seen in the man's eyes though. Some sense that he wasn't actually going to hurt her, but he was going to make everyone think he would.

She ran her fingers over Fontana's knuckles. It had been a long, quiet flight back to Venezuela and her uncle's little haven. The team had all been lost in their own thoughts. After Fontana shot Truckle, Officer Maxwell had pretty much told him to go home. That he'd done enough. So, here they sat on her uncle's noisy glider rocker, trying not to move it.

Jordyn didn't like the guilt he was feeling. It was written all over his handsome face. What he'd done to protect himself when he was in the camp years ago was completely up to him, and he shouldn't feel responsible for anyone left behind.

"You need to stop this," she told him. "The way it ended

was the way it needed to end. You got closure, and Truckle did as well. He probably wouldn't have survived being in another prison somewhere. Right?"

"No," Fontana agreed.

"I hate that he used you as a tool for suicide, but that's exactly what he did."

Fontana blinked and turned his head to look at her. "I realize that. And to a certain extent I expected it. Maybe even subconsciously... I was looking for the situation we found ourselves in. I really *was* sympathetic to his situation, and I have to wonder if he wasn't manipulating me a little. I thought he was naïve about our mental capabilities, but maybe I was the one that was naïve."

"I think you could have taken the same actions in that situation."

"Yes," he agreed. "Maybe since I gave Giraldi and the CIA my blood offering they'll leave me alone for a while."

Jordyn looked at him askance. "You really think so?"

Fontana shrugged, not sure about much of anything anymore. Well, he was sure of one thing. He loved holding Jordyn's hand. Her palm was textured, but not unpleasantly, and it was small enough that he just curled it up in his fist. It felt right. He held her hand up in the light, running his fingertips over her glossy nails. "You're kind of amazing, you know that?"

She snorted. "I don't know about that," she murmured.

"I do," he said firmly. "This hasn't been anyone's idea of an ideal situation but you've made the best of it and we prevailed. We completed our mission."

"Yes," she said softly. "Now to take the company down."

"I have a feeling Officer Rose is already working on it. Along with Wulfe and his secret informant."

"The CIA is going to be busy for a while."

Fontana nodded, his thoughts on things other than the

operation. This was the first time the two of them had had even the slightest bit of privacy. The men were out in the hangar relaxing with Pablo and his secret stash of homemade cookies the neighbor lady had made him.

"I want to take you out somewhere," he said abruptly. "Somewhere that you have to wear a dress."

Jordyn groaned. "A dress? Seriously? I'm not much of a dress kind of girl."

He looked down at her, smiling. He loved the look on her face. "Yes," he agreed. "A dress. Something that shows off that beautiful ass of yours."

Jordyn tipped her head back and laughed, and he had to cup her head in his hands and bring her mouth to his own. She tasted of toothpaste, one of the first things they'd done when they reached Pablo's place. She'd also taken a shower, and she wore a threadbare Wonder Woman t-shirt and a pair of black nylon running shorts. He thought he smelled some type of citrus fragrance, but he wasn't sure exactly what it was. Probably shower gel or shampoo. Jordyn wasn't much of a perfume type.

"You're beautiful," he sighed, rubbing his cheek against her own. "And you smell fantastic."

"You're hard up," she snorted.

He prodded her to her feet, spun her around with her hand and cupped her ass in his palms, pulling her against him where he sat. Jordyn took it one step further, though. She straddled his hips in the ancient glider, grinning down at him as she rested her heat against his hardness. The metal beneath them screeched in protest, jarring in the quiet night.

Fontana's brain shorted out as he held her cupped against him. Yeah, she was right, he was hard up. But it was her he wanted. No one else.

I still want to lick you.

Fontana froze as he heard her words in his mind. "Well, let's see what we can do."

Pushing up and out, he surged off the glider, holding her to him as he maneuvered through the door. Then he carried her down the hallway to the guest room he'd been given. Allowing her feet to touch the floor at the side of the bed, he waited for her to say something. Or to pull away. But she didn't do either of those things. Instead, she pushed closer and stretched up onto tiptoe to press her mouth against his own. Fontana got lost in the kiss, his emotions ricocheting around in his body. He wanted to fuck her and love her and just... *absorb* her. There was nothing about this woman that he didn't like or admire, and for the first time in his life he thought he could see a future with someone.

The situation they were in wouldn't allow them to relax their guard completely, but he felt like Jordyn Madeira accepted him for who he was. He was not a good guy, but he supposed he had enough decent characteristics that she could overlook his not so decent ones.

Her fingers were moving over his abdomen and one finger stroked just inside his waistband. If she went just a hair further she would find the tip of him, laying off to the side. Fontana knew that it would be all over if she stroked him there. It had been a long time since he'd been with a woman. Fontana stroked a finger down her chest to the tip of her nipple, pronounced beneath the soft fabric of the shirt and sports bra, then he cupped her breast in his hand. She had the boobs of a much taller woman, and he was dying to see them.

"Take the shirt off," he told her, voice rough.

Reaching across her abdomen, she did as he told her, tossing the shirt away. Yes, there they were. Cupping both of her breasts through the fabric of her bra, he stroked her nipples.

Jordyn dragged in a sharp breath, her stunning eyes going

soft with pleasure. He was glad this made her happy. It certainly made him happy. Squeezing a finger beneath the tight elastic band he lifted it up over her breasts to high on her chest. Her dark areolas were tight with pleasure and he leaned down to take one into his mouth.

Jordyn cried out, her fingers stabbing through his hair to hold his head against her. That was fine. He didn't want to leave anyway. But he did want to taste the other one, so he shifted. A fine quivering started in her body, and he wondered if she was wet.

He glided his hands down her ribcage and over her ass, pushing her shorts away. He pulled back enough to look at her panties. They were mostly maroon, but had big pretty designs across the fabric in other shades. "I love this color," he said as he stroked the maroon band.

"Noted," she whispered. Wriggling, she lifted the tight bra up over her head and let it fly into the darkness. There was light from the moon and the light in the hallway, but at some point the men would be coming in and he would need to close the door. He wanted to watch her as long as possible, though.

Jordyn had turned from him partially, and he caught sight of the burns down her side. Gently guiding her shoulders, he turned her away, then surveyed the damage. They ran from her upper neck all the way down her right side, almost like she'd laid in fire. "Damn, girl. That strong woman thing? Yeah, you just keep impressing the hell out of me. That had to have been excruciating."

She turned her head to him and he could see her perfect profile, but it was the damaged side. Without hesitation he pressed a kiss to her imperfect ear, and the fringe of odd hair growing around it. Then he kissed her cheekbone, and his lips caught salt. She was crying.

Fontana's heart ached with sympathy as he wrapped as

much of his body around her as he could as she cried. *You're going to be all right*, he told her over and over again. *I think you're beautiful.*

Her hands had been stroking the length of his arms over and over again where they cradled her, and the tears eventually stopped. "Thank you, Drake. I haven't felt that exposed for a long time. I guess I needed some affirmation."

"We all do sometimes. You helped me on the trail, you and Payne. I have a feeling you're going to have to help me more, too, if you hang around." He cleared his throat. "Or let me hang around."

"Hang around, huh? What does that entail?"

With his arms wrapped around her, he felt when she stopped breathing, and her heart began to race.

"Well, you know. Being together and learning about each other. Maybe ... learning to love each other."

He felt her draw in a shuddering breath, and he was very conscious of how he held her against him, her lush ass pressed into his groin. She seemed to realize it as well, because her breath sped. Cupping his hands in her own, she guided them to hold her breasts again, and he was very happy to do that for her, scraping his thumbs over her hard nipples. Jordyn groaned and began to sway her hips against him, very subtly. Then harder.

Fontana loved her breasts, but he wanted more. Running his right hand down her bare midriff, he skirted it beneath the elastic of her panties. With no hesitation, he slipped a finger between her puffy folds. She was hot and wet and gasped as he sank his finger in. Then he moved that finger in a searching sweep.

Jordyn gasped, her own hand coming down to cover his on the outside of her panties. Then she seemed to get frustrated. Shoving the panties down her thighs, trying not to dislodge him, she held his hand to her as she kicked the fabric away.

Then, aligning their fingers, she showed him what she liked. Her hips began to move, riding his hand, and it was all he could do to not grind himself against her ass. No, her first. *Always* her first.

Moaning, her hips contracting, Jordyn's body got wetter and wetter, but he knew what she needed. He angled his middle finger up just slightly, catching the hard bud of her clitoris. He flicked his fingertip over it, and she cried out long and low, her body dancing in his arms as she orgasmed. She would have fallen to her knees if he hadn't held her.

When she could hold her feet, she turned in his arms, her hands immediately going to his shirt. "Get rid of this."

He did as he was told, his body jerking as she went to his waistband. She unfastened his cargo pants and tried to push them down his hips, but he had to kick off his boots first. His erection throbbed as he bent over to untie the laces, and he finally ended up just ripping them off his feet. Jordyn laughed as he kicked them away and went back to pushing his pants down his thighs. Fontana kicked them away as well. Then her hands were on his cock, outlining his shape beneath the thin fabric of his athletic shorts. If she stroked him right like that, he could come within just a couple of minutes, he knew. It wouldn't take much.

With a direct look, she sank to her knees in front of him, and he knew the time had just shortened significantly. She began kissing him through the fabric, and he felt his body contract. Then she drew the fabric down over his body and down his thighs. Gripping him in her hand, she kissed the tip of his cock and he had to wonder how the fuck he was going to last if she did this. "Not a good idea, babe. Seriously."

She paused, then her tongue reached out to loop around the head of him. "Babe, huh? I might be able to get used to that."

Fontana almost went to his knees then as she drew him

into her mouth as deeply as she could and fisted the rest of him. His hips contracted and he worried about hurting her, but she didn't seem to mind. She took him deep only a dozen or so times before he had to pull back from her touch. His body quivered, aching for release, but he had to be inside her. It felt like it had been forever since he'd been dreaming about her.

For the merest second, as pulled her up and guided her onto the mattress, he felt her emotions, just to make sure that she didn't have any anxiety about what they were about to do. There was no hesitation there, or worry. Only joy and peace and need. She'd had the appetizer, now she wanted the meal.

She produced a little square packet from somewhere and blushed a little. "I think Zero knew something was going to happen because he made me take this."

Contraception hadn't even occurred to him. "Thank you, Zero," he said fervently, ripping the thing open and rolling it on. He kicked the door shut and turned back to her. Then, unable to wait any longer, he lowered himself into her waiting arms. For a moment he just looked down into her shining eyes. They fluttered shut as he leaned in to kiss her, and she reached down to guide him inside her soaked body. She stroked herself with the head of him several times before positioning him to sink deep. Shuddering, he tried to acclimate to the feel of her body gripping his. She was so fucking tiny beneath him that he worried that he would hurt her, but she only pulled him tighter as he tried to brace above her.

"You're not going to break me. I want you to make love to me, damn it." Breathing into his ear, she nipped at the skin of his neck. For the first time in a long time Fontana let his body go, plunging and withdrawing. Even with the layer of rubber inhibiting feeling, he knew his orgasm would be quick and hard. Gripping her lush ass in his hands he angled her hips up, looking for that magical spot women had. She had to come with him.

Jordyn cried out beneath him, her orgasm coming easier than he'd expected when he hit her G-spot, and the feel of her losing herself beneath him sharpened his own need. He could feel the release coming up through his balls, and he slowed to savor the rush. Even as Jordyn continued to twitch beneath him, Fontana tried to be *in* every second as the orgasm washed over him. He thought it would be quick and hard, but it was actually slow and hard, arching his spine and making him clench his teeth. Jordyn's movements beneath him drew the orgasm out, until he slammed into her as deep as he could one final time.

The room was dark when he opened his eyes enough to notice. He'd rolled off to the side, enough to not crush her with his weight, but he still held her in his arms. He didn't want to let her go, but he knew they had practical things that needed done. The rubber was in danger of leaking if he didn't take care of it, and he couldn't risk that.

The light from the moon was the only illumination, and it caught the flash of her grin. She ran her fingers up through the curls along his neck and he shivered. "Are you going to blow the lightbulbs every time you come?"

Fontana jerked his gaze around. "Did I do that?"

She nodded, still smiling. "I think the bed shook too. Do you make things shake?"

"Sometimes. It's your fault," he groused, kissing her on the nose. "You make me lose control."

She kissed him, licking at his mouth as if she couldn't get enough. "You make me lose control as well," she whispered, and her smile faded. "You make me feel more than any man ever has, Drake Fontana. And I love it. I don't want to freak you out or anything, but I'm totally falling for you."

His heart stuttered in his chest and he didn't have to drop

his shields to feel what she was feeling. It was there on her face and in her arms and her eyes. Throat tight, he rested a kiss on her lips. "I think I've already fallen for you," he admitted.

A tear streaked down her cheek, just a flash in the moonlight. "I thought you were going to be a pain in my ass."

"Likewise," he chuckled.

They held each other for a long time in the night, until Fontana had to get up. They were going to be laying in a puddle if he wasn't careful.

The light bulb was indeed shattered over the bathroom sink. He would have to clean that up first thing in the morning.

When he returned, Jordyn held her arms open for him, easily and naturally, and he sank against her just as easily. They fell asleep as one unit, holding each other as tightly as possible.

EPILOGUE

Leaving the next morning was bittersweet. Her uncle enjoyed the men, and she worried he would be lonely after they all left, but he waved her worries away. "The neighbor and I get along well. Maybe one day she will invite me for breakfast."

He glanced significantly to Fontana, then back to her. Jordyn felt her skin flush, and she grinned, giving him a kiss on the cheek. "*To quiero, Tío.*"

"Love you too, niece."

Fontana held her hand as they climbed onto the Terberger corporate plane. They chose two seats together, and the other men seemed to sense that they wanted to be alone. Zero had given her a questioning look when they'd joined everyone for breakfast, and she'd given him a wink, letting him know that she was okay. Everything was good.

For a few blessed hours today she and Fontana would be able to just be together, without a lot of outside interference.

She'd woken with Fontana's talented fingers between her thighs, teasing her to a slow morning orgasm. Then she'd had the pleasure of returning the favor. They were out of condoms until they got back to the States but creative nonetheless. They'd showered and dressed and cleaned the mess up in the bathroom, and she wondered if she was going to have to Fontana-proof her apartment. Maybe she needed to invest in more candles.

The thought made her smile as she leaned toward him in the seat. He met her partway and they kissed. She had to force herself to back away, because she just wanted to learn every single thing about him. She almost told him she loved him, but it was too soon. Their relationship was too new, and they'd gone through a lot of shit together in a short amount of time, which might be influencing what she was feeling. Jordyn would give it some time, but she had a feeling she was well and truly hooked on Drake Fontana.

The CIA basically promised to kiss the Dogs of Wars' asses for eternity if they agreed to turn federal witnesses.

It was strange walking into a room where so many people were happy to see him. Duncan and John shook his hand first, and quiet Shannon actually gave him a hug. Actually, she gave *everyone* a hug all down the line as she welcomed them back.

After a backslapping hug, Aiden had waved them into chairs around the conference room table. Then he slid a document across to Fontana. Everything that Fontana and Jordyn had mentioned was in there, smothered in legalese, plus more. In addition to prosecuting Damon Wilkes, they wanted a promise from the men that they would help convict anyone else connected to the situation in any tangential way.

"They really want to take these fuckers down," Fontana murmured, leaning over the document in front of him.

"They're covering their bases," Aiden confirmed. "In the

two years since Shu's information was valid, I'm sure they've brought others in to keep the program running."

Fontana's gaze drifted down the page. "We're going to be reinstated? Or offered other accommodation?"

"Yes," Aiden said slowly, "But not immediately. There are so many military suspects tangled up in this they don't want to send up any red flags by messing with our records until the hammer drops on them all and I completely agree their reasoning. For the moment, we will be listed as government contractors attached to the CIA."

Big Kenny guffawed, slapping the table. "Oh, that's rich. As much as you complained about the 'fucking spooks'." The rest of the men laughed as well, then quieted.

Fontana grimaced. "This isn't what I expected, Will."

Aiden shrugged. "I think it's more than we could have hoped for. We're not being drained in a government lab and injected with things meant to try to kill us."

Yeah, he was right about that. He really didn't have anything to bitch about.

There were protections in place retroactively to protect Lost and Found, and an allocation that they would be brought in as consultants as well when it came time to place the survivors. There was also a notation that the Dogs had discretion to hire whoever they needed to in order to complete their tasks.

"Flip to the second page," Duncan told him softly.

Fontana flipped the page. The contract was signed by the President of the United States, as well as several other high-ranking officials. Even CIA Officer Rose had signed the paper though Fontana wasn't sure how the man had gotten back to Washington so fast.

"Wow," Jordyn breathed, leaning into his arm. She squeezed his leg beneath the table. "I don't know how you can ask for anything more than that."

There were two lines waiting to be signed. Wulfe had scrawled his name on the third line.

"He signed it in Washington, before it was couriered to Colorado. He's lost contact with his informant, so he's trying to locate him."

Fontana nodded and reached for the pen in front of him. He scrawled his signature across the line and pushed it back to Will. He signed the paper as well, and Shannon took them from him. "I'll make copies for everyone. The courier is waiting downstairs for the response."

Damn. The courier had *waited?*

"Time is of the essence," Aiden said, obviously feeling his surprise. "So far Damon Wilkes is hiding out. His wife gave a small press conference yesterday, but she didn't really say much. Just that he's dealing with some issues behind the scenes and that they'd recover from this tragedy stronger than ever."

Fontana rolled his eyes. "Of course, they will."

"In the meantime, we're researching and standing by as back-up if Wulfe calls for us. Team Alpha needs to go home and catch up on sleep and food and whatever else you need."

Fontana's eyes drifted to Jordyn, and she smiled. *Sex?* She asked mentally.

Will's head jerked around and he stared at Jordyn, his mouth falling open. Then he looked at Fontana. *Did she...?*

Yup.

And you and she are...

Yup.

Fontana grinned, loving that he'd surprised his buddy.

I'm happy for you, Fontana.

And he could feel that through their connection. *Thanks, Will.*

They got up to leave the conference room, and Fontana realized he had nowhere to go. He'd been sleeping on Will's floor since he'd gotten into town. He leaned down to whisper into Jordyn's ear. "Can I come to your place? I'm kind of between apartments."

She laughed but nodded. "Of course, you can. I would love to have you there."

Again, he could feel that acceptance and excitement flowing from her, and it made his heart ache. He didn't know how the hell his fortunes had changed, but he appreciated that they had.

"We better pick up a box of condoms on the way," he whispered.

"Or two," she said, giving him a significant look.

Fontana shivered, and grinned. "And maybe some Swedish fish. And Oreos. Man I've been craving them."

They were laughing as they walked out through the conference room door. For right now they would get themselves healthy and settled and learn what they could about each other. Because tomorrow they needed to be ready for the exposure and implosion of the Silverstone Collaborative.

AFTERWORD

Stay up to date with my releases and cover reveals by subscribing to my newsletter!
www.jmmadden.com/newsletter/
I expect to release Wulfe's book, Retribution, in January!

ALSO BY J.M. MADDEN

The Dogs Of War

Genesis

Chaos

Destruction

Retribution

If you would like to read about the 'combat modified' veterans of the **Lost and Found Investigative Service**, check out these books:

The Embattled Road (FREE prequel)

Duncan, John and Chad

Embattled Hearts-Book 1 (FREE)

John and Shannon

Embattled Minds-Book 2

Zeke and Ember

Embattled Home-Book 3

Chad and Lora

Embattled SEAL- Book 4

Harper and Cat

Embattled Ever After- Book 5

Duncan and Alex

Her Forever Hero- Grif
Grif and Kendall

SEAL's Lost Dream-Flynn
Flynn and Willow

SEAL's Christmas Dream
Flynn and Willow

Unbreakable SEAL- Max
Max and Lacey

Embattled Christmas

Reclaiming The Seal
Gabe and Julie

Loving Lilly
Diego and Lilly

Her Secret Wish
Rachel and Dean

Wish Upon a SEAL (Kindle World)
Drake and Izzy

Mistletoe Mischief
Cass and Roger

Lost and Found Pieces

The Lowells of Honeywell, Texas
Forget Me Not
Untying his Not
Naughty by Nature
Trying the Knot

Other books by J.M. Madden
A Touch of Fae
Second Time Around
A Needful Heart
Wet Dream
Love on the Line
The Billionaire's Secret Obsession
The Awakening Society- FREE
Tempt Me

If you'd like to connect with me on social media and keep updated on my releases, try these links:

http://www.jmmadden.com/newsletter.htm

www.jmmadden.com

FB-Authorjmmadden

Twitter- @authorjmmadden

And of course you can always email me at
authorjmmadden@gmail.com

ABOUT THE AUTHOR

NY Times and USA Today Bestselling author J.M. Madden writes compelling romances between 'combat modified' military men and the women who love them. J.M. Madden loves any and all good love stories, most particularly her own. She has two beautiful children and a husband who always keeps her on her toes.

J.M. was a Deputy Sheriff in Ohio for nine years, until hubby moved the clan to Kentucky. When not chasing the family around, she's at the computer, reading and writing, perfecting her craft. She occasionally takes breaks to feed her animal horde and is trying to control her office-supply addiction, but both tasks are uphill battles. Happily, she is writing full-time and always has several projects in the works. She also dearly loves to hear from readers! So, drop her a line. She'll respond.

Made in the USA
Lexington, KY
27 September 2018